P9-CME-699

If
These
Wings
Could
Fly

If These Wings Could Fly

Kyrie McCauley

KATHERINE TEGEN BOOKS
An Imprint of HarperCollins Publishers

Katherine Tegen Books is an imprint of HarperCollins Publishers.

If These Wings Could Fly
Copyright © 2020 by Kyrie McCauley
Bird Illustrations copyright @ 2020 Vladimir Ceresnak / Shutterstock
All rights reserved. Printed in the United States of America.
No part of this book may be used or reproduced in any manner whatsoever
without written permission except in the case of brief quotations embodied in
critical articles and reviews. For information address HarperCollins
Children's Books, a division of HarperCollins Publishers,
195 Broadway, New York, NY 10007.
www.epicreads.com

Library of Congress Cataloging-in-Publication Data

Names: McCauley, Kyrie, author.
Title: If these wings could fly / Kyrie McCauley.
Description: First edition. | New York, NY : Katherine Tegen Books, [2020]
    | Summary: In Auburn, Pennsylvania, a farming community overrun with
    crows, high school senior Leighton struggles to keep herself and her sisters
    safe from their abusive father even as she starts a relationship.
Identifiers: LCCN 2019021411 | ISBN 978-0-06-288502-9 (hardcover)
Subjects: | CYAC: Family problems—Fiction. | Sisters—Fiction. | High
    schools—Fiction. | Schools—Fiction. | Dating (Social customs)—Fiction. |
    Crows—Fiction. | Supernatural—Fiction.
Classification: LCC PZ7.1.M42213 If 2020 | DDC [Fic]—dc23 LC record
    available at https://lccn.loc.gov/2019021411

Typography by David Curtis
20 21 22 23 24   PC/LSCH   10 9 8 7 6 5 4 3 2 1
❖
First Edition

R0459120348

For my little brother, Jackson,
who is like a star,
because he lights up the universe,
(and because he's so much taller than me).

For Kayleigh and Katharyn,
who never hesitate to brave the dark with me,
flashlights in hand.

And for survivors of domestic violence,
and those still in it.
It might feel like the end of the story,
but it is just the beginning,
and the rest is yours alone.

AUBURN, PENNSYLVANIA
SEPTEMBER 2

CROW POPULATION:
212

Chapter One

IT'S IN THE STRETCHES OF SILENCE that I wonder if she's dead.

My window is open, its wooden shutters thrown wide to welcome a breeze that doesn't exist. I suck in air thick with humidity and look at the night sky. Heavy clouds, no rain.

Mother Nature, you're such a tease.

Our town waits on rain to ease the drought. Rain to wash away the sweat that clings to our bodies each day as soon as we step outside. Rain to pummel the hard, dry dirt beneath withering crops in the fields. Rain is life. Rain is forgiveness.

Rain washes away sins faster than a priest can.

I hear it again: a deep, rumbling noise. Don't be fooled; it isn't thunder. His voice is as loud as God's and as mean as the Devil's. I try to ignore it, but then I hear the soft padding of feet on the hallway carpet. A moment later, my bedroom door opens, and the girls come in. The three of us sit under my window, one sister huddled beneath each of my arms.

As if I can protect them.

My arms curl around their shoulders. "It's okay," I whisper, to them and myself.

A scream fills the house. It isn't Mom. It's the opening shriek of a classic rock song. When the bass drum hits, the door to my room quakes.

It's a full-volume night.

There's a slight rush of air from the open window above us; the thin lines of muscles in my sisters' arms tighten in fear. The dark silhouette of a bird appears on the far wall of my room.

"It's just Joe," I say, and untangle myself from their grasps. I turn to face a fierce, shiny black eye. His beak looks wickedly sharp this close. He doesn't usually come to the window. He likes to sit on the mailbox. Or on the fence near our bus stop at the corner. Or on the lowest branch of the tree in our front yard. Joe is singular among other black birds, distinguished by the gray feathers on his abdomen and back. Distinguished as well by his dedication to being near us, always.

Joe caws. He shakes his wings in a show of bravado and turns.

"Bye, Joe," Juniper says as he flies away.

Something crashes downstairs.

"Mom," Campbell says. I imagine Mom hurt. Crying. I look into Cam's eyes, and my own terror is reflected back at me.

"I'll go check on her." There's no such thing as whispering

over the music, so I almost shout it. I squeeze their bony little hands, a single drumbeat of reassurance, and rise.

When I get to the stairs, he's playing Guns N' Roses's *Greatest Hits* so loud my teeth ache, and yet I can still hear him. I steal a glance over the banister, and I find him in the kitchen. If I weren't used to the sight, I'd wonder if the dark red tone of his skin was the sign of a medical emergency. But it's rage. The powder keg tonight was an upcoming mortgage payment. The spark that lit him up: an energy bill twice the normal amount. It was a dry, hot August, and the AC worked too hard.

I can barely see the rounded gray metal on top of the fridge. He keeps his gun where it's easy to reach. He says it won't be much help if he has to go find it during a home invasion, but it's the thing I think about every time he gets like this. It's always the same question in my mind: Is tonight the night he reaches for it?

Mom comes into view. Her long red hair is loose, disheveled. She heads for the stereo.

He runs after her, each footfall a tiny earthquake in the old house. He's a solid wrecking ball, and he tears across the room after Mom when her hand touches the volume dial.

He shoves her into the door of the entertainment center, and it flies back into the wall. A chunk of plaster breaks off where it hits. Mom rubs her shoulder, says nothing.

My fear is trapped in the cage of my chest. It flaps its

futile, frightened wings as I sneak upstairs.

"She's okay," I tell the girls. "But I need to call the police."

"The phones are out," Campbell reminds me. When it starts, he rips the phone cord out of the wall. He hoards it on the kitchen table—in plain sight but rendered useless.

"I'm going for help." I eye the window, and Cam notices.

"It's not too high?" she asks. If she's scared, she masks it. Even at thirteen, Campbell is the picture of control, her face calm, her voice even. She understands the danger we're in. She also knows how to hide it from Juniper.

"Not at all." I climb out my window, onto the roof that covers our porch. The air is still heavy, laden with things it cannot hold much longer. I know how it feels to carry something that isn't yours. Soon the sky will break.

Outside I pause, assessing. Maybe he won't find them out here. At least not right away.

"Come out here," I tell them, and point to the far corner of the roof, where it meets the house and forms a little nook. "It's okay. It'll be an adventure."

Campbell swings her legs over the windowsill and crawls to the corner of the roof.

Juniper hesitates.

"Leighton, I'm scared," she says. Some twisted little part of me is grateful she's scared. That she could spend so many nights of her nine years tucked into shadows like this, and still know it's not normal.

"Hey, babe, look at me. It's gonna be okay. You are just

going to snuggle up with Campbell for a few minutes. Here, take Ava-bear."

I move into the room again, doubling over the windowsill and reaching for the foot of my bed. Soft down fuzz fills my hand when it finds the toy. I lean out the window and offer my beloved stuffed bear to Juniper.

She shakes her head no.

Something rumbles downstairs besides the music, and my stomach tightens in response. He's so angry tonight. I drop the bear and crouch at the window, finding Juniper's dark eyes filled with tears.

"How big is your brave?" I ask her.

I've stolen it, right out of our history. I've cannibalized it from my own gentler early years, when Mom would use the phrase to get me on a bike or a roller coaster. And I've brought it here, into this awful night. But I need it, for Juniper.

"So big," Juniper says, and climbs out the window. I walk her over to Campbell.

The tree in our yard sways, though there's no breeze.

Crows.

Birds fill the branches. There must be a hundred of them. More. Juniper's soft whimper forces the crows from my mind. I swing my legs over the edge of the roof and drop before I can think about it. It's a short fall, but I hit the ground hard and lose my balance. My hands scrape the walkway where I catch myself, drawing blood. I look up and find Campbell peering down. "I'm fine," I say. "Get back." I melt into the shadows of our yard, just as he passes the kitchen window.

When he turns away, I run. There's only one other house on our road. If we always felt safe in our home, I might call it scenic, with the mountains as a backdrop and nothing but idyllic Pennsylvania farming hills for miles.

But we don't feel safe, so instead I'd say it's isolated. Detached.

Alcatraz.

But there is one neighbor. Mrs. Stieg. Just a few hundred feet away in a farmhouse that's easily a half-century older than our house, but meticulously maintained. Racing across the road, I steal a backward glance at my house. I check for two shadows on the porch roof, but my gaze is drawn higher.

Crows cover the top of our house. Dark shingles shrouded in even darker feathers.

When I reach our neighbor's house, I close my fingers over the sting of my freshly skinned palm and slam my fist on the door. When a light flickers on upstairs, hope swells inside of me.

The light turns back off.

I knock harder, but I don't think she's coming.

Fear claws inside my chest, wanting *out*. No one else lives close. I can't leave my sisters long enough to walk a few miles into town. I cross the road again. Back in our yard, I start to sidestep the dozens of crows on our lawn, when the front door swings open.

"What the hell do you think you're doing?" He fills the

whole doorframe. Two-hundred-plus pounds of anger now directed at me. I run through the answers in my head, playing outcomes as fast as I can. Which response is the safest?

"I called the police," I lie, and it's a big one. He will know in minutes that it's untrue.

My father stares me down for a moment, as though he's daring me to speak the truth. Then he turns into the house. The music finally cuts out, and the silence is surreal. Like everything before now was a nightmare, and I've just woken up.

If only.

He moves through the kitchen, and the birds shuffle around me, cawing softly. Or maybe they're loud, and it just seems soft in contrast with how loud the music was a moment ago.

"After all I do for you," Dad says as he collects his essentials: wallet, keys, gun. "So fucking ungrateful."

He strides to his truck, slamming the door shut. Moments later, he's leaving, and I know why. He likes to scream and scare us, but he's always been careful not to land himself in jail. It's a thin line, but he walks it well.

I move down our front path, through the grass, and stop at the edge of the road. He'll come back tomorrow, but tonight we're safe. I watch until his truck turns, and I lose sight of it as the sky cracks open overhead.

Rain pours down, scattering crows in the dark.

AUBURN, PENNSYLVANIA
SEPTEMBER 3

CROW POPULATION:
3,582

Chapter Two

IN THE MORNING, THE CROWS ARE still here. And by here, I mean *everywhere*. Crows on every branch of the tree in our front yard, until it is more feather than leaf.

I stand at my bedroom window watching the birds rustle and twitch on the branches. They're on Mrs. Stieg's roof, too, shuffling along her rain gutters.

Our front door slams.

He's back.

I hurry out of my room and into the shower, desperate to normalize the morning, to remind him we have school. Sometimes if we do things just right, he matches our calm. He migrates toward our normal. As the scalding water hits me, I hope that this is one of those times.

I love school, but this year is different. It's the last year. My countdown has officially begun, and last night was a more ominous beginning than I'd wanted. One year. I have one year to find a way to keep my sisters safe if I want to go to college.

When I get to the kitchen, he's not there, but Mom is. She startles when I walk in, and coffee slips over the lip of her mug, splashing her fingers. She doesn't seem to notice.

"Good morning, Leighton," she says. She smiles, but it's not a *Mom* smile. It doesn't quite reach her eyes. Mom used to smile at us like we were all in on a joke together. Now I get the same hollow one she flashes to strangers.

"Morning," I say.

He's brought her flowers. Scarlet roses that sit in a chipped vase next to the sink. He likes to apologize with small gestures that never match the gravity of what he's done.

It seems to work.

I hesitate, wondering if this is a morning to provoke or let go. "He's back?" I ask.

Now even the hollow smile is gone.

"Drop it, Leighton," Mom says.

This is a morning to *let go*.

"He slept at his office. What more do you want?"

I rattle off the list in my head. His arrest, his apology, his relocation, his kindness. His death. It depends on the day, the hour, the moment, and my mood, but there's a lot more I want than him sleeping in his office.

"I have work today," Mom says. She's always grabbed a few shifts a week waitressing at the diner, but she's been picking up more lately. Trying to make up for the construction business not doing as well. "Will you come right home after school for the girls?" I ignore the abrupt change in subject. Walking into the living room, I begin to pick up framed photographs from the floor, hooking them back on their nails.

It's like the house itself knows when these nights are coming. There are clues, if we watch carefully: a subtle darkening in the corners of the rooms; the picture frames tilting on their nails, preparing to fall at the first commotion; the sudden compulsion to whisper, as though the house will carry our secrets to his ears. The pressure inside builds for weeks, until it is so palpable I can taste it on my tongue— metallic and biting. Like blood. The taste of anger.

I step back into the kitchen and lift the last frame from the floor. It's a photo of two teenagers wearing crowns. They've been named king and queen. I study the girl in the photo, my eyes gravitating to the things we have in common. Same pale white skin with a few copper freckles across the bridge of the nose. Same wide smile. I wonder how we're different. Her hair is vibrant red, where mine is a lighter, strawberry blonde. And what about the things you can't see? Like her capacity to forgive so much hurt. Do I carry that in my bones, too, like I do the shape of her jaw?

Instead of hanging this photo up, I lay it on the counter beside the roses.

She has to decide whether to put it back on the wall.

The last thing I do before it's time to usher my sisters

outside to the bus stop is reach past Mom to plug the phone in. This stupid, useless house phone. He told Mom and me that we could have cell phones last year. Then he remembered that cell phones call police and cost money, so we never got them. There's just this one phone, with a cord that does nothing to help us when he tears it out of the wall.

I slam my finger down on the receiver and hold the phone to my ear.

"Dial tone's back," I say.

Chapter Three

TO EVERYONE ELSE AT AUBURN HIGH, summer means freedom.

That's not the case for me.

At least here, I know what to expect. I know who I am. For the next eight hours, I know Campbell and Juniper are safe in their classes. I can pretend everything is normal. So when I step off the bus on our first day back and wave to the girls as it pulls away, I know they are thinking the same thing: *thank God summer is over.*

Sofia finds me before first period. She tears down the hall and throws her arms around me. "Leighton! You beautiful person, where have you been? We haven't talked in a week!"

"Sorry, Sof." *I've been in a domestic nightmare.* "I was . . . *way* behind on my summer reading. I spent the last few days catching up." We make our way through the crowded hall together, bumping into so many people that it becomes silly to keep apologizing. It's a stampede of wide-eyed freshmen, and we are caught in the fray.

"Well, me too. At least we could have suffered together," she says, her long dark hair bouncing in its perpetual cheer-leading ponytail. Sofia is the happiest person I know, and I'm not sure how, but even her features are happy. Her cheeks are low, round, and rosy. Her eyebrows arch dramatically, and she leaves them to grow naturally, adding to the drama. Her smile is a little off-balance—the right side of her mouth curls up higher. It makes her always look like she just stopped laughing a moment ago. And usually she did. After nights like last night, I'm so grateful she's my friend.

"So what do you have first period?"

Sofia unfolds her schedule and crinkles her nose. She holds the paper away from her body like it's contaminated. *"Physical Education."*

"Wow. That's unfortunate. You're gonna have to shower all over again."

"And have wet hair all day."

"The scheduling gods did not smile upon you."

Sofia groans, leaning her head on my shoulder. "What about you?"

I pull out my schedule to double-check.

"AP English."

"Oh good, you get to read about people killing each other for stupid reasons first thing every day."

"Still better than gym."

"Good point. Bummer that none of our classes overlap this semester."

"Seriously. But we have newspaper. And first dibs on assignments now that we're seniors. Do you still want sports? They better not give it to Chris just because he's a guy—"

Sofia stops walking so fast I bump into her. We've reached the large windows that face the soccer field.

"What the hell." Sofia doesn't swear much, and the "hell" comes out on a sigh, like she didn't mean to say it out loud.

Crows cover almost every inch of the field.

"Didn't you notice them earlier?" I ask.

"A few here and there, like usual. Nothing like this."

We pause at the windows, letting freshmen bump into us in their haste to beat second bell. Across the street is the football stadium, and I can make out small dark shapes filling the bleachers. The crows are in constant motion, taking off and landing, circling overhead. There must be thousands of them. And they've all decided to come here.

God knows why any creature would choose Auburn.

Especially one that can fly away.

Chapter Four

IT ISN'T UNTIL AFTER SECOND PERIOD that I have a chance to find my locker. It's not in the senior hall. I follow numbers down, rounding the corner into the junior hallway.

Warm.

Warmer.

Hot.

Great. I get to spend senior year banished to the juniors' hall. They must have run out of lockers for seniors. Which means no hanging out at the Senior Wall, which is literally just a *wall* that seniors alone get to stand at and lean against to talk between classes and yell at any lowerclassmen who get too close. Every year the senior class decorates the wall with a gigantic "CLASS OF" banner with the graduation year, and everyone writes curse words and smutty messages on it until the administration takes it down because it's too vulgar. One class didn't make it past homecoming.

All I really need out of senior year is a diploma, but I still feel a pang over missing out on another normal high school thing. I've already missed so much. Nights I've chosen to stay home because he was in a bad mood. Birthday parties I knew to never ask for.

I open my half-size locker and start to cram all my textbooks inside. I'm still trying to convince myself that Senior Wall is a dumb tradition anyway when someone grabs me from behind.

Well, doesn't grab. *Tickles*. My ribs.

"What the hell!" I yell, spinning.

"Oh shit." The hands are off and the person steps back. Liam McNamara is standing there, looking every bit like he knows he messed up. "I'm so sorry. I thought you were Lyla Jacobs."

"Who?"

"Lyla. She's a junior. Your hair looks a lot like hers. And she's my cheerleader."

"I didn't know they were considered property." I know what he means. Sofia's been doing this for a few years. But I want to let him squirm.

"No, they're not." He runs his hand over the top of his head. "I'm really screwing this up."

"Um, yeah," I say. I know Liam. I know *of* Liam, I should say. We move in different social circles. Or rather, he moves in a circle and I'm more of a solitary dot.

Liam McNamara: fellow senior, student council vice

president, member of the varsity football team. His super-
lative should be Most Likely to Score a Modeling Contract
While Running for Congress. Liam has always had a lot of
girlfriends and a lot of charm. But thanks to my home, I've
seen the flip side of the charming coin, and it isn't a prince.

"Lyla is *the* cheerleader, who I respect and do not consider
property in any way, shape, or form, who is paired with me
for the season. She'll, like, decorate my locker and make me
cookies and stuff."

I don't roll my eyes. I don't. But it takes a long, conscious
mental effort not to do so.

"Okay, well. It's fine. You just startled me."

"Yeah, I'm really sorry. Lyla is my friend. I swear I don't
go around touching strange girls. Not that you are *strange*,
I just mean—"

"It's okay, Liam. I'll see ya around."

"Well, actually, my locker is, uh—" He points to the
bottom half-locker that's under mine. Because of course.
Let's draw this awkwardness out for the whole year.

I move to the side, letting Liam crouch down at his locker.

"We should at least ask them to switch us. Wouldn't want
one of our star players to injure himself stooping over for
his books, would we?"

"Ah, thanks, but that wouldn't be very chivalrous of me.
Besides, it's just football."

"Did you say *just* football? In this town that's practically
blasphemous."

"Yeah. But there's not much else to do around here, and it'll look good on college apps." Our conversation has taken a surprising turn, and I try to quiet the surge of curiosity I feel. *Let's move along here.* But Liam doesn't move along. He stands at our shared locker space and leans against mine.

"We have first period together, right, Leighton?"

Leighton.

"Didn't know you knew my name, Liam. Let alone how to pronounce it."

"Leighton. Like Peyton. Like Peyton Manning. Easy enough to remember."

"Do I remind you of a professional football player?"

He laughs.

"No. You're a shrimp. You would literally get crushed on a football field. But seriously, there's, like, two hundred kids in our class. I know who you are."

"Just not from behind."

"I'm never gonna live that down, am I?"

"Probably not. But it's only been five minutes. Give it time."

"Leighton's a cool name," Liam says.

I pause while adjusting my bag.

"Thanks. It was a birthday present."

A dad joke. Seriously? But Liam laughs, and I soften a little. *Calm down, Leighton. Not everyone is out to get you.*

"So, Advanced Placement English. Should be a fun semester," I say, sarcasm infused in every syllable.

"Yeah, no kidding. Our summer reading was depressing.

But I liked *Beloved*. You headed this way?" Liam nods his head toward the senior hall. "We should get moving before the bell."

Liam takes my heavy calculus book and starts walking. It takes me a moment to realize he isn't stealing it but carrying it for me. I blink stupidly a few times before catching up.

"You liked *Beloved*? It was really sad."

"Sure, but it was important. Stories matter. Representation matters. Besides, it's better than reading *Romeo and Juliet* freshman year. Enough about rich white kids already."

I laugh. Liam is one of very few Black students in our school, and I'm caught off guard by his candor.

"Fair point," I say. "Didn't care for the romance?"

"That wasn't romance. That was idiocy. I don't know who said 'all is fair in love and war,' but I'm calling bull. When you love someone, you don't treat them like that. You don't end up dead."

I know we are talking about a book, but in my mind I hear the crack of the door hitting the wall last night. I see that same wall this morning, perfect, as though the plaster never broke. I remember how my eyes slipped past it as I hung up frames, like they were unwilling to accept the way our strange house erases his violence for him.

I've stopped walking, and when Liam notices, he stops, too. The air around me feels cold. I can't remember what was funny or cute or charming about our conversation.

"Can I have my book back?" I ask, my tone cool and crisp, as controlled as I can make it. I can't help it. The alternative to cold is crying, and I don't want to fall apart. Not here.

"Um, yeah, of course, Leighton," Liam says, handing my book back. "Is this about earlier? Cuz I'm really sorry . . ."

"I just forgot a notebook. I'll see you in class," I mutter, and I'm gone, walking down the hallway as fast as I can without getting called out for running. I try to ignore the burning throat and stinging eyes so they'll go away. Just act normal.

Normal.

Normal.

There.

The word has lost all meaning.

Chapter Five

IF THERE WAS EVER ANOTHER VERSION of Campbell Grace Barnes, I missed it. As far back as I can recall, she's been the serious one. I'm a reader, sure, but Cammy is a thinker. She thinks while she brushes her hair, her fingers ruthlessly detangling knots in the shiny, straight red strands. She thinks while she eats her cereal, one hand holding a spoon, the other one tapping against the table. A staccato beat to accompany her thoughts. She thinks when he yells, and when he throws things.

Most of the time, I have no clue what Campbell is thinking. I know her better than I know anyone, but her mind is the Mariana Trench, and there are depths I'll never see. And that's okay. She can contain the secrets of the universe and keep every last one to herself for all I care, as long as she's still a kid sometimes. That's all I want. And it's there when she leaves on her bicycle.

Campbell loves Mom, Juniper, me, and her bike, and I'm

not sure the bike would come fourth if she ranked us. She *covets* it. Every day after school, she is in the house only long enough to ditch her backpack, and then she's off, riding down Frederick Street, turning left at the corner. She goes to a richer neighborhood—one that almost passes for suburbia, though the houses still have a ton of space between them. She rides with her friends, zipping in and out of streets, ignoring helmet laws. Campbell on her bike is *not thinking*. And that is good for her.

On our fourth day of school, Campbell has already been gone a half hour when there is a knock at our door. I spring from the kitchen table, where I had been stress-reading some college brochures and wondering if I'd ever set foot on one of those ivy-covered campuses.

Mrs. Stieg is standing on our front porch. Mrs. Stieg is probably in her mid-seventies, and I don't know how long she's been a widow, but I never knew her husband. She is sweet and gray and grandmotherly. She likes to wave at us from her front porch when we walk to the bus stop. Mrs. Stieg likes roses, and they grow in abundance around her home every summer. Mrs. Stieg likes to ignore knocks at her door in the middle of the night.

"Can I help you?" I ask. I'm wondering where I get this compulsion to be polite to someone who couldn't bother to help me call the police. I miss what she says. Something about Campbell.

"Sorry?"

"My garden on the far side of my house. Your sister and her boys rode through it yesterday and ruined my Mister Lincolns."

Her boys. Campbell's bike-riding friends happen to be mostly boys. Mrs. Stieg likes to strongly imply her disapproval.

"Mister Lincoln?" I repeat.

"My roses. They destroyed a patch of roses."

"Oh. I'm sorry, Mrs. Stieg. That doesn't sound like Cammy."

Yes it does.

"I didn't think so, dear. It's those *boys* she spends her afternoons with. Shouldn't a girl her age have girlfriends?"

"I think a girl her age should just have friends, actually."

My rebuttal earns a stern look.

"I'm sorry for the flowers. Can we help fix them? I'll bring Campbell over first thing tomorrow, and we will clean up any mess."

Mrs. Stieg considers the peace offering, which I'm still not sure she deserves after the other night. I try to forgive it. Maybe she wasn't sure what she heard. Maybe she was scared.

"Very well. Seven a.m. You girls should bring some gloves."

We arrive at 7:15 the next day, holding gardening gloves we dug out of the garage and large coffee tumblers. Campbell isn't usually a coffee drinker, but an early Saturday playing with thorns warrants some caffeine.

When I confronted her about the garden mishap last night, she said it was an accident. Her friends biked home with her, and they were all going down the hill too fast to stop, so they crashed into a flower bush. She tugged up her shorts, showing me the thorn scrapes.

"Why would I bike into thorns *on purpose*, Leighton. It hurt."

I relented, unconvinced. Campbell was out on the roof when I went for help. She would have seen Mrs. Stieg's light turn on and then off again. If any thirteen-year-old in the world believed in vigilante justice, it would be Campbell Grace.

Whether the damage was done on purpose or not, we'll be spending the morning cleaning it up. We get our instructions from Mrs. Stieg and dive into the scramble of branches and wrecked flowers.

"You guys really demolished this thing," I say, tugging on a stubborn piece. Mrs. Stieg wants us to remove all the broken branches, and then she will see if the thing is salvageable. If it isn't, we owe her a bush. "Did you just run through it once?"

Campbell doesn't hear me—or at least, she pretends not to. She has her arms buried in the bush, and there are little lines of blood where the thorns have already gotten her.

"Why don't you go home and put on long sleeves? You're going to get shredded up."

"I'm fine."

"Whatever," I snap back. This is her mess. I'm just trying to help.

We work silently from then on, sweat and blood mixing on our arms and legs where the thorns nick us.

Why roses? Of all the flowers someone could obsess over, why choose one with a built-in defense system? It would be like trying to domesticate a garden full of Campbells—a constant battle, and one likely to draw blood.

We finally finish pulling apart the broken bush around nine and go get Mrs. Stieg for her evaluation. The bush does not look good. It is missing huge patches of branches. But she studies what is left, pushing and pulling at it. Testing its roots.

"It'll live," she says. "Though we'll have to wait and see how rough it looks next bloom."

Next bloom, meaning next year. I'll take the reprieve.

"Great, thank you, Mrs. Stieg."

I elbow Campbell.

"Thanks," she says, halfheartedly.

"And here," Mrs. Stieg says. "Take these home for your sweet mother." She hands me a freshly gathered bouquet of roses, from a non-trampled bush. They are bright yellow, and they smell even stronger than the Mister Lincolns did.

"Young lady," Mrs. Stieg says, facing Campbell. "Running wild around this town isn't going to get you very far. You have to respect your elders."

"I do," Campbell says, but I grind my teeth at the statement.

Not *all* elders deserve our respect.

"Did you girls know I was married for forty years?" Mrs. Stieg asks. I feel Campbell straighten beside me. It's subtle, but there's a tension there that wasn't a moment ago, and it's echoed in my own body.

"That's great," I mutter.

"My husband wasn't perfect, you know," Mrs. Stieg presses on. "Men aren't perfect. But it is their job to provide for their families, and that is stressful for them. Do you know what a woman's job is?"

Campbell's hands clench at her waist, and I fold my arms over my chest.

We know where this is going, and it has nothing to do with the roses or Cammy's bike or her friends that are boys, and everything to do with the other night. When I think of how scared we were, I feel like I could be sick. The combination of bile and the sweetness of roses is overwhelming.

"To support their husbands," continues Mrs. Stieg, unaware of how close I am to throwing up in her rose beds. "To forgive them. To *manage* that stress. And to do so privately. Without embarrassing them or causing a fuss. Do you girls understand?"

And this is when quiet, always-thinking Campbell decides to speak up.

"That's really fucking stupid, Mrs. Stieg."

She turns on her heel and marches across the road and into our home, slamming the door behind her.

Mrs. Stieg's mouth is open. She turns to me, and I know

she's waiting for my apology. Or maybe my *apologies*, plural.

I'm sorry for the noise.

I'm sorry for the disturbance.

I'm sorry for Campbell swearing at you, and I'm sorry I ever knocked on your door for help.

"Thanks for the roses," I offer instead, and follow Campbell home.

Part of me knows it's stupid. We've made an enemy where we needed a friend. But another part of me knows that Mrs. Stieg was never going to help us. Her generation was taught that appearances mattered most. That being a good wife is somehow better than being happy. Or safe.

Mom puts the yellow roses in a vase on a table at the bottom of the stairs, next to the wilted red ones our dad gave her earlier this week. They smell so strongly as they wither and die that I nearly gag every time I pass them. I smell the roses and think of women let down by other women. Women who are told their obedience is more important than their voice, not by their husbands, but by their mothers, their friends. Women willing to watch each other get hurt for the sake of image and tradition.

After a few days, I can't take it anymore, and I march the vases out to the trash cans and dump the flowers on top. I want to leave them there so Mrs. Stieg can see them in the garbage, but I don't. I bury them under a bag, and even the trash is a more welcome smell than the rotting sweetness of those flowers.

Chapter Six

ON MONDAY, WHEN WE WALK PAST Mrs. Stieg's home to get to our bus stop, something catches my attention. Beyond the crows lining her fence, in the far corner of her garden, another bush has been decimated. Not just broken like the first bush, but pulverized. All that's left is disturbed dirt and pieces of crimson petals, smashed branches . . . nothing is intact.

When I point it out to Campbell, she shrugs, but there's something there—something in Cam's big brown eyes that shine with pride—and I know that if I checked her bike right now, I'd find matching bits of crimson petals on the tires.

I don't check.

Chapter Seven

SOMETIMES IT FEELS LIKE I'M STANDING on a precipice, and there's nothing below to catch my fall.

When I feel like this, I reach for someone else's words to pull me back. To remind me that the world is bigger than my home. Bigger than Auburn. It's the best thing I inherited from Mom—her love of words. She loves classic literature and poetry, and every memory of my childhood smells like the stacks of paperbacks she'd stash all over the house. She made books our home in a way our house never was.

But now I can't stand the classics. She always said they were romantic, but someone always ends up brokenhearted or dead. Or brokenhearted and *then* dead. As though tragedy is the only ending that has meaning.

These days, I'll take journalism over literature. I'll take truth over grief. Leave romance at the door, I'm a newspaper girl.

But I still have to take lit class, and we are learning *Tess of the d'Urbervilles*, so I'm not done with the tragedies quite yet. I slip into class early, flipping through the chapters we were supposed to review this weekend. When Liam enters the room, we make eye contact, and he nods at me.

I quickly look down at my book.

But when he sits at the back of the room, I can't help glancing at him. Naturally, Liam sits with the most popular kids, but in AP English it's a special subset. The *very smart* populars. They sit with their desk pushed up to their boyfriend or girlfriend, somehow always just at the periphery of following the rules. Alexis and Brody are on-again, off-again, but today their desks are pressed tight, and his arm is wrapped around her shoulders. They are both tall and blond and leggy and athletic. People always stereotype popular teens as dumb, but they're just teens with better-than-average social skills. Why stop at homecoming court when they can have Harvard? Especially when there's nothing that would keep them from actually *going*.

On the other side of Brody is Amelia. She is *definitely* Harvard material. She has perfect teeth and parents who are surgeons, and she can probably quote both Austen and the latest *Glamour* magazine. The truth is, I've always been a little envious of Amelia. It seems like she's friends with everyone. She's approachable. Even if I wanted to be warm, inviting, I wouldn't know how to untangle myself from all the barbed wire I've placed around me. It's in the set of my jaw. The way my shoulders turn away from people. "Proceed with Caution" screams my body language, and it's the only language I know anymore.

When my gaze returns to Liam, his desk is like an island. I guess he isn't really a lone wolf when he's the kind of guy who perpetually has a girlfriend, but somehow he still looks alone. Set apart. Like he has a little buffer around him. I think by senior year in such a small town, our social interactions are almost on autopilot. It's been a long time since any of us has looked up. Or at least that's true for me. Which is why I probably wouldn't be noticing Liam if he hadn't mistaken me for Lyla Jacobs.

Mrs. Riley launches into our *Tess* lesson, and I try to stop thinking about Liam and focus on her. Mrs. Riley teaches with Ms. Frizzle–level enthusiasm. She's eccentric and loud. She runs the newspaper, too, so I'm used to her antics, but it feels a little offbeat when we are discussing gender inequality in the nineteenth century.

"The social commentary is considered way ahead of its time, especially when it comes to women. Any thoughts on this?" Mrs. Riley asks.

"What was he, like, a feminist? Can guys even be feminists?" Brody asks. He's reclining in his seat now, and manspreading so hard that his leg blocks the whole aisle between desks.

He says *feminist* like it's a dirty word.

"How do you define feminism, Brody?" Mrs. Riley asks.

"Uh, frigid bitch—I mean—chicks in pink hats?" Brody says, and chuckles break out throughout the room. I mess with my copy of *Tess*, folding the corners of pages like I'll need them for something. If Mrs. Riley asks, I'll tell her I was marking every time some pompous, entitled ass tried to ruin Tess's life.

"Anyone else?" Mrs. Riley opens the question up to the room. "Leighton?"

"Sure, ask the ice queen about feminism," Brody mutters.

My cool, collected exterior precedes me. *Ice queen*. Last year, I turned Brody down for junior prom, and he's been making snide comments ever since about me being too cold for any guy to thaw out. He didn't just ask me out, he *promposed*, getting down on one knee in the lunchroom and giving me a box that held the dance ticket. And I said no. In front of everyone. Public rejection didn't sit well with Brody, and he's called me an ice queen ever since.

"Guys can be feminists," I say, and thirty sets of eyes turn in my direction. I'm feeling sharp around my edges today. "But probably only the more evolved ones."

"Like me," Liam says. "I'm a feminist."

"Great," Mrs. Riley says. "Define it."

He falters. "Uhh. Wage gap. Wonder Woman. Bra burning?"

"Oh God, please stop," I say.

"Thank you," Liam says. "That was all I had."

"You probably *are* a feminist, though. It just means you think women deserve equal rights. It's not that complicated or scary. The hats aren't mandatory," I say.

"Sounds stupid," Brody says.

"What's stupid is thinking a girl is obligated to go out with you just because you asked her."

"Retract your claws, kitty cat, this isn't a protest," Brody says, puckering his lips and blowing me a kiss.

"Go to hell, Brody," I snap.

"All right, that's enough," Mrs. Riley says. "Let's get back to *Tess*."

The conversation veers back into the nineteenth century, but there's still some commotion in the back of the room. "Leave her alone," Liam says, kicking at Brody's outstretched leg so that he pulls it back under the desk.

Liam.

I steal one more glance.

Something about him keeps drawing me in, curiosity outweighing my typical caution. Liam is self-assured, but it doesn't come off as an ego trip like it does with most guys our age. He's cute, but not a jerk about it. His brown skin is smooth, his complexion perfect. But it's the less obvious things about him I'm starting to appreciate. Like how his jawline is so sharp, but when he smiles his whole face softens. Like how he smiles a lot. Like how his eyebrows are full and he uses them to his advantage, quirking them up, furrowing them down. His expressions are funny and warm, and I feel like they would make anyone want to be his friend. And I like his eyes, too. They're kind.

I like that he calls himself a feminist and cares about representation in books. Liam's dad is white, and his mom is Black. His dad grew up in Auburn, which means he knows everyone, and his mom is the assistant principal at the middle school, which means everyone knows her. Liam is far from a stranger to me, even if we've never really talked before. There are no strangers in a town this small.

I even landed in Mrs. McNamara's office a few times when I was in eighth grade. My grades were slipping, almost in direct correlation to the first few failures of Dad's business—and the resulting anger we saw at home. But Liam's mom didn't lecture me or make me feel bad because of my grades, she just encouraged me to focus on school because it *was the path to any future I desired*. Her words stuck with me. An illuminated path was what I needed. The next semester I got a 4.0. I couldn't control what was going on at home, but if I worked hard enough, I could control my grades. My future.

The McNamara family moved to Auburn from Philadelphia when the elder Mr. McNamara retired from his law practice, and Liam's dad took over. I remember thinking that Liam and I had that in common—being stuck here because of our grandfathers' businesses. But it was more complicated than that for Liam, coming to a town with so few people of color. On Liam's first day at Auburn Elementary, we were all sitting at a long lunch table. I was at the far end, book open in front of me, but Liam, the new kid, was right in the middle, the center of attention. He was outgoing and funny, and everyone liked him and wanted to sit near him. He'd just told a joke that even made me crack a smile and put down my book and wonder about this new boy who had everyone laughing so hard.

Then another kid in our class said that he had a joke, too. But when he said it, it wasn't funny. It was racist.

When I looked at Liam, I saw this moment of hesitation. I think he was waiting to see if anyone else was going to speak up.

"Dumb joke," nine-year-old Liam said. "I've got a better one." Within moments he had the entire table laughing again. But I've always felt ashamed of that moment. Of everyone's silence. Of mine.

And looking at Liam now, I wonder how many things like that have happened since. The comments made, and the quiet that follows. I wonder if he ever hates Auburn, too. It's hard to reconcile because he's one of the most popular kids in school, but that doesn't change what this town is like. Here they label ignorance as tradition and carry on as though they've earned the right to be cruel.

Chapter Eight

WHEN IT STARTS, I AM IN my room. My calculus book is open, but I haven't finished a single problem when the voices rise from downstairs. I'd hoped to get my homework done before it began, but there's been a ball of lead in my stomach all evening just from *knowing* it was coming. It's been building all week: he gets quieter before he erupts. Tonight, the house felt as somber and soft as a graveyard, and I've been sitting for two hours in dread with my legs curled beneath me, listening as voices turn angry. My pencil is still sharp where I abandoned it on my desk.

It's when the voices suddenly go quiet that I rise from my desk. Some perversion of fear that feels like curiosity wins, and I pull open my door an infinitesimal degree. A perfect, practiced angle—just enough to listen, stopping before it creaks.

I know why people open doors and check darkened basements in horror films. Why they look for the monster. It's because sometimes it's the anticipation that hurts the most. So much that I want to do some awful, stupid thing to piss him off and just *make it start*, because if it starts, then it can end. Because somehow right after is when I feel safest. A few hours of grace. Of not feeling like my nerves have been tugged line by line from my body and replaced with hot white electric wires, burning me from the inside out.

I move to my bedroom window and pull up the blinds. He's in the yard now, carrying a trash bag to the can outside. His truck is parked out front—a massive thing that he uses for work. The logo pressed to the side of the truck reads "BARNES CONSTRUCTION, *family owned & operated for more than 50 years.*"

The sign implies that he wanted his father's business, but that isn't true. My father wanted to leave Auburn, to go play football at state college. He had a full scholarship. He dreamed of going pro. And perhaps he could have done all of that if he hadn't messed up his knee in his second-to-last game senior year. They were *this close* to a state championship. Unheard of in a school district like ours. The town still talks about it. His greatest failure a local legend. The punch line for every drunk joke at the bar.

He takes pride in that truck, though. It's cherry red, and he keeps it shiny and clean all year. It's probably a beautiful truck to anyone who cares. I don't. Not when the business is failing and there's no food in the fridge and we aren't sure if we'll be able to fill the oil tank when it gets cold in a few weeks.

Right now, it is not a beautiful truck by anyone's standard. It is covered from headlight to bumper in crow shit. I want to find it funny, but I know who will face the consequences for this act of defiance, and it isn't the birds. Mom's car is out there, too, parked just behind the truck, but it's clean.

He sees the filthy truck. I can almost feel his anger, the tension pulsing in his arms. He lifts the trash bag and throws it at the tree. It catches a few branches as it falls back to earth, and they tear at the bag's underbelly, spilling its garbage guts as it descends. His rage isn't spent, though, so he reaches for another trash bag, and another after that. Some of the crows take flight. Most of them ignore him, which only fuels his rage. The drapes move aside in Mrs. Stieg's window across the street. *Curiosity killed the . . .*

Joe lands on my windowsill. I tap on the glass softly in greeting. *Hello, Joe.*

Downstairs, the front door slams. He finally ran out of anger. Or bags. Our garbage hangs in the branches of our tree, on full display. It's like our own special variation of Christmas ornaments. I spy with my little eye a banana peel, a cigarette carton, the end of a loaf of bread that no one ever seems to want. Used tissues abound, and the ones caught in the trees almost look like little doves.

I tap the glass again. *Why were you up here the other night,*

Joe? Tap, tap, tap. *Why do you watch us?* Tap, tap. *Can you help us?* TAP.

A silver line appears on the glass. I've broken it. I tap again, and again, and the line grows, stretching up, slowly, a little with each tap, until it branches into three. Three little slivers of air, searching for the path of least resistance in the glass. Tap. Tap.

The silver lines hit the pane. I press my finger to the line and follow it up.

Sssht. I hiss a sharp intake of breath and shove my cut finger into my mouth. I taste the metal in my blood and the salt on my skin. When I look up, I can't find the crack in the glass, even when I shift side to side, thinking a different angle will reveal the thin lines again. It's gone. Or fixed, I guess. Just like the wall downstairs.

I want to see it again.

I slip out of my room. As I pass the girls' door, it opens, and my sisters' soft faces appear.

"I'm gonna check on Mom," I tell them. "Why don't you two go sit in my bed."

Downstairs in the living room, I cross to the entertainment center. The voices in the kitchen are agitated but muffled by the sound of running water in the sink. I can't hear what they're saying.

I reach the wall where the plaster broke and run my hand over its surface. Smooth. Unmarred. No sign of fresh paint.

It's like it never broke.

The sound of shattering glass makes me jump. I run into the kitchen. Mom had been washing dishes, and one must have slipped from her hand. There are shards of glass all over the floor. She gets the dustpan and brush.

"What a mess," he says, walking around the perimeter of broken glass. "What a fucking mess."

"It's just broken glass," says Mom as she kneels, sweeping up the pieces.

It was the wrong thing to say.

"Just broken glass? It's everywhere. So I guess we'll just step on glass every time we have to use the sink. I guess this doesn't matter, either." He reaches into the sink for another glass and throws it to the floor next to Mom. It shatters into crystals that reflect the light in a million directions. If it were anything else, I'd say it looks beautiful.

I step back into the living room as he reaches for another. And another.

There are bits of glass flying everywhere, and Mom recoils, pulling her hands in to her chest. A piece must have hit her.

"Stop it!" I yell at him from the living room, and he whirls.

He reaches down and grabs Mom's arm, hauling her to her feet.

"Leave her alone," I say, running into the room and pulling at his hand where it's squeezing her arm so tight.

"Leighton, don't," Mom says.

He releases her suddenly, stepping away.

"Yeah, well, I guess that makes me the fucking bad guy again." He reaches for his wallet, keys, gun. It's only in his hand a moment, the distance from the top of the refrigerator to the waistband of his jeans, but I can't breathe until it's away.

"I'm going to the car wash," he says. "Those goddamn birds made a mess of the truck."

He is gone a moment later, truck engine revving as he pulls away.

"You okay?" I ask Mom. She nods quietly and starts to clean up the glass again. I hop onto the kitchen counter and put my feet in the sink. I run the warm water, washing out the slivers of glass stuck in the soft bottoms of my feet. When she's done cleaning the floor, my mom wordlessly gets tweezers and checks me, finding two more pieces of glass embedded in my skin.

"He didn't used to be like this," she says as she squeezes the bottom of my foot, trying to get an edge of the glass shard to stick out enough for her to catch it with the tweezers.

I think Mom wants us to walk on the proverbial eggshells. But I've never been good with subtlety. I want to throw the eggs at the walls and let them smash to bits. I want the house to look as terrible as it feels on days when we get home and he's waiting for us with violence in his eyes. I've often wondered, Does he need us here? A tree falls in the woods. . . .

Where would his rage go with no one to witness it?

Because I feel like I'm always here when the tree falls, and I don't just hear it, I'm crushed by it. Branches snap my ribs. Leaves fill my nose and mouth until I choke. I hear the tree groan and rumble as it transforms into a monster.

Mom finally gets the last piece of glass out of my foot.

"I know he wasn't always like this, Mom. I remember. But he's like this now."

I scoot off the counter and wobble upstairs on the sides of my feet, careful not to get blood on the carpets.

To be honest, I think he'd yell even if we weren't here.

He just likes it better when we are.

AUBURN, PENNSYLVANIA
SEPTEMBER 15

CROW POPULATION:
16,980

Chapter Nine

LIAM MCNAMARA FINDS ME AT LUNCH. He folds his long body into the booth across from me, sitting next to Sofia.

"How goes it, ladies?" Liam asks, acting as though this behavior is perfectly normal.

Sofia meets my eyes across the table, and they narrow. I've been keeping something from her, and the jig is up.

"Tater tots," I say, pushing my tray away. "It goes *cold tater tots*, Liam."

"Yum," he says, snatching two off the plate. "I don't mind them cold."

"Cold like an ice queen?" I ask.

Liam looks up from the tray.

"Brody is an ass. And I told him exactly that after class yesterday."

"Yeah, he is." I pull out my newspaper binder and flip through it.

"Seriously, and I've never laughed at the stupid ice queen

thing." I stop flipping and look up, trying to figure out how serious he is right now.

"Hey there, remember me?" Sofia asks, waving a hand in front of my face. "What happened?"

"Brody Thompson was being a jerk in lit class," Liam says.

"Oh, well. That's hardly news to anyone." Sofia rolls her eyes.

"Thank you for saying something to Brody." I don't speak up in class much, and I haven't spoken to Brody since I turned him down, so it was really nice to have support yesterday.

"No problem," he says. "So . . . wanna go out with me sometime?"

Sofia chokes a little on her chocolate milk.

"Um, sorry, but no thank you."

"Wow," Liam says. "You aren't even gonna think about it."

Just for a moment, I imagine bringing Liam to my house. A wave of nausea hits me.

"I don't see the point of dating right now."

"Wait, you don't date *at all*?"

"I have to focus on getting into college."

As Liam and I talk, I try to ignore the wild gestures that Sofia is making across the table. Thank God Liam is doing this thing where he focuses only on me. Forget the charm, or how damn funny he is, or those kind eyes. It's his attentiveness that I find nice. So different. He's really looking at me and listening to what I say.

That's what makes me want to say yes.

"There's no chance you aren't getting into college, Leighton. Don't you have, like, perfect grades? You're super smart."

The blunt compliment surprises me.

"It could be fun," Liam adds.

I fiddle with the bracelet on my arm—a leather cuff bracelet with my initials on it. Campbell and Juniper each have one, too. Our grandpa made them for us just before we lost him, a few years ago. It reminds me of him, and my sisters.

But then my thoughts inevitably shift to our house, and I turn my happy little heart back into stone.

"I don't have time for fun. I have homework to do." That's true, at least. Senior year, advanced placement classes, college applications, newspaper. How can anyone have a social life when we have six hours of homework every night?

"You can just tell me I'm not your type," Liam says. "I can take it."

"You aren't my type, Liam," I say.

Liam blinks a few times, then lets out a long, low whistle. His perfectly pursed lips almost make me take back my rejection.

"Wow. That, uh, that cut me deep, Barnes. Cut me real deep." He sighs and leans forward, resting his forehead on his hands on the lunch table.

"Liam?" I ask, and nod at Sofia, who reaches over to shake him a bit. Sofia can't stop giggling, and it's taking everything I've got to not cave in and laugh, too. Liam sits up again, stone-faced and refusing to break his character of heartbroken teen. I give him my best I'm-not-falling-for-your-games look.

"Gotta respect your decision. Might take me years to get over this moment, though, Barnes. Decades. I will pine. I won't go full Romeo, but I'm thinking the word *catatonic* might apply here," Liam says as he slides out of the booth.

"You are ridiculous," I say, but my reproach is weak coming through the gigantic smile on my face.

"All right," Sofia says. "Now please go away so we can talk about you and I can convince this amazing, stupid girl to go out with you."

"There's hope?" Liam says. "I'll take it. See ya in English class, Barnes."

He grabs one last cold tater tot, tossing it in the air and catching it in his mouth as he walks away.

"The way he calls you by your last name makes me feel like I'm intruding on something . . . intimate."

"Ew, Sofia. Don't say *intimate*."

"Whatever. It's true. Do you hear the way he says your name? He likes you, Leighton."

Dammit.

Every interaction with him is so fun. And light. I feel happier talking to him at our lockers than in any other part of my day. And in a parallel universe, I would recognize this for what it is: I have a colossal crush on Liam. Maybe in that universe we could date. But in this one, no such luck. I have a countdown. A deadline. Less than a year to get things fixed at home so that Campbell and Juniper are safe. Or I can't go.

The last thing in the world I need is to set myself up for one more heartbreak. Because in my living room there is a framed photo of Auburn High's Homecoming King and Queen from nineteen years ago, and it's a constant reminder of what *ever after* really looks like. Maybe classic lit had it right all along, and the romances just haven't gotten to the real end of the story yet.

If you wait long enough, all hearts get broken.

Chapter Ten

THE CROWS DON'T STOP COMING. I feel their shining eyes watching us wherever we go. And every day, the eyes multiply by two and two and two, until the twos form thousands. They perch on fences. They cling to trees. They watch from rain gutters and church steeples and broken weather vanes spinning on barns. The rusted roosters turn not with the wind, but with the inconsistent, shifting weight of feathers.

One afternoon they arrive like a black cloud over Auburn, thousands at once.

I hear the complaints whispered everywhere I go—in the grocery store line, and by the secretaries in the school office. *A mess. A nuisance. Why don't they leave?* And maybe it's because we already had Joe, the strangeness of the bird a constant presence in our lives, but I find that I like the birds. I like their noise and their watchful eyes. I like the way they pay attention to the people of Auburn.

The first time I noticed Joe was two years ago this autumn;

I remember because we'd just buried Grandpa, and even though our view hadn't changed, everything felt different. We used to stay with my grandparents all the time. Their old farmhouse was our second home, our safe retreat from my father's anger. It always worked in a cycle—the rage, the apologies, a few weeks or sometimes just days of peace, and then the buildup would begin again. And Mom was usually good at reading those signs, and casually suggesting we go stay with her parents for a night or two. But occasionally even she missed the signs, and we wouldn't know the storm was coming until it was on top of us and Mom was ushering us out to her car and bundling us into car seats and showing up at my grandparents' house in the dark of the night. Sometimes we would arrive crying and still scared, but most of my memories of our huddled walk into their home are marked by silence. A quiet understanding among the adults, and a familiar acceptance for us girls. Besides, by the time we got there, we were feeling safe.

But then two years ago a heart attack wrecked that carefully orchestrated balance. Grandpa was gone, and Nana slipped fast. Without Grandpa there filling in the gaps, we realized that Nana wasn't doing very well on her own. So their house was sold to pay for an apartment in assisted living. I begged Mom to leave him then. To move us in with Nana, so we could take care of her.

When she refused, we didn't speak for a month.

We visit Nana every few weeks, but I like to supplement those visits, so sometimes I tell Mom I'm staying late after school, and I wait on the corner for a bus that takes me thirty minutes to the neighboring town of Lincoln, where Nana's apartment is. Today everything is gray outside the bus window: the clouds overhead, the building she lives in. There is a flash of black and gray on the building's sign. Joe. It isn't the first time he's followed me here.

I step from gray into yellow. The walls are goldenrod, and in the waiting room is an ancient sofa covered in lemons, faded and soft on their edges where the fabric has been worn. I sign in, and the receptionist waves me up, recognizing me.

Nana greets me with a long hug. "Leighton! What a lovely surprise. It's been weeks since you last visited."

"Hi, Nana. I'm sorry. School started."

"Don't you dare apologize. Let's have tea. When's your bus?"

I put her kettle on for tea and crack her windows open for fresh air.

"An hour," I say, and settle on the chair across from her. Some days she's every ounce the woman I've always known, and today is one of those days. Her mind sharp and her memory untouched. "Mom doesn't know today."

She nods her understanding. She knows I sneak here.

"The girls?" she asks.

"The same," I say.

"Your mom?"

"The same," I say, but my voice catches. It's all the same. Actually, that's not true anymore; it's worse.

I don't tell Nana that part.

"Tell me about school," she says, and our chat is easy and warm. There's a lot I miss about their old farmhouse and, of course, Grandpa, but these last two years have brought Nana and me closer, too. There's a softness in our understanding of things at home and my parents. I don't have to be guarded in how I speak. It's how I imagine talking to Mom would feel if we didn't have my father like a wedge between us, making us dance around the most crucial thing, the thing we can't talk about. But with Nana, there are no topics to avoid.

Our hour goes too fast.

I clean our mugs and straighten her kitchenette. I close her windows. It's just a sampling of what we had at her old home, but the warmth is the same. The smells. A hint of her favorite perfume on everything.

"Things will get better, Leighton," she says as she hugs me goodbye.

"I know," I say. It's an easy lie for both of us.

"Before your grandpa passed, I used to pray to God every night that you girls would stay with us. Where you would be safe."

"And after Grandpa died? Did you stop praying?"

"I started praying to your grandpa instead. I'm hoping he has some pull up there. I keep waiting for some message from him."

"I'll look for a message, too."

"You do that, dear."

And I do. On the walk to the bus stop, and on the ride home.

There is one highway into Auburn. When we cross into the town limits, there is a large green sign that reads, "Welcome to Auburn, Pennsylvania. Population: 2,378." And at the bottom of the sign, the town's slogan: Auburn Born, Auburn Proud.

I keep looking for a message from Grandpa, some hint of that feeling I always got when I stepped into their home. That things would be okay.

But when I get off the bus and look around Auburn, there's nothing but crows.

Chapter Eleven

I THINK I LOVE BRAND-NEW NOTEBOOKS for the same reason people love babies. For a moment in time, they are *perfect*. Unblemished. Pure potential.

Then we make it our job in life to ruin them.

We add to them, encumber them. Erase and try again, never quite able to fully obliterate the original mark. We fill them up with our words and wishes and desires. It is an imperfect, imprecise process, and we don't always get it right.

I got what I wanted for the newspaper this year: my own column. But our first issue will be published online at the end of the week, and I haven't figured out a theme yet. Sofia has sports, so she's been busy cheerleading and covering football games. Our team is the high school equivalent of a Greek tragedy every week. Everyone is hoping for a better ending than what is delivered to them, yet they keep coming back for more. You wouldn't know they lose by how this town loves the game, though. We almost won state *once* nineteen years ago, and our football players are still treated like All-American Gods.

I think of Liam McNamara.

And then I deliberately *don't* think of him.

I tap my ultra-sharpened pencil on the blank page in front of me. The tip breaks off. I side-eye the pencil sharpener on the other side of the room. No hurry, brain. No important things to write. No looming deadline. I drop the pencil and hit the power button on my computer's monitor instead—our newspaper is operating on some ancient behemoth desktops—and wait for it to power up. My desk faces the windows, and outside are the baseball fields. They are covered in crows. I can't hear them from in here, but I see their open beaks, and I know they are cawing. The crows are always cawing.

Sofia sits on my desk.

"Hey," she starts. "Were you ever gonna tell me that you and Liam are a thing?"

"We aren't a thing," I protest, but Sofia holds up her hand.

"I didn't say what kind of thing, but you most certainly are a thing, because that at lunch yesterday was not a nothing."

"Sorry, Sofia . . ." I stand and stretch. Maybe movement will help me figure out this column. "What are you working on?"

"Don't change the subject," she says. "What is going on with you and Liam?"

"We've just been talking—" I pause while Sofia squeals. I smile. Leighton alone would put the whole Liam thing in a tiny box and not open it until later, if at all. Leighton alone doesn't have time to think about a guy when she has an article due. She has a portfolio to round out if she wants to get into one of the top journalism schools in the country. Acceptance to college—and escape from this town—depends on that tried-and-true Leighton focus. No distractions.

But Leighton with Sofia is different. A little less intense. A little more *seventeen*. This Leighton opens the box, and peers inside. What *is* going on with Liam?

"Our lockers are on top of each other," I explain.

"Dirty," Sofia says.

I raise my eyebrows. I'll turn this car around.

"Sorry. Go on," Sofia says.

"So we started talking between classes, and we have lit together, and, I don't know, he's so smart. Did you know how smart he is?" I circle my desk while we talk. I walk over and crack the window. Now I hear the crows. The cawing is louder than I expected.

"It's finally happened," Sofia says. She sighs behind me.

"What has?" I ask over the sound of the birds.

"My little Layyyton has a guy!"

"I don't!" I say.

"Only because you haven't said yes, yet. Which you will."

"I won't."

"Loooooovebirds," Sofia serenades as she retreats to her own desk, her mission complete. Who needs instruments of torture to get information when you could just send in Sofia Roman? She could make anyone sing, even a raspy, mangy old—

There it is. An idea for my column blooms in my mind, taking shape quickly. I'm going to write about the crows. They don't seem to be going anywhere, and their numbers have already been newsworthy. Our local news ran a segment on them last week. I could pick up where it left off, following the numbers, interviewing a bird expert. Maybe I can even figure out what the hell they're doing here.

While I wait to pitch Mrs. Riley my column idea, I scan the news bulletin board that hangs on the wall. All things Auburn and anything potentially newsworthy goes up here. A pink flyer pinned to the corner of the board catches my eye. "Scholarship" is in bold letters across the top of the page.

Auburn Township Senior Scholarship Essay Contest. Shit. The scholarship is $5,000.

My dad wants me to go to state college. It's where he would have been if he hadn't lost his football scholarship. It's where Mom would have been if she hadn't decided to stay here with Dad when he proposed. But I hate it. Maybe I could have liked it if I'd found it organically, but they've been pushing this school since I was in diapers. I want to get out of rural Pennsylvania. I want to live in a city. And study journalism at one of the best schools for it: New York University.

We'll never have the money for it. If I do get in, it'll be on scholarships and loans. Which means every little bit of money I can put toward it will help.

I scan down the flyer. "Submit two thousand words answering the following prompt: What does *Auburn born, Auburn proud* mean to you?"

Chapter Twelve

IN SCHOOL WE ARE TAUGHT TO begin our papers with a thesis statement.

I like the logic of it. The structure. I write one sentence, and every word thereafter must support that claim. I never could get lost in poetry, the way it can't seem to follow rules. Mom likes that about it. The sentence fragments and the way it shrugs off proper grammar like an ill-fitting coat. The way words are felt, until that's all that's left. No reason. No logic. Not even self-preservation. Mom's thesis statement became, "My life has meaning because he is in it." And now every move she makes supports that claim.

I refuse to write in feelings. Journalists seek the truth. They use proper grammar and sentence structure and some goddamn facts.

But tonight, when I sit down to do my homework for lit class, I don't begin with a thesis statement for my *Tess* paper. I begin with one for me: *I will leave Auburn and go to college.*

Now everything I do must support that claim.

Like writing the winning essay for Auburn's scholarship contest.

Chapter Thirteen

AT HALF PAST THREE IN THE morning, the door to my bedroom creaks, and I'm wide awake the same instant, blood coursing hard into my heart as fear floods my veins.

It was a nightmare. It wasn't real. His gun isn't out. The girls are safe. Mom is okay. I try to slow my breathing.

Light from the hallway filters in, casting beams across my carpet.

"Leighton?" The shape in my doorway is small and slight. Juniper.

"Yeah, babe?" I ask. My voice shakes, and I clear my throat to cover it. The rush of adrenaline has left me jittery.

"They're fighting. Can I sleep with you?"

"Course," I say, scooting over. With the door open, I can hear it, too. Not all-out yelling, but agitated voices. The foundation of a bad night is there.

Juniper runs through the dark room and dives into bed. I'm about to ask her where Campbell is when another shadow crosses my carpet. She closes the door behind her. The voices are subdued to a dull murmur, but now that I'm awake, the muffled sound irritates me, like having a song playing with the volume turned down low.

"Want to go back to sleep?" I ask.

"Too awake," Juniper says. Her eyes always make her seem older than she is, but her detached voice in the dark reminds me that she is so little.

"Then let's play a game instead," I say.

"Anywhere But Here," Juniper says.

Campbell sighs heavily and turns away from me. I elbow her, a little harder than I mean to.

"Play with us," I tell her. I need her. She's my partner in this—in keeping Juniper distracted.

A softer sigh this time, and she turns around.

"Okay," I whisper. I run my fingers over the seams of the dragonfly quilt Nana made me, comforted by the texture. In the dark, their blue wings look black, and they remind me of the crows.

I wrap an arm around each of my sisters, one settling toward me, the other ever so slightly resistant. Juniper can still be little, and I have college to look forward to. But Campbell is trapped. And she's old enough to know it and be angry.

"The Galápagos Islands," I begin. "There are turtles a hundred and fifty years old. The sun dries their shells after it rains. Soft waves hit the pebbled beaches."

I don't actually know what the beaches of the Galápagos are like—rocky, sandy, pebbled? But that's all right. Anywhere But Here is about escape, not accuracy. "Huge red flowers, bigger than your head, bloom in the forest."

The house rumbles under us as he runs across the floor downstairs. My mind plays its favorite game: Worst-Case Scenario. What if he's running toward her? What if he hurts her?

"London," Campbell says. Her tone could cut a wire. "We pass Big Ben and the Tower of London. We see churches older than the United States of America. We drink tea, and then we take a ride on one of those double-decker buses."

Something crashes downstairs. The girls jump in my arms, and a small sound catches in Juniper's throat. Like for an instant she wanted to scream, before she remembered there's no point. That it could even make things worse. Bring him upstairs.

"This isn't working," Campbell says.

"Shadows?" I ask. But they are already climbing out of bed, moving to our grandmother's armoire. It was the only thing I wanted from their house when it sold. It's absurdly big in this little room, but I love it.

Some nights we take our time before opening the doors, pretending that we will discover a pathway to Narnia. This isn't one of those nights.

We squeeze inside, and I reach for the kerosene lantern that I have stashed behind an old box of books. I leave the door partially open to let clean air in and carbon monoxide out. The lantern was Grandpa's and looks like it survived an actual war, but it works well, and it's lasted us a lot of nights like this. My gestures in the dark have been rehearsed a dozen times before. My fingers close on a lighter that I keep hidden in a shoe. I turn the dial on the lantern to lower the wick into the vase of kerosene.

Tiny space, lots of books for kindling, small children, and flammable liquid.

I really do have all the great ideas.

But when I light the lantern, I'm greeted by two tired but eager pairs of eyes.

A warm, familiar glow fills the closet. Now it's an adventure. There's a twinkle in Juniper's eyes. The smallest hint of a smile tugging the end of Campbell's mouth. We are explorers camping on a mountain. We are astronauts, and we've just landed on another planet. Any sounds of the house are gone, masked by door after door we've put up to keep them out. Masked by our sheer, stark will to not listen to them any longer.

"All right," I say as we crouch down in the armoire, folding limbs over each other until we find some semblance of comfort. "I'm ready. What've you got?"

"A horse," Juniper says.

I think for a moment, then place my palms together with two fingers extended out to form a nose. My thumbs make ears, and the silhouette of a horse appears on the wall. Juniper giggles softly.

"That's pretty good, Leighton," Junie says.

"How about a cat?" Campbell asks. "But not just a head and ears. The whole animal."

I sigh. Some people might say that midnight kerosene-lantern shadow puppets in a tiny space as we hide would be enough of a challenge, but not my sisters. They try to stump me with increasingly complicated requests.

I put my arms lengthwise against each other, one hand up and one down. I extend two fingers on top for ears and one on the bottom for a tail.

A black cat sits on the wall, twitching.

"Here," Juniper says, reaching out. She gives the cat some whiskers, too.

"No helping," Cammy says. "That's against the rules."

"There are no rules, Campbell; the game is made up," I say.

"Just because they aren't written down in a set of game instructions doesn't mean they don't exist."

"I wasn't helping," Juniper says. "I was impressizing."

"Improvising," I say.

"Improvising," Junie says.

Juniper and I give Campbell our saddest faces.

"Okay, okay, I like the whiskers," Cam relents.

I play the game for nearly an hour, until finally my request for another shadow challenge is met with silence. They are asleep. I consider moving them, but I would wake them up untangling our arms and legs. Besides, my arms are tired from so many shadows.

Dad taught me this game, when Campbell was still a baby and Mom was busy with her at night. He'd use a flashlight propped on the table by my bed and show me how to twist my fingers until a picture formed on the ceiling above us.

But that was a long time ago.

Tonight I make one last shadow. The head of a crow, its sharp beak formed by the tips of my nails. Then I twist my hands together and make the shape of a bird flapping its wings, rising. Another bird joins the first, a second small shadow on the wall. And then a third shadow bird flies with the others. I lie there in the dimly lit space, too warm thanks to the hot lamp and hot bodies, waiting for another noise from downstairs.

I let my hands fall to my sides, but the birds go on. Flap, flap, soar. Flap, flap, soar. They cross the wall of the armoire, back and forth, pulling me toward sleep. Lulling me into forgetting why we are hiding. I turn the dial on the lantern, lifting the wick from the oil, and blow out the flame. I keep my eyes open in the pitch-black, fighting sleep, and losing fast. Now everything is one shadow, and this shadow takes the shape of a closet. This closet takes the shape of a sanctuary. This sanctuary takes the shape of three girls who are flapping their wings but going nowhere.

AUBURN, PENNSYLVANIA
SEPTEMBER 28

CROW POPULATION:
22,367

Chapter Fourteen

THIS TIME HE APOLOGIZES WITH PANCAKES instead of flowers.

On Saturday mornings, the Auburn Diner is the most popular place in town. We have to wait thirty minutes for a table, which means a lot of small talk. Something my father excels at. The Barnes family has lived in Auburn for three generations, and my grandfather created Barnes Construction from nothing. His business is responsible for a lot of the buildings still standing, including our house, which my dad grew up in before buying it from his aging father.

Legacy is a strange thing.

My grandfather's legacy in this town is literally carved in stone—his name and the dates of construction are chiseled into cement blocks on almost everything built here over the two decades when his business was booming. The legacy of the people he employed. But I'm starting to wonder how many men have two faces. One for inside their home, and one for outside.

"Hey, Erin." Our waitress, Christine, greets Mom first. They work together here. "No shifts this weekend?"

"No, not in again till Tuesday, actually."

"Lucky girl," Christine says, her eyes falling on my dad. "You been watching these games, Jesse Barnes?" Christine is an old friend of Mom's from high school. She would have watched the entire rise—and fall—of Dad's football career.

"Sure am," Dad says. "Auburn proud, right?" My father orders pancakes for everyone, because they're cheap. But he adds coffee for him, Mom, and me, and hot chocolate for the girls.

"Aw, what a special treat," Christine says.

She turns back to Mom. "So if you aren't working, do you want to join us for girls' night out, for once? Nothing special, we're just meeting at Jimmy's Tavern for a few drinks."

Dad speaks first.

"That's nice of you, Christine," he says, and she flushes a bit when he says her name. "But Erin can't tonight."

"Aw, well. Maybe next time," Christine says, still talking to Dad.

"Maybe," Mom says, and Christine takes our order to the kitchen.

That won't happen, either. Next time. One by one, Dad has found reasons to push people away. *Your friends always hated me. They aren't good influences on you.*

Eventually, she just let those friendships slip away.

Our food doesn't take long, but right as it arrives, someone else stops by our table.

"Hey, Jesse! It's been a while," Mr. DiMarco says. Officer DiMarco. He's on duty, wearing his police uniform.

"Bill, how are ya?" My father stands and greets him. He hasn't been over in a long time—his own kids are really young—but when I was little, my father's best friend from high school was at our house all the time. I used to call him Uncle Bill.

He greets my mom and then looks to us girls.

"Wow, they're all so big," he says with a laugh.

"Crazy, right? Leighton's applying to college this fall. Perfect GPA."

"Ah, wow. Let me guess. You're hoping she picks state college."

"What kind of fan would I be if I didn't?" Dad says.

I turn my attention back to my plate and take a bite of pancake. It's covered in butter and syrup and sprinkled with confectioner's sugar, but when I take the first bite, I gag, something sour flooding my mouth. Everyone else seems to be enjoying the meal. Juniper's grin is huge and real.

I hate the bad nights. I hate how loud and cruel he can be. How scared he makes us.

But it is mornings like this that hurt the most. When we are expected to pretend that everything is okay. Because my legs are sore from how we slept in the armoire, an entanglement of limbs and fear, and the bite of pancake that I managed to swallow refuses to settle in my stomach.

"Hey, listen," Bill says. "I heard the council didn't pick your company for the library renovation. Tough break, man, I'm sorry."

My mom and I look up in surprise. This is new information. Dad worked on that proposal for months.

"I didn't realize—" Mom starts to speak, and my dad's hand falls to her shoulder. He grips it, pats her back a few times. Squeezes again. All with a smile on his face. But there's white tension in his knuckles, and a look that crosses Mom's face. He's hurting her.

"Yeah, well, what can you do? You win some bids, you lose some bids. That's the job," Dad says.

Juniper and Campbell sit forward in their seats.

Juniper's eyes stay fixed on Mom, like she's watching for a signal from her. How do we react? Do we smile and nod?

We do.

We smile.

We nod.

We say pleasant goodbyes.

But the milk in my coffee tastes curdled, and the sugar turns to salt on my tongue, and I'm bolting from the table, barely making it to the diner restroom before I throw up flour and sugar and salt and grief.

Chapter Fifteen

JUNIPER AND I ARE SPRAWLED ON a blanket in our backyard. There is a slight chill this early in the morning, but it will warm by the afternoon. I'm eager for the crispness of Pennsylvania autumns, but this year summer refuses to loosen her hold.

Campbell loves this weather. Bike-riding season is extended, and that's where she is now. Mom almost called an early end to it after she learned about the rosebush accident, but I convinced her to let Campbell ride while she can. She needs her wolf pack on bicycles.

Juniper brought her book outside, and I'm alternating between calculus homework and newspaper research. I've brought my art folder out, too, but mostly so I can glare at it occasionally and wish it would spontaneously combust. I'm very terrible at it, and regret registering for the "easy" elective.

For a while we work quietly—or at least, we are quiet. There are crows all around us, and they make themselves known. The cawing of crows is the new Auburn Township soundtrack.

I finish up my calc work and reach for my crow research. I found out that this has happened before in other towns. In New York and Oregon. Even another little town in Pennsylvania.

"Experts estimate the murder of crows has reached fifty thousand or more," I read to Juniper from that other town's local paper. "Birds are still arriving by the thousands as they migrate south from Canada."

"Fifty *thousand*?" Juniper yells. "How many are here?"

"No clue," I say. "Not that many. Not yet, anyway."

I turn over the *Auburn Gazette*, our local paper, which is barely more than a penny flyer. Front-page news this week is our football team's win last night.

"Weird," I say.

"What is?" Junie asks.

"Just our football team. They're . . . winning. They've won every game so far this year, actually." I would wonder if the headline was a prank, but Auburn takes football too seriously for that.

There are crows lining our fence, and I pull a box of raisins from my backpack and start to chuck them across the lawn.

"That's against the rules," Juniper says. "You said so in your paper."

"You read my column, Junie?" I always bring home a

paper copy for my writing binder, but the paper mostly exists online. I didn't realize Juniper even had access to it.

"Yeah, Campbell always prints out your articles, and she lets me read them first."

I like watching the crows flutter off the fence and land near us to snatch up the raisins. I like how they hop around. And honestly, I like breaking a rule for once. I'll break the hell out of Auburn Township Ordinance 3417. I'm a rebel with a cause. Filling up Corvidae bellies, one raisin at a time.

"Here, Junie. Give it a try." I hand her a few raisins, but then notice her bare wrist. The three of us always wear the leather cuffs Grandpa gave us, but hers is gone. "Hey, your bracelet is off."

She looks guilty. "I lost it. I'm so sorry. I thought it would be at home in my room, but I can't find it anywhere."

"Don't worry. I'm sure it will turn up. I'll look for it later, okay?"

I turn back to the pages in front of me. "It says here that this town hired wildlife experts to try to scare them off," I say, mostly to distract her. I shouldn't have said anything about the missing cuff.

"Scare them how?" she asks. She throws an entire handful of raisins at once, and a bunch of crows swoop down from a nearby tree.

"Flares, loud noises. They brought in falconers to haze the crows. With live hawks. They also opened up a crow-hunting season for several weeks."

"Like a bird-killing spree?" Juniper takes the box from me and throws a raisin as high as she can. A crow catches it in midair.

"Pretty much," I say. Hunting is popular around here. We even get off school when deer season starts. It's never really bothered me, but I feel a weird twinge at the thought of the crows being shot. Juniper figures out the feeling before I do.

"I hope they don't do that here," she says. "The crows aren't that bad. And I'd be so worried about Joe."

"Joe's pretty smart," I tell her, pushing aside my own discomfort. "Besides, there aren't nearly as many crows here. It says that there were so many crows in this other town that they blocked out the sun. We don't have *that* many crows. Don't worry."

Juniper turns onto her back, looking up at the clouds like she's imagining the sky filled with black birds. I don't want her to be anxious about Joe, so I change the subject.

"What are you reading?" I ask. She passes me the book without taking her eyes off the sky.

It's a young reader's collection of fairy tales and fables.

"This was mine," I say, paging through it. "I loved these stories."

"They're really good," Junie says, turning to face me. Now I've got her attention. "I can't believe it's just been sitting on your shelf all wonderful and unread for *years*."

She makes me laugh.

"Sorry, Juniper. It's all yours now."

"Really? Thanks."

She opens up the front flap of the hardcover, where a faded scene of trees, flowers, and woodland creatures is printed.

"Can I borrow a pen?" she asks.

"Um, sure."

She grabs my pen and puts a line under my name, which I must have scrawled into the book a decade ago, and then adds her name underneath it. "There, now it's official."

"Well done."

"Can I have a piece of paper, too?" she asks.

I tear her a sheet out of my notebook.

I catch sight of the first two words she writes at the top of the page: *Dear Joe*.

"Writing to Joe?" I ask.

"Yeah, well, the animals in these stories are really smart, and I think Joe is smart, too, so I've been writing him letters."

"Are you expecting a response?" I ask. If I could catch her leaving the letters, I could write responses for her. It would be a little lie—like the tooth fairy, but with crows.

"That's stupid, Leighton. Birds can't write."

Oh, well, never mind the letter plan.

"But he might leave more gifts."

"What?" I turn on my side to face her, curious.

"I left Joe a letter last week, and when I checked it was gone, and he left me a present."

"What kind of present?" Juniper has a good imagination,

and I don't usually call out her stories, but this doesn't sound like one of her games.

Juniper reaches into the pocket of her jeans, and then opens her fist to reveal a shiny blue marble.

"Joe left you this?" I take the marble and roll it between my fingers.

"I didn't see. But I think it was a crow. I left the note and some crackers. You won't tell I fed them, right?" I shake my head and hold up the raisins as evidence of my own guilt. She continues. "I came back and they were gone, but there was a marble and a feather."

It feels like a stretch to me, but I reach for my notebook and write another note to ask an expert about crow behaviors. They're really smart. Maybe it isn't a coincidence. Maybe Juniper is getting presents from the crows.

"He's not leaving presents, Juniper. He's dropping garbage," Campbell says from behind us.

"Well, aren't you a little ray of darkness," I say. "Don't listen to her, June Bug. I think it's possible Joe is leaving gifts, and I'll even find a bird expert so I can ask them."

"Thanks, Leighton." She stands up with her letter, but Campbell reaches out, snatching it from Juniper's grasp and holding it above her head.

"'Dear Joe,'" Campbell reads. "'My teacher says it's bad for the town that you are here now because you are loud and messy, but I'm loud and messy, too.'" Campbell pauses and rolls her eyes. "You've got that right."

"Stop that! Give it back!" Juniper jumps, trying to get her letter back.

"'Tell your friends they should stay. When I see you I feel safe'—"

On the last word, Campbell stops short, her arm lowering enough that Junie can grab her note back.

"Cammy," I say, but the look on her face tells me that she feels bad already.

"Here, Leighton, you believe me, so you're allowed to read it," Juniper says.

I read the end of the letter silently.

Your fethers are pretty. I found six so far and I'm starting a collecshon. One is gray so I think it is yours. Love, Juniper Barnes, Age 9

"It's a lovely note," I tell her as I return it. "Joe is gonna love it." Her frown softens at my words, and she's off, folded note in hand, running toward the tree at the far end of our property. She kneels under the branches and looks up. Her mouth moves, but I can't hear what she's saying to the birds.

"You've gotta be nicer to her," I tell Campbell.

Campbell starts to walk away. "Don't worry, I'll take care of her when you go to college."

There's so much resentment in her voice. I struggle to think of the right thing to say to her this time.

"Campbell, I won't—"

The sound of a truck roaring onto our road distracts us.

"Oh no," Cammy says, running. She races around to the front of the house, but she's barely rounded the corner when I hear a horrible screeching sound.

I leap to my feet and follow her. He's back, his truck thrown into park but still on, and he's in front of it, tugging on something.

Campbell is frozen in the yard.

"What is it?" I ask, but then he wins his battle.

Campbell's crushed bicycle is pulled out from under the front of the truck.

Shit.

"What the fuck was this doing where I park?" he yells, throwing the mangled bicycle into our lawn. "The front bumper is fucking scratched to hell. Dammit, Campbell!" He screams the last at her as he passes, storming into the house and slamming the door as he calls for Mom. But Cam doesn't flinch, or even act as though she's registered his existence. She's just standing in the yard, looking at her bike where it lies bent in half. She stands there, and I see it: how hard she is thinking. She's probably thinking of how to fix it—impossible. Thinking of how she can save money for a new bike—unlikely. Thinking about how her best friends ride their bikes, and if she doesn't have a bike—

Campbell thinks. She thinks so hard. And I realize that's all she'll be able to do now that her bike is gone.

Chapter Sixteen

I HAVE CREEPY-BASEMENT-INDUCED INSOMNIA.

Sometimes I lie awake at night and think about the crawl space in our basement. It isn't anything special—a little creepy, but it's nothing more than a hole in one of the stone walls. It's maybe six feet off the ground and opens into a space as wide and long as the foyer it lies beneath. There are some pipes visible inside, and a floor made of insulation and years of dust.

I don't know why I fixate on that crawl space, but I do. Maybe because it is dark and moist and feels like it's hiding things. Maybe because it is behind the staircase, so that most people would miss it entirely. Especially if something were covering the opening.

Maybe it is just because I am in a shitty situation and was blessed with an active imagination.

So I lie awake, waiting to see if anything is going to happen. And even when the house stays quiet and calm, I can't sleep. Even when his mood is good and money is okay and he laughs with her and brings her flowers, I can't sleep. Because I know that maybe tomorrow night it won't be darkness and the deep breathing sounds of a peaceful house. Tomorrow night might be all of the lights in the house turned on. The trash bin hurled across the kitchen, leaving a trail of eggshells and crumpled bills and cigarette butts. His incessant, angry voice, repeating the same words over and over as he moves around the house looking for more things that will piss him off even harder, because once he gets going, I swear to God, he loves it and tries to feed that flame.

I'm not scared of the dark. I'm scared I won't make it to morning. So I lie awake at night and I think about that crawl space. I think about how it might be where he hides our bodies one day.

Chapter Seventeen

MY VISION BLURS AND I READ the same sentence for the fourth time.

It was a weekend of unbroken tension in our home. The voices arguing Friday night, the lost construction bid, Campbell's bike. More problems to solve. Less time to do it.

Tension like that works its way into every nook of the house, until it feels small and tight and so full you can barely breathe with all of that worry packed inside the walls.

I'm balancing a huge stack of loose papers, still warm from the library printer. I've been running back and forth because the newspaper room printer is down. The pages in front of me contain crow myths and folklore, from almost every historical period and major geographic region in human history. Medieval. Babylonian. Celtic. Crows have been used as symbols for as long as we've told stories.

I'm not looking where I'm walking.

"Whoa there!" shouts a voice from the floor, too late.

I walk into Liam where he was crouched at his locker.

"Jesus Christ," I mutter as my pages fly everywhere.

"It's a little late for a prayer on this one, don't you think?" Liam scoops up my scattered pages and climbs to his feet. We talk every day when we exchange books, and we debate each other in lit class all the time, and I like how familiar he is to me now. How I'm starting to think of him as a friend. His eyebrows shift into concern.

"You all right?" he asks.

"I'm really sorry. Sleep deprived."

"Studying too much?" He shakes the papers in his hands.

"Kind of. Newspaper article."

"That's a lot of work for an extracurricular," he says.

"Says the football player with the perfect grades," I say, cocking my head to the side. "How much do you practice? Three hours a night? And then you study?"

"That's different. It's all for those college applications."

"Not so different. Me too."

"You want to do this in school?" Liam shuffles the pages, straightening them. We start walking together, my notes tucked safely under his arm.

"More like in life. But yeah, school to start."

"That's cool. I've read your articles. They're really good."

"Thanks, Liam. But flattery doesn't really—"

"It isn't flattery."

I squint my eyes at him. *Isn't it?*

"Okay, it's flattery, but it's true. And you can't say the same, because you don't come to football games."

"How on earth could you know that?"

"Because Sofia knows that, and she told me. Sofia is wise. Sofia knows all. *Sofia* thinks I'm nice."

"Very smooth use of the best friend card, Liam."

Dammit. I really do like him. And for a moment, I let myself have the daydream. The one where he asks me out again, and this time I say yes. The one where we go see a movie, and I lean my head on his shoulder.

It's a perfect night.

It's an impossible night.

We've reached the newsroom.

"Sorry I ran into you, Liam."

"It's cool. Pretty girl tripping over me is kind of the opposite of a problem for a seventeen-year-old guy."

I reach for the classroom door.

"Hang on," he says. "I do want to ask you something." He looks into the room, like he's checking whether anyone can overhear us, before he speaks. "I'm not gonna keep asking you out, Leighton. I don't want to bug you. But if you ever wanna just . . . talk? I'm a good listener."

Goose bumps prickle my arms, and tears threaten my eyes. It's hard to keep it under control when I'm tired. It's even harder when Liam McNamara is looking at me like he already knows my secrets.

I swallow hard.

"Thanks, Liam. That's really nice. But I'm fine."

I start to walk into the classroom but turn back, feeling some weird, strong urge to be honest with him. To stop using school as the dumb excuse that it is.

"I *do* like you, Liam. If things were different, I'd love to go out with you. But my life is a little more complicated than it might appear here at school. I have sisters, and they, ah, they really need me. Next year they won't have me, and this year I need to be with them."

I don't know what else to say. I can't be specific. It's too much.

It hurts too much.

"I have a little sister, too, Barnes. I . . ." He hesitates, leans up against the wall. "Listen, I get it." He holds out my notes for me, and I want to take my rejections back. I want to say yes. But I don't.

Because the truth is that I don't need Liam, but Campbell and Juniper still need me.

Chapter Eighteen

WE RECEIVE OUR PROGRESS REPORTS IN final period
on Friday. I'm picturing city lights and studying with real
journalists and—I frown.

AP English: 100.

Honors Calculus: 97.

Chemistry: 96.

Art I: 79.

I have a C. In *art class*. I buzz through the crowded hall-
ways, hell-bent on getting out of school as fast as possible. I'm
a drone bee, and the honey that calls me is a book and Lorde's
new album and pulling the curtains closed and lying on the
shaggy carpet in my room. Art class. That was supposed to
be my easy class. My break in the day so I could put more
time into Newspaper and college applications. Dammit.

I shove my books around in my locker, trying to remember homework assignments for the weekend in the haze of
frustration. I finally give up and start putting all of my books

into my bag. Better to have them and not need them. I can always work ahead. Except for art. I can't work ahead in art.

I slam my locker shut with all the force I can use without being called out by a hall monitor for "exhibiting aggression" and sent to the school counselor.

"Hey, Peyton Manning," says a voice behind me.

"Cute," I say, sarcasm ringing like a bell. I don't even turn my head. I'm eager for my weekend. It isn't official until I step through the doors.

"What's up with you?" Liam asks, reaching out to take my backpack. With the weight gone, I buoy upright, unaware until that moment that I'd been walking at a tilt.

"Thanks," I say, rubbing my shoulder and dropping the sarcasm this time.

"Sorry, Leighton, I didn't mean anything—"

"It wasn't you." I fall into step beside him. His height advantage makes our paces hard to match. My shorter legs have to take several little steps to keep stride with his long ones.

"Progress report troubles?" he asks, and I grimace.

"Wait, really?" He laughs, then catches himself. "Sorry. I'm not making fun of you. I'm just surprised."

"It's nothing," I say, glancing around. Someone could hear him.

He extends his hand, palm up. I hesitate for a moment, and then decide to humor him. I hand over the report.

"Tsk-tsk," he says, shaking his head as he reads. "Looks like you might even need—" Liam stops walking and looks around, his eyes darting to the classmates filing past us. "A tutor!"

He whispers the words, but it's an obnoxiously loud whisper.

"Okay, okay, enough," I say, tugging on his arm to make him start walking again. "I don't need a tutor."

"I'm just teasing you, Leighton. You have time to get your grade up. It's gonna be fine. It's just art."

"I'm terrible at art," I say. "It was meant to be fun."

"Maybe I could be your tutor," he says.

We've reached my bus outside.

"You can't be my tutor, Liam."

"Sure I can," he argues. "I can draw."

"No, you can't." Liam McNamara acts like he's good at everything. But I'm starting to smile. Why do I like this about him?

"Seriously, Leighton. I like art. I'm good at it. Like *really* good."

"You aren't even taking art," I accuse, pivoting on my foot at the edge of the sidewalk, facing him head-on while my bus idles next to us.

"I'm taking Art IV," he counters.

Oh. Maybe he *is* good at everything. How annoying.

"I can help, really."

"Um, okay," I say. I don't know why I've said yes. Or maybe I do know why: because I wanted to. I want to see Liam outside of school. I've wanted to for a while. Art feels a lot safer than a date.

"Great."

"Um . . . tonight?"

"Tonight's the football game. Versus Eagleville. Our sworn rivals. And I don't know if you heard, but we are undefeated."

"Oh, right." Since they've been winning, I've had to make the conscious choice to not follow the team news.

I'm feeling a little rejected, which is stupid. It isn't even a date. It's an art-tutoring session. It might even qualify as the exact opposite of a date.

"You should come to the game. There's gonna be a bonfire at James's place afterward. We could hang out . . . find another time this weekend for art?"

"I don't really go to parties . . ." I begin, reaching for my bag. The first bus is pulling away, and I've got to go.

"Come with me," he says, releasing my bag. "It'll be—"

"Wild? Cool? We'll get wasted?" I supply some of the words I've heard used to describe their parties.

"Fun," Liam says. "It'll be fun."

Stop being such a buzzkill, Leighton. Maybe you'll actually make a second friend before you leave this school. The bus driver adjusts her mirror and places her hand on the gear. *Move along, ducklings,* her expression says. I feel put on the spot, and I just *know* that Campbell is watching every moment of this from the bus window. Too much pressure, and I falter.

"Sorry, I just can't." Cool, Barnes. You are super cool. Keep turning down this super-cute, terribly nice guy who is interested in you. But Liam doesn't call me on it. He tries one last time.

"No party. But maybe I'll see ya at the game. And maybe we can work on art at my house Sunday?"

Heavy sigh from the bus driver.

"I've gotta go." I climb onto the bus, doing my best to ignore the glare I get from the driver as she shifts the gear and closes the door behind me. I squish in beside Campbell and reach over her to pinch the releases on the window, lowering the top.

Liam is still on the sidewalk outside.

"Okay. Maybe I'll see you tonight. And art on Sunday sounds good."

His smile is the best thing. I feel like I could act stupid for that smile. The thought is sobering. I'm not that girl. I'm not going to forget myself over a boy.

"But it's still not a date," I add, my voice harsher than necessary.

"I'll call you Sunday," he says, unfazed. Still smiling.

When the bus lurches forward, I whip around and sit in my seat before I can call out and cancel our just barely made plans.

"Who is *that*?" Campbell demands as soon as I'm sitting.

"Just a friend," I answer. "Barely even a friend. He's going to tutor me."

"He's tutoring you?" Campbell asks. Clearly, she doesn't

believe me, so I hand her my slightly crumpled progress report.

Campbell reads it.

"Oh my God, you have a C. This is a first."

"I know," I groan. I rest my head on Campbell's shoulder. "In freaking art."

"New York University isn't gonna take a student who gets C's, Leighton."

I purse my lips. "How'd you know about NYU?"

"I know everything," Cammy says, carefully folding my progress report.

"Don't tell him," I say, meaning Dad, but of course she knows not to.

"Duh," Campbell says. "Not that it matters anyway. Grades like this and you'll be stuck here with me after all."

Her comment is like barbed wire. It isn't meant to hurt me. It's meant to protect her.

"You'd just love that," I say.

Campbell doesn't answer, but she rests her head on mine in a silent kind of apology. I sneak my hand over one of hers and squeeze it. I don't want to ever leave her. But I don't know how to stay in this town one second longer than I have to, either.

How big is your brave? I think.

It isn't very big. It's small, and it's shrinking.

What will it take to leave them: courage or cowardice?

Chapter Nineteen

OUR BUS DRIVES PAST THE FOOTBALL fields, where little boys practice for their flag football games. They can't be much older than seven or eight, but the coaches are yelling, and the fathers on the sidelines are grim-faced.

What happens when you tell little boys every day of their lives that they must be the *most*? The fastest, or the tallest, or the strongest. Maybe you tell them to be bravest, like that's better. Like they won't take their fear and bury it down deep in an effort to please you.

But there isn't so much room at the top, and while it might feel like disappointment when they're seven, it starts to feel like failure when they're seventeen. And then some of them become a different *most*. They become the meanest. The loudest. The angriest.

You'd think I was programmed to love this game, but I never could. My dad loved it so much it destroyed him. Why would anyone give something so stupid that much power over them?

But when I pull out the *Auburn Gazette* on the bus, the front page is the same it's been for weeks: a full spread talking about the last game's win and the next game's challenge. I might not understand what goes into the sheer force of team spirit exhibited in this town, but it's getting harder and harder to deny one thing: this team is newsworthy.

And if I want to be good at my job, I should try to understand why. Besides, Sofia loves cheering for the team and covering the games for the school paper. Maybe she can help me see it in a new way.

I finish homework at the kitchen table while we wait for my father to get home from a construction site out of town. Mom and the girls are cooking dinner and laughing. And things feel so calm, it makes me feel like I've overreacted to the other nights. This is what normal homes look like, isn't it?

When he gets home, we can tell it was a good day, and there is a soft, but distinct, release of tension as Mom welcomes him.

Campbell and I set the table, and she smiles at me over the glasses. We are a few short, so we grab some of Juniper's old plastic toddler cups instead. We know why there are too few glasses, but we brush the thought aside like a mosquito at our ear. Something we could forget instantly if it would just leave us alone.

Juniper climbs into her chair. "Cool, princesses! I missed these cups! Thanks!"

She grabs her plastic mug that we've filled with milk,

unaware that we would switch her cup for any other reason than to bring her joy.

I get the spaghetti and meatballs while Mom fixes a salad. Dad's construction jobs have been steady the past weeks; he just has to drive an hour away for them. It's been a relief at home, and he's been too tired to be mad, and there's been some more money. A full fridge.

Dad showers the construction dust off quickly before joining us.

"Feels like I haven't seen you guys in a week. Fill me in."

Juniper talks about school. She's excited to start a living history project, the same one I did in third grade, where we interview an Auburn resident over the age of sixty-five.

"Maybe we can stay with Nana overnight," Campbell says. "So you can ask her your questions."

I stare at my plate, not trusting myself to keep the worry from my face at her words. We only ever stayed with Nana when things were bad. When we were running away.

But Dad smiles. "That's a great idea, Cammy," he says. "I bet she misses you girls like crazy these days."

He tells us about his construction job. It's salvage work, so it's messy and unpredictable. A fire in an apartment building, and they're gutting the ruined parts and deciding whether the building can be functional again. It reminds me of the rosebush and Mrs. Stieg's close inspection of its roots, and what a strange question it is to ask of anything: *Is it worth saving?*

I wonder how our family would fare under such close scrutiny.

"I was thinking of going to the game tonight," I say quietly.

"*You* want to go to a football game?" Mom asks.

"Yeah, um, they're doing well? And Sofia is cheering *and* covering the game, so I thought she could use an extra newspaper person on hand."

"They've been in the paper a lot lately," Dad says. "The most in years."

Nineteen years, probably.

Winning streaks are few and far between.

"All right, it's been a while since we've been up there," he continues. "Let's all go."

It's not the answer I expected, but I realize it's a better one. I'd rather be out of this house anyway, and have Campbell and Juniper with me.

"Great." I excuse myself quickly and go to get ready.

Campbell joins me a minute later.

"Football?" she asks.

"Yeah. Go Wolves!"

"You hate football."

"Yes, I really do. But I like news. And the team winning is news." I pull a blue cardigan from my drawer.

"No. No, no, no. You aren't going to the library," Campbell says, taking the sweater from my hands and throwing it into the back of my closet.

She roots around in my drawers for a few minutes.

"Here," she finally says. She drops jeans and a T-shirt and a long-sleeved flannel shirt onto the bed. "Hair?" she asks.

"Will you braid it?"

She closes both her eyes for a moment, like she does when Juniper is annoying her and she has to dig deep to collect her patience.

"Just take the messy bun out. It'll have some curl. Your hair is pretty, and you never wear it down." She doesn't wait for me to do it, but reaches over and tugs at the knot until my hair falls loose.

I reach for my hairband, but she pulls it on to her own wrist.

"No way. If you have it, you'll put it back in that bun."

Campbell starts to leave.

"Thanks," I say. "Do you need help, too?"

She laughs. "No. But you have to answer a question."

"What is it?"

"Does Liam play football?"

"I'm not answering that because it's irrelevant."

"Liar," she says on her way out the door.

I hold up the shirt Campbell chose for me and smile. It was a private joke between us when I found it at the thrift shop, with its big gold letters on the front that say GO SPORTS.

We used to joke that it was the closest thing to an Auburn jersey we'd ever wear.

Chapter Twenty

THE COWBELLS ARE RINGING.

The football stadium is packed. *Auburn proud.*

The first quarter is about halfway through when we arrive, which means the regular lot is full, and we have to park on the side of the road. It's chilly, so I help Juniper put on gloves and a hat before we walk over.

As soon as we buy tickets, Juniper spies the food trucks.

"Funnel cakes!" she shrieks, and looks up at Mom.

"Okay, *one treat*," Mom says, and lets Junie tug her away.

We wait silently with Dad until they come back.

"Let's find a spot along the fence to watch for now—the bleachers look crowded," Mom suggests.

We line up at an open spot not far from the cheerleaders. I manage to make eye contact with Sofia and give her a little wave. She drops her pom-poms and comes running over.

"Do my eyes deceive me or is Leighton Barnes at a *football* game?" she asks.

"Hey, Sof. How's it going?" I keep my hands snug in my jacket pockets, but lift a shoulder toward the field. There are too many men at the fence, and I can't see the game.

"It's bumpy tonight," she says. "I think they're starting to feel the pressure of these wins."

"No kidding," I say, looking around. It feels like the entire town is here. "Need help covering it? I figured since you're cheering, you might need a hand."

"Yes! I'm so glad you asked. There's this one player that is doing really well so far this season, and I have a vested interest in tracking his specific moves tonight."

"Sofia, please don't say—"

"Could you watch out for number thirty-six for me?" She doesn't let me answer, instead calling over her shoulder to her squad, "What, you can't call next cheer without me? I'm so loved and missed that the squad is crumbling without me? I'll be right there!"

She turns back to me. "Thanks for the help, Lay, you're a lifesaver! *Thirty-six*!"

Sofia jogs back over to the cheerleaders just as the announcer says, "A promising start so far tonight from Auburn High's number thirty-six, Liam McNamara. Certainly one to watch as we head into the second quarter."

I close my eyes for a moment in quiet annoyance, and then realize I must look exactly like Campbell did when she was helping me pick out my outfit. Sure enough, when

I turn on my heel, Cammy is two feet away from me on the track. "Want some company covering *number thirty-six?*"

"Why not?" I answer, scanning the fence until I find our parents and Juniper. "They seem okay?"

"Weirdly okay," she says.

"Enjoy it while we can?" I ask.

"Heck yes."

We link arms and start circling the field. I dig change out of my purse, and we have enough for one hot cocoa, so we take turns sipping it as we go.

"It's getting cold," she says. She doesn't just mean tonight. She means in general, autumn is going fast. She's missing her last bike-riding days.

"Are your friends here, Cam? You don't have to babysit me," I tell her. "I'm gonna have to go up into the bleachers to be able to see anything, anyway."

"Oh, I'm not. I just wanted the cocoa." She holds up the cup.

"Take it. Be good," I say, and we part ways at the bottom of the bleachers. I watch until she reaches a pod of fellow eighth graders gathered down the track.

I'm about halfway up the bleachers, hoping that the only open seat isn't next to the band, when I hear my name.

"Leighton!"

I turn and see Amelia waving shyly. Her outfit is coordinated from her headband to her shoelaces, and I feel a wave of self-consciousness at my worn boots and thrift store shirt. But she gestures at an empty seat next to her, encouraging me to join her. *Be social,* I tell myself. *It won't kill you to try a little.*

I shuffle into the crowded seating and make my way to Amelia.

"Thanks so much," I say when I join her.

"No problem," she says, smiling. "I don't think I've seen you at a game in, like, two years, Leighton."

"Yeah, it's been a while."

"Anyone in particular you came to see?" she asks.

"Um, not exactly, but I'm helping Sofia cover the game for the paper." Amelia shifts, setting a designer handbag in between us and tucking her straight black hair behind her ear. I've never once seen her hair in a messy bun. I tug my hair over my shoulder on the other side, away from her view.

She lifts her hands to her lips and screams, "Yeah, James!"

Right. Should probably actually watch the game.

Amelia is petite, but her voice is loud, and she enthusiastically cheers for our team the entire quarter. I'm amazed her voice isn't hoarse from the yelling. I keep an eye on the maroon jersey with "36" on its back, watching how Liam's movements are so fast and sure. I don't scream like Amelia does, but I do feel a rush of excitement when he scores a touchdown. He said he plays because there isn't much else to do around here, but he's good. Maybe Sofia wasn't just messing with me when she asked me to watch him play tonight. Touchdowns are news.

I hear another voice ringing clear in the crowd, cheering for thirty-six.

A few rows of bleachers down and across the aisle is Liam's family. His little sister, Fiona, is yelling for him.

I watch the McNamaras cheering for Liam for a few minutes. It makes me smile. It's just such a normal, easy family thing. Supporting someone you love.

"I'm gonna go check in with my family," I yell to Amelia over the cheering.

"Okay!"

I try to spot them while I'm in the bleachers, but it's impossible in the crowd that pours off the stairways to get food and drinks during half-time. I follow the push of people until I have to stop to let the football team cross from the field to the locker rooms.

Number thirty-six stops short in front of me.

Liam lifts his helmet off.

"Nice to see you here, Barnes," he says.

"McNamara!" yells his coach.

"Go," I tell him, smiling.

"Going," he says. He starts jogging backward. "Sunday?"

"I said yes already. Stop asking, or I might change my mind."

Liam laughs and ducks into the locker room.

And that's where Campbell finds me, staring at the closed locker room door with a stupid smile on my face.

"Leighton, I need you," she says, grabbing my elbow hard. I know that voice. She's worried.

"What's up?" I say, but she's already moving through the crowd, twisting her body between the bruising crush of people. "Cam, wait!"

I have to push through people to keep up with her, apologizing for my rudeness, but not stopping. Something is wrong.

When we emerge on the other side, our dad is talking to Mr. Dillard. He's the father of someone our parents went to school with, and he happens to run the *other* construction business in town. The one that got the library renovation. He also always brings up Dad's knee injury when they talk. I try to figure out if he's said anything yet.

"Could've gone pro! I know it! The whole town knew it. Would've been our claim to fame."

Dad's expression is pained, his smile forced. "Yeah, well, some things aren't meant to be."

"You're telling me you were meant to run your daddy's business?" He laughs. "Run it right into the ground in this economy, am I right?"

My stomach drops. This is bad.

Mom knows it, too. "Jesse, we should get Juniper home soon. It's late for her."

She pulls on his arm, but he's immovable.

"Stop it, Erin," he says.

His whole body has gone tense. His knee injury is always a rough topic. A reminder of what could have been. But the business is like a gaping wound. He's doing everything he can think of to keep it moving, but it was never his dream to run it.

Mr. Dillard doesn't know when to shut up.

"Takes a special kind of drive to run your own business," he says. "Some people got it, some don't. Kinda like running the ball, don't you think?" He shrugs at the field. I'm vaguely aware that halftime is ending. The players are lining up, and people are climbing back into their seats.

"Jesse, let's go home," Mom says again, tugging harder.

He lifts his arm fast in response, drawing it back, and then almost instantly dropping it to his side.

He remembered where we are.

My stomach turns, embarrassment flooding me. I feel like the entire town is watching this moment.

"Hey, everything okay down here?"

It's Bill DiMarco. He isn't in his uniform. Off duty, just enjoying the game.

"Fine, Bill, thanks," Dad says, but his face hasn't softened. Bill sees it, too, taking in the whole scene. Mom's tense withdrawal from my father's side. The way Juniper's lower lip is trembling.

But then he turns his gaze back to Dad, and claps him on the shoulder. "Just wanted to say hi. Kind of wild to see the team doing well, huh? Reliving the glory days."

The tension shifts, melts. Dad turns his attention from Mom, finally.

"Damn straight. Maybe this time they'll actually go all the way."

Bill smiles, but there's sadness in it. Or pity.

Dad's smile slips again.

"We're gonna head out early, though. I've got a job a borough over tomorrow."

"Of course, yeah, good luck with that," Bill says.

Bill's attention turns to my mom. I can almost hear the question as it forms in his head. *Are you all right?*

I've never wanted anyone to ask a question more. To acknowledge a thing they just saw with their own eyes. To do something about it.

"Good to see you, Erin," he says, and turns away from us.

Good to see you, too, Uncle Bill.

AUBURN, PENNSYLVANIA
OCTOBER 5

CROW POPULATION:
29,433

Chapter Twenty-One

LIAM CALLS ON SUNDAY, JUST LIKE he said he would.

He invites me to his house, and even though Mom covers the phone before she hands it to me and mouths *It's a boy*, she doesn't say no when I ask her if she'll drive me over. As I get ready in the bathroom, Juniper lifts herself up and sits on the bathroom counter. She watches in silence while I draw on eyeliner. When I reach for my gloss, she purses her lips, and I gloss her up, too. She smacks her lips together, checks her reflection, and wipes the back of her hand across her mouth.

"What is even the point if it's not flavored something yummy," she says. But she lingers in the bathroom, pouting a bit into the mirror.

"Something bothering you, Juniper?" I ask, my mouth forming an involuntary O while I put on mascara.

"Who is Liam?"

"A friend from school," I tell her. I blink too soon, and

mascara stripes line the top of my cheek. Juniper licks her finger and wipes at the marks, smearing spit and makeup.

"Ew, Junie." I pull away from her, laughing.

"A boy friend," she says. I can tell *boy* and *friend* are separate words the way she says it. Like Campbell's bike friends.

"He's helping me with art class. It's homework."

"Hmm," she murmurs. It's a heavy *hmm*. I drop the mascara on the counter and give her my undivided attention.

"Yesssss, June Bug?"

"Nothing. Just that maybe 'art homework' is code for something else."

"Juniper! What would it be code for?"

"How should I know? It's something Campbell said, and I never know what she's talking about."

Ugh, Cammy, stop growing up so fast.

"Talking about me?" Campbell asks from the door.

"'Homework' is code for something? She's nine, Cam."

"I'm not a baby," Juniper says.

"You are such a baby," Campbell says. "And a tattle."

"Am *not*!" Juniper shrieks.

"Enough," I say. "Campbell, stop antagonizing her. Junie, please tell Mom I'll be ready to go in two minutes."

Juniper hops off the sink, slamming her shoulder into Campbell as she passes by.

Campbell drops the toilet lid and sits down. She pulls her legs up and crosses them.

"He's really just a friend?" she asks, then makes a kissing face at me.

"Campbell."

"Is he nice?" And there it is. That's what she wanted to ask. She tries to be subtle, or to trick Juniper into asking me things, but we can never pull that off with each other. Her forced casualness is so familiar to me.

"He's very nice. And if he's ever *not* nice, I will stop hanging out with him." She holds my gaze for a moment, then shifts, nods her head. The tension eases from her shoulders.

It's visible to me, even if others can't see it. The things Campbell carries. The worry.

"You like him?"

Campbell deserves honesty if I'm leaving her all evening to hang out with him.

"Yeah, I do."

"Okay," she says. She leans forward and holds out her hooked little finger.

"Swear you'll be careful."

I reach to link my pinkie finger with hers and tug down. "Pinkie promise."

We should go. Mom and Juniper are probably ready to leave. I grab my backpack, but I pause at the door.

"Hey, Cammy, we're gonna find a way to get you another bike, okay? I don't know how yet, but we will."

"It's my own fault anyway."

"For leaving it out front?"

"No, for being mean to Juniper that day."

I drop my backpack and shut the door, moving right over to Campbell and crouching in front of her. People think she looks like Mom, but it's just the red hair. She has the hard set of Dad's jaw, and his eyes. "Hey. That's not how any of this works, Cam."

"No? It felt pretty karmic to me," she says. She stands up and moves to the vanity, lifting a tube of toothpaste and starting to squeeze it all toward the opening, lid tight in place.

"You think it's a punishment? You do something mean, so you get something bad back? I don't think there's anyone keeping a tally, Campbell."

"I guess not. I've just always wondered . . ."

"Wondered what?"

"What we did to deserve . . ." Emotion makes her voice crack, and she stops talking. She's rolling the toothpaste now, so it's all condensed at the end. Pressure built. Ready to burst when opened.

"Nothing, Campbell." I take the tube from her hand and set it on the counter. "That's why it isn't real. There is no magical ledger of good and bad."

"Maybe it's too bad there isn't, though."

"Why's that?"

"Because that means no one will ever punish him."

Chapter Twenty-Two

BY THE TIME WE ARE CROSSING town to where Liam lives, the sun has started to set. Auburn has a lot of flaws, but it does sunsets right.

As the sun sinks, the colors change, and remind me of the time Juniper got into my desk and used highlighters to color in my copy of *The Bell Jar*. I remember trying to read it after and being unable to—the colors were so bright against the chaos of Plath's words. The contrast kept pulling me from the pages. Neon pink and lemon yellow in layers, just like the sky looks now. Dark words covered in highlighter. A stifling town blanketed by pretty sunsets.

Just before the sun disappears, it glows red like a fireball over Auburn. Like it could make everything its light touches burn.

Liam's family lives up against the mountains, and every house we pass is a looming, but pristine, Victorian. Wraparound porches and dog houses in the yards. No weathered gray siding or neglected flower beds on this side of Auburn.

"So, you're really sticking with the tutoring story?" Mom asks as we pull into the driveway. The girls came with us even though Dad is home. Or maybe because he is.

"What do you mean?" I ask as I haul my heavy backpack into my lap. I probably could have left some books at home.

"I mean, you've never needed a tutor before." Mom smiles at me. "Sounds made-up."

I laugh. "Here, I have proof."

I dive into my bag and pull out my art portfolio. I produce for her inspection my latest project: a still life re-creation of a photograph. The picture is paper-clipped to the corner—a bowl of pears that should have been simple, or so I thought. Turns out pears are an impossible shape to draw. In the photo, they look full and juicy and appetizing. Mine look like they are from an online quiz called "What Kind of Fruit Is Your Body Shape?"

Mom is quiet for so long that I look up and realize her struggle. She isn't sure how to agree that I probably do need help with art class without offending me.

"It's okay, Mom. I know they suck. That's why I'm here."

She laughs. An honest-to-goodness laugh, and it's like gold.

Juniper snickers from the backseat, delighted. I catch a glimpse of Campbell in the rearview mirror, and even she's smiling.

"They don't suck. They . . . could use some direction,

that's all." She's teasing me, but she ends with a smile, and I already feel the beat of the inside joke. The word *pear* gets tucked inside my stone heart for safekeeping.

I pause with my hand on the door handle, then turn back and kiss her cheek goodbye. *Hi, Mom. I see you in there.* I get out of the car, and wave to Campbell and Juniper as they pull away. There are a bunch of autumn decorations on the porch. Pumpkins and signs, and even a full-size, grinning scarecrow. He's probably useful to have around this year.

Liam's sister, Fiona, answers the door. She is a sophomore, so probably fifteen, but she's tall like her brother. She's dressed in a leotard and slim-fitting athletic pants, and I remember that she danced in the talent show last year.

"Leighton! Hi, come on in." She is smiling wide as she ushers me in. "I'm so glad you are here. Liam is bored, and when he's bored, he torments me."

"That sounds about right," I say. "Maybe he needs more hobbies."

"Oh, he has them. He says they aren't as fun."

"Well, if it makes you feel better, you aren't his *only* target; he teases me, too." Fiona laughs and rolls her eyes dramatically, and I like her so much already. It would have been easy for her to make me feel out of place in her home, but she's warm and friendly, and it's impossible to feel weird.

"LIAM, YOUR DATE IS HERE!" Fiona bellows up the stairs, and I startle beside her.

Well, *now* I feel awkward.

"Oh, we aren't—I'm not—" I sigh. I don't know what this is, but it isn't a date. "I'm just here for art."

"Well, that's fine, too," says a voice behind us, and I turn to see Mrs. McNamara.

I'm surprised to realize I'm now at eye level with her. Liam is a lot taller than his mom, but otherwise he takes after her. Warm, kind eyes that look exactly like his. Her eyebrows are impeccably arched, but when she narrows her eyes at Fiona, there's the same expression on her face that I've seen on Liam's.

"Fiona Marie, must you yell?" she asks.

"He always has his headphones on," Fiona says.

"Then go upstairs and let him know his friend is here."

Fiona dashes up the stairs, and Mrs. McNamara smiles at me. "Leighton Barnes. It's been years. Last time I saw you—" She holds her hand up to our shoulder height. "Anyway. You've grown up. I can't believe you kids are *graduating* soon." She leads me to the kitchen. "Coffee? Tea? Maybe some hot cocoa?"

"Whatever is easiest," I say.

"It's all easy, dear."

"Tea sounds good."

"Mmm, I agree. I think I'll join you." She gestures toward a stool that is pushed up to the kitchen island, and I climb up. There's a yard sign leaning against the island, and I accidentally knock it over. It's one of those equality signs, with block letters in bright colors on a black background. *We believe in science. No human is illegal. Women's rights are human rights. Love is love. Black Lives Matter.*

I hop down and prop the sign back up. "I like your sign," I say.

"Thank you, Leighton. It's hard to be a blue dot in a red county, isn't it?"

"Definitely leads to some tense conversations." I think of Liam proudly declaring himself a feminist in lit class, and smile. "I can't wait to go to college, and hopefully live in a more progressive place for a while. Do you miss living in Philly?"

"Oh, every day. It's tough to move to a town that has, what, fewer than five percent people of color living here? *But* it means I can really shape the discourse in the middle school. Add some inclusive school programs, get more diverse books in the library. Those are good changes for a little town like this. And it was hard to teach in the city, too. Most schools are underfunded and overpoliced. That's a tough environment to educate in."

"That sounds like a hard job to have."

"It was. So is this." Mrs. McNamara nods her head toward the windows, gesturing at all of Auburn, it seems. "And speaking of hard career choices, Liam tells me you want to study journalism."

"Very much so."

"That's an important job. Now more than ever."

"I'll probably end up covering Liam's senate race one day," I say, only half kidding.

Mrs. McNamara laughs outright. "That may be. He's got enough charm for it. Liam's dad would love if he went for law, but between you and me, I hope Liam pursues the thing he really loves: art."

I smile. "Liam could probably excel at both."

"Well, he's stubborn enough to try it. That's for sure."

The electric kettle has finished heating up, and Mrs. McNamara pours steaming water into a mug. She passes me a basket of teas to choose from.

"Thank you, Mrs. McNamara," I say.

"You are very welcome." She leans against the other side of the kitchen island, blowing on her own tea. "Liam should be down soon. He had football practice all afternoon, so he had to shower and primp a little."

I laugh at the word *primp* being used for Liam.

"You doubt it? He's worse than his sister some days!"

"This tea is so good," I say, taking another sip and smiling at this new insight into Liam.

"How are your parents these days, Leighton?"

I take a huge gulp of tea, scalding my tongue.

"Um, the same as ever." *A lie.* "My dad still has the construction business." *For now.* "My mom is still at the diner."

"Oh, bless her. I waitressed for years, and I swear it was the hardest job I ever had."

"She says that, too. But she says everyone should do it."

"I agree. I'd love to see them again sometime, your parents."

I'm saved from responding because Liam steps into the sunset-warmed kitchen. He's wearing a white T-shirt and athletic shorts, and the scent of his shower wash arrives with him, fresh and earthy, with a hint of mint. Mouthwash, probably.

The sight of him makes me wish this were a real date.

"Hey, Leighton," he says. He smiles like my presence there is the greatest thing, and I wonder if he could turn off the flirting if he wanted to, or if it's part of his actual genetic code.

"All that time, and he comes down in a plain old white tee," his mom says, shaking her head. "There are cookies, chips, whatever you want in the pantry. You can have the basement if you don't mind Fiona dancing and need more space. But she's switching from ballet to hip-hop soon, so the music might be a bit much."

"Thanks, Ma," he says.

"What'll it be," he asks me, pulling the cabinet open. "Salty or sweet?" He is holding up Twizzlers in one hand and white cheddar popcorn in the other.

"Um, sweet. We'll need clean hands."

Liam chuckles, and my face and neck turn warm as I

realize the implication of my words. "For the pencils . . . for the . . ." I falter. There's no recovering. I turn around, but thankfully Liam's mom has gone into another room.

"If you say so, Barnes," Liam says. "Are you okay with working in my room? Fiona is a perfectionist. She'll do the same piece twenty times in a row until I'm ready to, like, fill my ears with superglue rather than listen to that same song one more time."

"Your room is fine."

We gather snacks and books and head up. Liam's room is huge and midnight blue. His walls are covered in posters— a bunch of X-Men posters with Wolverine on them. A few of the latest Marvel movies. There are framed shadow boxes displaying *Black Panther* comics that look pristine. A basketball net hangs over his laundry basket, and he has a giant bookcase next to his bed. When I step closer I realize that it's almost entirely filled with graphic novels.

On his bed there is a large, very well-loved stuffed bear, wearing a purple vest. Liam must realize why I'm smiling, because he goes to his bed and lifts the brown bear, bringing him to me. "Leighton, I'd like to introduce Mr. Jelly."

"You named him Mr. Jelly?" I ask, laughing.

"The Third," Liam says.

"Was there a Mr. Jelly the First or Second?"

"No, there was not. But I am the third William McNamara, so when I was five I thought that's just how names worked.

Also, peanut butter and jelly sandwiches were the only thing I'd eat for, like, three straight years."

"Ergo, Mr. Jelly the Third."

"Ergo."

I return the bear to the bed and move to Liam's desk, where, sure enough, there is a sketch pad open to a drawing of a town. The town is on the moon, surrounded by barren craters, against a backdrop of darkness and far-off stars. Liam follows me over, and his fingers start to tap out a beat on his stack of textbooks.

"Wow." I run my fingertip over the edge of the page. "Liam, this is beautiful."

"Thanks," he says.

"Lonely place to live," I say.

His fingers stop drumming. "Yeah, it would be."

There are a few pamphlets on the corner of Liam's desk, and I recognize the crests and perfectly landscaped paths. College pamphlets. And not just any colleges.

"Harvard, Yale, Stanford . . ." I read the three names that are exposed, then realize how invasive that was. I step away from his desk. "I'm sorry."

"It's cool. I would have put them away if I cared. They're my future; might as well embrace it."

"You make it sound so ominous."

"Nah, not ominous. They're the best."

"They are the best. So what's wrong?"

"Nothing," Liam says, but there's this hint of apprehension in his voice. "Just competitive as hell, ya know? I want to get in."

"To which one?"

"All of them," he says, and he isn't joking. He's determined, the sheer want shining in his eyes. I see the moment he realizes that I'm studying him a bit more closely than I usually do.

He laughs.

"Isn't that the dream? Get in everywhere? Have half a dozen golden paths laid out, ours for the choosing."

The golden path comment reminds me of what his mom said to me in middle school, to encourage me to get my grades back up. I wonder how many times he heard that talk at home.

I smile. "I'm good with one golden path, actually."

"Okay, honestly, I just don't want to take any chances of being stuck here next year. I'm really over this town."

"I get that." But for once I'm not thinking of what's going on in my home. I'm thinking about my conversation with Liam's mom, and living on a little colony on a lifeless moon. I've been so caught up in my own stuff for years, head down, eyes on the floor, selfishly assuming I was the only one in Auburn dealing with anything.

"So I'll apply to these amazing schools, and some good schools, and some okay ones—just to be safe. And some art programs. My parents have money to help me with school, so it's just on me to get accepted, and, you know, figure out what to do with my life."

"No pressure." I note the way he mentions art programs with a forced casualness. Like he wants to downplay how important it is to him. I know that tone well. It's the same one I use with my mom to broach the topic of leaving. Like if you don't let anyone know just how much you want it, it won't hurt as much when it doesn't happen.

"None at all." Liam laughs.

"So is that what you want to do? Create stories like that?" I nod toward the framed comics on his walls.

"Yeah, I mean, this town is so small, and *so* white. That's why stuff like this matters so much to me—" Liam gestures to the graphic novels on his bookshelves. "I've always loved superhero stories, but now there are finally characters on screen that look like me. It makes me feel like a career creating that kind of art isn't such a long shot after all, if that makes sense."

"That makes a lot of sense. And you are really talented."

"Anyway." Liam shrugs. That little buffer shifts back into place. "Speaking of art . . . we should probably actually do that now."

I wrinkle my nose at the reminder. "Yeah, okay. Let's do art."

I pull out the ugly pears and hand them over. Liam reaches

for the pencils on his desk and a small case. We sit down on the floor, and he opens it, pulling out a pair of glasses.

"You wear glasses?"

"I'm very, *very* slightly farsighted. Sometimes reading is hard. And drawing goes better when I'm wearing them."

"Shouldn't you just wear them . . . all the time?"

"Don't need to. My vision is perfect otherwise."

"I'm pretty sure that's not how it works."

"I'm pretty sure it's how I work," he says. "Can we not dwell on this? I'm not good with admitting my flaws."

"It's hardly a flaw, Liam. Those glasses look great on you."

He turns, his typical smile slipping into place. "Is that right, Barnes?"

"Liam."

"Okay, okay. Making a mental note that you like the nerd type, and we'll move on." He chuckles. I spot a Superman comic on the chair by his desk.

"Clark Kent wears glasses."

"Not when he's flying," he says. But then he shrugs. "But now that you mention it, a Black Superman would be pretty cool."

He reaches for my pear drawing. "May I?"

"Be my guest." I doubt the thing can be salvaged, but I watch as Liam begins to color in the edges of one pear, making just the right parts of it darker with lines, drawing out the round shape of the fruit. When he's done, the pear looks almost real. I feel like I could pick it up.

"That's amazing. Wow. How do you know how to do that?" I ask.

"How do you know which words are right in your essays, or your column?" he asks. "Same thing. Just a thing I can do. And a lot of practice."

"I guess. But you could easily learn to write better. I can't learn to do that. That's witchcraft."

"Try," he says, and hands me my paper.

We work at it for an hour, and by the end, my pears look somewhat decent. Nothing like his, but my report card might say "Shows progress" next to a solid B+ if I can keep this up.

We are sprawled across the floor of his bedroom for elbow space, though we still keep bumping into each other while drawing. Liam leans over, his finger following the dark edge of a pear, and tells me how to fix it. I look up at him and smile. I'd forgotten the glasses for a moment, and he looks distractingly cute in them. It's like the softness of them just accentuates his strength. One little vulnerability that throws the rest of him into sharp focus. Athlete. Academic. Ivy League–bound, apparently. But then I remember the set of his jaw when he talked about getting accepted everywhere, and that pinprick of annoyance over his glasses. Perfect. Too perfect. He's trying *so* hard, and I want to tell him that I see it. I see him.

He finally catches me looking at him, and knocks his

shoulder softly against mine.

There's a knock on Liam's open door, and we spring apart.

"Liam," Fiona says from the doorway. "Oh, sorry."

Liam collects himself first. He gives me a half smile, quirks his eyebrows at me. More charm.

I want to hate it.

I don't.

"It's fine, Fi, we're just practicing pears."

"Is that something dirty? Because if it is, I really don't wanna know."

I hold up my sad drawing as evidence of our innocence.

"Ah, pears," Fiona says, coming into the room. "You guys have art together."

"No way," I say. "I'm struggling through Art I."

"These are good!" Fiona says. "I'd totally eat one if it wasn't paper."

"Thanks," I say, laughing.

"What did you need, Fiona?" Liam nudges his sister.

"Oh, right. I think I figured out that last part of my routine, which means I am so ready for this competition."

"That's great, Fi. Does this mean I'll be hearing that song less now?"

"No. More. It has to be perfect, and I have less than two months."

Fiona tells me about dance and this big trip their family has planned so she can compete next month, and what a big deal it'll be if she does well. She's easy to talk to and easy to laugh with, and it feels totally normal to be hanging out with Liam and his sister. I'm even a little relieved by her presence, because this was always meant to be about art class, and leaning into Liam's shoulder was making it hard for me to remember that.

Fiona takes a stab at the pears, and even hers are better than mine, but I pay attention to how she moves her wrist, and the shading, and when I try another I really am doing better.

Liam walks me out a few minutes before my mom is supposed to pick me up, and we stand on his driveway in the chilly fall air.

"Thank you, Liam, that was nice of you."

"Ah . . . no it wasn't." He stretches his arms, rubs his hand over his head. He didn't wear a jacket outside, and his arms are bare. I always thought I'd go for the slim, nerdy, quiet type in college. But Liam is a football player, which I swore never to date. He's the popular guy with all the charm. More strikes against him. He's loud and funny and comfortable being the center of attention in a way I never will be. And yet . . .

"Of course it was nice. You helped me a lot."

"Maybe. But it wasn't with a pure heart. Listen, I'm not exactly hiding the fact that I like you. And I'm totally cool with us being friends. It'd just be nice to see you outside of school sometimes."

Oh.

"I told you, Liam, I don't have time."

There are so many things I don't say.

"You're right, you don't have time."

Exactly.

Wait.

"What?"

"You've got this college thing in the bag, Leighton. Why don't you just, ya know, have a little fun? Do you *ever* have fun? Because I haven't seen any sign of it. It doesn't have to be anything serious. Let's just hang out. Get to know each other more."

I know there are a thousand reasons to say no. And I'm needed at home.

But Liam is smiling down at me, and I just spent a few hours in the warm, safe haven of his lovely home, and I'm seized by the desire to be selfish. The desire to say yes.

"Okay."

Liam grins, and I'm already glad I did it.

"Okay," he says. "So, next Friday, James is having another bonfire. Shouldn't be too wild or crazy. Sound all right?"

"Okay," I say again.

"Oh, and . . . do you want a ride to school?" he asks. "I drive right past the turn to your house to get to school, so it's on my way. It'll give you a break from a crappy bus ride. Plus . . . maybe you kinda sorta like my company?"

"Kinda." I smile. "Sorta."

"Yes?" he asks.

"Um. Yeah. Yes, I can do that. I mean, thank you."

A minute later, Mom arrives and picks me up. And for most of the night, I feel great about saying yes. All the way home, and while I review my calc notes at our kitchen table. As I say a soft good night to Mom where she's already fallen asleep on the couch, and as I get ready for bed.

But when I get to my room, I find Campbell and Juniper asleep in my bed, and I feel a pang of guilt so strong it physically hurts.

They stir as I climb in with them.

"Hey, Cammy," I say into the dark, my voice low. I don't want to wake her if she's already drifted back to sleep.

"Yeah?"

"Do you mind if I go to a party Friday night?"

"Ha. I *knew* it wasn't about art," she says. I don't have to see her face to picture the smile on it. Brat.

"He offered to drive me to school in the morning, too."

"That's good, Leighton. We'll be fine. You never would have said no to my bike rides. You need things, too."

I should make a point of talking to sleepy Campbell more often. She's so nice.

"Besides, all you ever do is study. If you read too much, your head will explode."

And there she is.

I laugh and press my feet up against her bare legs.

"Jesus, Leighton, your feet are icicles." She grabs an extra throw pillow and shoves it under the blankets, between our legs. "There. The pillow can defrost you."

Maybe this will be okay. I can't make a habit of it, but it's one night. One party. Not even a real party, just a bonfire with friends.

One night to feel seventeen.

Before I miss it altogether.

Chapter Twenty-Three

THE BONFIRE IS WELL-ENOUGH CONTAINED IN a pit dug into the earth and surrounded by a ring of stones, but the flames don't know it. They spit and lick at us, red and gold claws searching for something to catch on. They strike me as something hungry, and I imagine them catching prey in the form of an old white house on Frederick Street. They would consume it all, crackling with ravenous delight as they fed on wood and painful memories.

The heat of the fire is too much. My face is hot and flushed, and I suddenly feel like I'm the thing on fire. The thing that splinters and burns from the inside out.

"You okay, Leighton?" Liam leans in, brushing hair out of my eyes and tucking it behind my ear. I lean into his weight, away from the fire. When he drops his arm around me, it feels like an anchor. Like maybe I'm not about to fly apart into little bits of ash.

"Yeah," I mutter, pulling my gaze from the flames. I look

into warm brown eyes framed by lashes so curled they should seem feminine. On Liam, they look . . . exceptionally good. The intensity of his focus catches me off guard. He's got that full-attention gaze down, like we aren't surrounded by his half-drunk friends. Like we are alone.

Maybe that's not a bad idea. "Hey," I whisper. "Wanna get out of here?"

Those brown eyes widen. He seems to realize something is off, but I'm betting he hasn't guessed that I freaked myself out as I sat here daydreaming about my house burning down.

"Yeah, okay. Sure, Leighton."

I don't know what made me think we could just sneak off, because as soon as we rise, we are noticed.

"Where you going, lovebirds?" Alexis sits directly across the fire from us, wearing Brody's varsity jacket and flashing us a mocking smile. When Brody comes back with a fresh beer, he throws his arm around her shoulder.

"Home," I say. "Curfew."

"It's eight fifteen." Her smile drops.

"She's lying," says Nick, a junior who plays on the football team. "She wants the D."

Well, Liam's friends are super cool. I try to ignore the comment.

"Ice queen? Doubtful," Brody says.

A few guys laugh. I'm grateful that the red glow of the flames probably hides the rush of blood to my cheeks.

"And that's our cue to leave. Good night, assholes." Liam pulls me away from their laughter.

"Your friends are jerks." We reach the car but stand outside of it, unsure, and I shiver. It's finally chilly at night, and away from the fire I wish I had a jacket.

"They're drunk," he says. Then he pauses after he opens his door, and looks at me over the car. "Nah, you're right. They're jerks. I'm sorry."

Inside, he starts the car but leaves it in park.

"Leighton, do you want to go home?"

"Two hours early? God, no."

"Then where to?"

It's a good question. The few options we even have around here will be closed before we can get to them.

"New York City," I say. "California. The moon."

Liam laughs, shakes his head at me.

"Do you want to just drive around?"

"Yes, please."

On the dark back roads, the two beams of the headlights stretch out so far ahead of us. There are no streetlights on these roads, and sometimes there's a mile between houses. The lights are like bright neon arrows, showing me the way to go. Anywhere but home, they beckon.

"Let's pull over," I say, and the words surprise me as much as I know they surprise Liam.

Pulling over means parking. And parking means the two

of us alone in the dark.

Liam doesn't say anything, but in a few minutes we pass the high school, and he pulls into a parking lot that leads to some hiking trails. We're surrounded by trees.

"Do you want to—"

"Should I turn off—"

We stop talking as quickly as we started. Any other time or place, we might laugh at our own awkwardness, but the darkness feels like a blanket weighing down our words. I drop my hand to where Liam's rests on the gear stick.

"Yeah, turn it off. Let's hang out for a bit," I say.

The car engine quits, and the silence is even more profound. It's just our breathing and the obnoxious thumping of my heart. I turn and blink at him in the dark, waiting for my eyes to adjust. Liam shifts in his seat, turning toward me, and I lean in, impulsive and brave, and just like that our lips meet, warm and wonderful. He responds immediately, his hand flying to the back of my neck, tangling in my hair, tilting my head back to just the right degree to deepen the kiss. Yes. This is what I need. To just get lost for a little while.

I can smell the dab of cologne he must have pressed to the underside of his jaw. And I can taste that hint of mint that always hovers around him. There are so many bits of him to learn, and for several minutes, there is nothing in the world but this warm, building exploration of each other, until I feel the gear stick pressing into my hip, painfully.

"Hang on," I say, breaking the kiss as I shift my weight off it.

"Shit, sorry," Liam says, his hands going to my hips to help me move to a more comfortable position. I'm surprised when he pulls, moving me right onto his lap instead of back to my own seat. It takes me a second to catch up, but I'm a pretty fast learner. Instead of sitting, I swing one leg over his hips.

Too fast, a voice inside whispers.

Shut up, I whisper back.

"Barnes." Liam's tone is surprised, and I smile into our next kiss.

His hands move up and down my sides, and then, on the next motion up, slip under the edge of my shirt. I expect some lightning strike of nervousness or embarrassment, but it doesn't come. It just feels . . . good. Safe. He pulls back from our kiss, and his eyes are wide open. They glint in the dark. He's breathing hard, and I smile to think that this response is for me. Not perfectionist Leighton. Not straight-A Leighton. Certainly not *Ice Queen* Leighton.

Just Leighton.

"Is this okay?" he asks, and his hands move tentatively, softly, giving me every chance to ask him to slow down or stop. I want to say it's fine. I want to stay lost. Or at least, part of me does. Another part of me is terrified, and a little overwhelmed by it all.

"Actually," I say. And that's all I have to say. Liam's hands are out from under my shirt and resting on my waist without another word.

"Thanks," I whisper, but we're too close and it's too dark to read his features. "Just a little—"

"Fast. Too fast. It's fine, Leighton."

"Want to sit outside?"

We get out and he gestures toward the hood of the car, helping me up to sit on it. It's warm from the engine, and he grabs his varsity jacket out of the backseat and offers it to me. The design is different, but the school colors haven't changed, and somewhere in our attic is the one my dad used to give my mom to wear.

But it's cold, so I accept it, draping it over my lap instead of putting it on.

Liam climbs up beside me.

"It's so quiet out here," he says. We are facing the woods, and the moon is just a slice of silver in the sky, but it isn't as creepy as I would have thought. The crows are still here. I recognize the sound of them shuffling on branches.

We are quiet a few moments, and I feel some of the awkwardness of our first kiss finally hitting us.

I look up at the night sky.

"Look, a satellite," I say after a moment of tracking the movement.

"A what?" Liam asks.

"It's a satellite." I lean into his side, drawing my arm up

beside him to direct his gaze. "You know Orion's belt? Those three stars there?"

"Yeah, I see that," he says.

"Now watch for a minute, it's gonna pass right through them, right . . . now."

"Oh wow, yeah, I see it. It looks like a star."

"Yeah! But it's too fast for a star, too slow for a meteor. Sometimes you have to watch a while to catch them moving up there, but they're there."

"I've never seen one before," he says. "I didn't know to look."

"Yeah, my mom showed me that when I was little," I say.

"That's cool," he says. He lies back against the hood of the car. "Bet I can spot the next one before you."

I purse my lips. "Does everything have to be a competition?"

"Makes it fun. I'm gonna win."

I lean back, too, resting my head on his arm. It isn't exactly comfortable on the car, but it's still warm. Warmer next to Liam.

He finds the next two satellites.

"Show-off," I say.

He pulls his phone out. "It's getting late. We should head out."

"Yeah, all right."

I'm sad as we leave the tucked-away parking lot. It felt

like we could hide from everyone in there. I realize how much I want a repeat of tonight, to spend more time with Liam, like this.

"So, was tonight okay?" he asks as he parks outside my house.

"More than okay," I say.

"What's wrong?" Liam asks.

"Tonight was great," I say. "I know you said we could just be friends, but maybe—"

"I'm in," he says.

"But I didn't even finish," I say.

"Whatever you want. You call the shots. I'm in."

We turn to face each other, and he leans in slowly this time.

It's a soft, brief kiss, nothing like before, and when we pull away, we're both smiling. Somehow, I feel more shy now.

"Now *that* is how I imagined our first kiss. Sorry for getting carried away earlier," Liam says.

"I got carried away, too," I say, but my mind is echoing the phrase *imagined our first kiss*. "Good night, Liam."

I have to force myself to climb out of his car before I ask him to take me somewhere else.

Somewhere not here.

Chapter Twenty-Four

I WALK INTO THE HOUSE WITH a smile on my face. I'm still replaying the evening's events—with a special emphasis on the kissing parts—when the lights over the counters flare bright for an instant, a surge of energy that draws my attention. That's when I see the sink, and the warmth on my lips is overtaken by dread, cold like a bucket of ice water dumped on me.

A dish is shattered—pieces are in the sink and on the floor. I think it used to be a plate, but now it's nothing but shards of yellow ceramic. There's uncooked pasta still in its package on the counter. I smell burnt chicken, and see a blackened pan in the sink among the shards. There's a pot of water still boiling furiously on the stove, and I quickly move across the kitchen and turn off the blue flame. When the water calms, I realize how quiet everything is.

I walk into the darkened living room, and then I hear it. A whimper. I drop my bag and jacket on the floor and climb over furniture in the dark until I find Campbell and Juniper huddled up together in the corner of the room.

"Are you okay?" I ask, but my voice echoes off the walls. It's like the house is amplifying the sound, making it feel dangerous to speak.

"We needed you," Cam says.

"I'm so glad you're home," Juniper adds.

I can't make out much in the dark, but Cam's eyes shine where the light from the kitchen catches them. *Dammit.* I should have been here.

"I'm so glad, too, June Bug. What happened?"

"We burned the chicken," she says. "So he threw the pan into the sink and shattered the plates and then Mom told him to stop and then . . ."

"And then" is enough. I can figure it out. He was mad. And she got mad. So he got madder. That seems to be an unspoken rule in our house: no one is allowed to be madder than him. I walk to the bottom of the stairs and listen, but I can't hear anything. It's awful and scary when he is screaming. But it is always worse when things are quiet.

"Did he take anything upstairs?" I ask Campbell.

"Anything?"

I glance at Juniper.

"Like a knife? His gun?"

Campbell's eyes widen. I regret the question, but she answers anyway.

"Not that I saw."

"Stay with Junie," I say, and step onto the first stair.

"Don't go up there!" Cam hisses.

I don't want to.

"I've got to check on Mom."

"Please, Leighton," Juniper says, her voice catching.

"Okay, okay." I back down the stairs. "I'm staying."

I squat down beside the girls, and we sit still and quiet in the dark for several minutes.

"Hey, Juniper, how was school today?"

Juniper climbs into my lap before answering.

"Goooood," she draws out.

"What did you learn?" I ask, my fingers fiddling with the soft strands of her hair. She needs a trim.

Junie seems to think hard about my question. The floor creaks upstairs, once. Then all is silent again.

"I learned about Amelia Earhart," Juniper whispers.

"You did?" I ask. "What did you learn about her?"

"She was one of the first ever women to fly planes, and she flew all over the world."

"That's great, June Bug."

"Leighton," Juniper whispers. "Do you think Amelia was fearless?"

A voice raises and then quiets abruptly upstairs.

"Yeah, Juniper, I think she had to be fearless."

Campbell's eyes are fixed on the ceiling.

"What about you, Campbell? What did you learn in school?"

Cam ignores me. I reach over and squeeze her hand. "I'm here now, Cam. I'm sorry."

She keeps staring. I can't help but glance up, too. Even if I had X-ray vision, I don't know if I'd want to look. My mind filters through the what-ifs. The worst cases. The nightmares.

She is hurt. She needs me, and I'm sitting down here. She might be crying or scared. He could have a knife, or his gun out. He could be threatening her.

She could be dead.

The floor creaks, and I look back down.

"Cammy? What did you learn about?" My voice is barely audible, but I know Cam hears me.

"I don't remember, Leighton," Cam says, her voice soft like mine, but cold.

We hear footsteps upstairs, and three necks crane back to look at the ceiling in unison. One set of footsteps.

No, two.

The door opens fast, slamming into a wall upstairs, and I startle, scaring Juniper in my lap. I hug her tightly and briefly—in reassurance and in apology.

"She's okay," I whisper to the girls as our parents come down the stairs. I can see their faces only in part. Half in shadow, half illuminated by the far-too-bright lights in the kitchen. He looks smug. A stupid smirk on his face. I know it's better than his anger, but I hate this face he makes. My eyes leave his ugly look and go to Mom. She's tired.

"Hi, Mom," I say.

"Oh, Leighton, you're home," she says.

"Are you okay?" I ask. He scoffs, crosses the living room.

"Of course I'm okay," she says.

Of course.

"We were worried about you," I add.

Mom sighs, opens her mouth to respond, but is cut off by "Welcome to the Jungle." He twists the knob until it's as high as it goes. Level: 100. The house is moving with the bass.

He goes into the kitchen, and something crashes into the sink.

"And no one thought to clean up the fucking burnt food," he yells. More dishes clatter, and Campbell jumps to her feet.

"Coming," she announces, her voice steady and clear, cutting through the music. Her voice holds none of the fear that had her so still and serious and soft a moment ago.

For some reason, Cam's enthusiasm for cleaning up burnt food makes me furious. Mom's casual *of course* makes me want to scream. I count to three in my head, my jaw shut as though it were wired that way. *Don't make it worse. Don't make it worse.* I need these words tattooed on my arm so I always remember. I stand up and deposit Junie on the sofa next to Mom.

"Tell her about Amelia," I yell over the music, and step past a kitchen lit so bright it hurts my eyes. I am sure the damn light is getting brighter and brighter, until I have to turn away from it, the outline of Campbell at the sink washing broken dishes imprinted on my eyelids. I blink, and the light is fine now. Back to its normal level of still-too-bright. It's like the house wanted that image to stay with me, burned into my retinas.

I walk around the living room picking up the frames. I hang them on their nails, letting them swing back and forth until they find their own resting place. When I pass the window, there is a flash of gray, and Joe lands just outside in the grass. I keep going, hanging a frame by the stairs. I step into the bathroom and pick up the towels that fell to the floor. And then in my bedroom I fix the posters on my wall, which don't hang on nails at all but on sticky tack, and I don't know why they are always down, too. Why this house falls apart without being touched. In the girls' bedroom, I unfurl stained-glass window stickers that have fallen to the carpet like dead flower petals and stick them back on the window. They used to form a butterfly, I think. Now they are just parts of an incomplete whole. The pieces we haven't lost yet.

Joe lands on the windowsill outside, and this time I pause because it feels like he's following me from window to window for a reason. I slide the window open slowly, giving him time to fly away. Then I reach my hand out, one finger extended, and he stays still as I brush my fingertip down his feathered side. Once, twice.

He turns and drops something onto the windowsill, then flies away.

I reach for the object.

It's Juniper's leather cuff, with her initials pressed into it. It looks a little weather-worn, but it's intact. Joe brought it back.

It's strange how some things are lost to us forever, and some find their way home, and we have no way of knowing which ending it will be until and unless they return.

A long time ago, Amelia Earhart flew away and never came back. She's always described as being lost. But now she reminds me of a piece of crow folklore I read for my column. The Babylonian flood predates even Noah. In the older story, when the whole world floods, those who survive on a boat send out birds to seek dry land. First they release a dove—but the dove, unable to find land to rest on, returns quickly. The second bird they send is a swallow. Again, with no land to rest on or fresh water to drink on the wide, endless sea, the swallow returns. Finally, they send the crow, who flies off toward the horizon, the third bird entrusted to find land. She does not come back.

Maybe Amelia wasn't lost to an endless sea. Maybe, like the crow, she found dry land, and decided to stay where she felt safe.

Maybe surviving can be fearless, too.

AUBURN, PENNSYLVANIA
OCTOBER 13

CROW POPULATION:
34,702

Chapter Twenty-Five

THIS HOUSE IS UNBROKEN THE WAY a healed bone is.

Something was bent at an unnatural angle, pushed too far, until it snapped, or shattered. But then it got better again.

When I was eight, we had a snow day. Mom was waitressing by then, and the diner didn't close, so she went in, hugely pregnant with Juniper. Dad slept in, his body tired from long hours all weekend spent trying to get a roof job done before the snow arrived. I made breakfast for Campbell and myself, and we were watching cartoons when he finally came downstairs. The trash was overflowing in the kitchen. We didn't take it out—I don't know that I even could have lifted it—but when he saw it, he got so angry, and he threw it across the floor, spilling it everywhere. Then he grabbed a cabinet door we'd left open, slamming it back the wrong way so that it tore off the hinges, the crack so loud it felt like it broke inside of me. I grabbed Cammy and we ran to my room, hiding in the closet.

Mom found us there in the late afternoon.

When we came downstairs, the trash was still everywhere, and he was asleep on the couch. But the cabinet door wasn't broken. I tried to explain to Mom, in confused, urgent whispers, that the wood had cracked right at the hinges. But it was intact, like it had never broken. I decided I must have seen it wrong. That it had just been the noise of the cabinet hitting the wall. But I know Campbell saw it, too, because when Mom went to change her clothes, Cammy leaned in close and whispered, "It was magic."

It was two years before the next explosion like that. There used to be so much time in between them. He's always sorry. He says it won't happen again.

I know now that the last is never true. It will happen again. And he probably does love us, but it's never been enough to make him stop. Instead, it makes it worse—his love for us. And ours for him. It makes it impossible to leave.

It took me a while to remember the cabinet door, and the way doubt had erased what I saw. I forgot until it started happening again, and more frequently. The house always repairing the things he breaks.

The house doesn't make sense, but neither does the way he splinters into something unrecognizable when he's mad. It's incredible what you learn to accept when so few things make sense, and Campbell and I learned to observe it in silence. To note the patched walls and fixed frames, and then fold that strangeness into a soft corner of our minds, where it could be ignored.

Chapter Twenty-Six

LIAM STARTS DRIVING ME TO SCHOOL. Every morning, he parks his Ford at the end of Frederick Street—across from the mailboxes that are now always covered in crows. He waits there while I walk my sisters up and make sure they get onto the bus okay. If the habit seems odd or unnecessary to him, he doesn't say anything.

Within a few weeks, it feels like we've been doing this forever.

Liam couldn't know it, but his consistency might be my favorite quality of his. I let myself look forward to Liam, and that anticipation starts to replace my fear of the crawl space at night. I fall asleep easier. It's just a fifteen-minute ride to school every morning, but it's a *good* fifteen minutes.

These drives aren't like our first date. We haven't even kissed again. We just talk, and laugh, and trade favorite songs.

On the second Friday of morning drives together, we have an exam in lit class.

"G'morning," he says, yawning. He's exhausted, thanks to football.

"Morning," I say, and pass him the extra tumbler I brought. "Mine is coffee, but I noticed you never drink it, so yours is hot chocolate. Hope that's okay. Or we can trade?"

"Perfect," he says. "Thanks. So, what'll it be?" He reaches for the stereo volume, turning his radio on.

"Used to Love Her" by Guns N' Roses is playing, and a sour taste fills my mouth.

"Not this," I say, reaching out my hand and turning the radio off.

Liam looks over at me, curiosity sketched across his face. "Not a fan?"

"Really not. Especially that one."

"How about no music?"

"Thanks." I drink some coffee and wait for the tightness in my chest to ease before I reach for my literature notebook. "Want me to quiz you while you drive?"

"Yeah, let's do it," he says.

"Okay—" I flip to the page with my study guide. We have a major exam on all of our summer reading books today. I browse for a good starter question, but these are all from our *Tess of the d'Urbervilles* curriculum from early September, so they're kind of depressing. "How much did the end of *Tess* suck?"

"Is that a quiz question? Damn, I'm gonna ace this thing."

"Just my question. Okay, focus. How does social class play into Tess's ability to navigate her world? How integral was her social station to the outcome of her story?"

Liam seems to ruminate on the question while he executes a very safe stop at a four-way and turns. I like how unhurried he is. Nothing is an emergency. No rushed, frantic movements. "Because, if she'd been rich, she would have had options. Money means choices. If you have no resources, then the tiniest little thing goes wrong and you're toast. Totally at the mercy of others. Also, she could have hired a sweet-ass attorney to defend her."

The end of his answer makes me laugh.

"How'd I do?"

"Good, but I wouldn't use the phrases 'sweet ass' or 'you're toast' in your short essays."

"Psh, where's the fun in that? Give me another," he says. "Quick, we're almost there."

"Ahhh, okay," I say, browsing my page. "Discuss the relationship of men and women in the novel. How are these social constructs different today?"

"Oh good, an easier one," Liam says.

On the page in front of me, I have bulleted points for this one. Six neat lines condensing gender discrimination over the course of a century into bullet points. It's absurdly simplified. I miss what Liam is saying.

"Sorry, what?"

"I said it isn't all that different, is it? It's all over the news. There's, like, a lot of harassment and assault, and I don't know. It's different, but it's a lot the same."

I glance at him sideways in the car, a little surprised by his answer. I didn't really think guys my age were paying attention to those things. And I thought he was half joking when he called himself a feminist. But he notices a lot.

"You okay in there, Barnes?" We've pulled into his parking spot. "I feel like you're anywhere but here this morning."

Of course he doesn't mean it, but I think of the game I use to distract Juniper on bad nights. Anywhere But Here.

"I'm fine."

"Too much studying," he says. "And too much football."

"You like football," I say.

"I like you a lot more," he counters. "We are so overdue for another date."

I smile. "I'd love that. But neither of us is going to have a social life if we don't get through this lit exam."

"Fair enough," Liam says. His face brightens. "Hang on, stay right there."

He gets out of the car, running around the front of it and tugging the collar of his fleece up to protect his neck from the bite of cold in the air this early. He opens the door for me.

"There. Some chivalry. To make up for what jerks guys are."

"Chivalrous knights burned women as witches."

"Yeah, I know, but this conversation about poor Tess is stressing me out."

"Same," I say, and we head into school together.

I try to focus on the review questions, but the phrase "poor Tess" is stuck in my mind. Tragedy, the classic plight of the classic heroines.

I don't want to be like Tess, poor Tess, or any of these women in books who are trapped. Or worse, they fight back, and they are killed for it. Because that part of it is too true. Speaking up can be dangerous. If you look for them, and I have, there are news stories every single day that tell you how dangerous it can be. I know how many hours of fear are contained in the phrase *domestic dispute*. There is an entire history of heartache there. And when I imagine myself as a reporter, I hope I can make those words worth their weight on the page. I hope that one day I can tell the stories that deserve to be brought into the light.

But as much as I hate saying nothing, it's the only way I know how to keep them safe.

For now.

But I won't be quiet forever.

Chapter Twenty-Seven

AFTER SCHOOL, I TAKE OUT MY frustration with literature in the place where I think best: the newsroom. Sofia is sitting at my desk, and when we make eye contact, it's like she reads my mind with one little glance.

"What's wrong?" she asks.

"Just a long day. Lit exam." I drop my research files onto my desk and dig for the scrap of paper I threw into my bag with the name and number of an ornithologist at a nearby college. "Move your butt, I have work to do."

Sofia doesn't move, so I sit on her lap.

"Very mature," Sofia says, sputtering as the messy knot of my hair flies into her face. "Just like real journalists."

"Real journalists do their work in the office, Sof. They don't just hang out talking and making googly eyes over crushes."

"I refuse to believe that's true. Swear to me we will never be too grown-up for googly eyes or crushes. Who are you calling?"

I'm already dialing, but I cover the mouthpiece with my hand. "A bird expert."

Sofia pushes me up and sneaks out from my chair. I collapse back into it as the number I've dialed starts ringing.

There's no answer, so I start to leave a message, but Sofia comes running back over to my desk, waving a sheet of paper and jumping up and down. I glare at her and stumble through the end of my message.

"Sofia!" I yell after I drop the phone down. "That message was incoherent. What is so important?"

"Winter formal announcement," she says, and drops the flyer onto my desk. A dance. She interrupted my phone call because of a dance.

"I wasn't gonna go," I tell her. The winter formal always falls on New Year's Eve—our district's attempt to slow down drinking and driving, as though flasks and molly and vodka bottles stashed under passenger seats don't exist.

"It's *eighties* themed, Leighton. It's going to be amazing. Besides, Liam's gonna ask you," she says. She puts her hand on her hip and tilts her head. "And you will say yes."

"Sofia . . ." I don't argue with her. It's pointless. "I'm hoping to set up an interview with the ornithologist this afternoon. Will you come along? We can practice our interview skills together."

"Yeah, yeah. You just need a ride."

Now I tilt my head. "Pleeeease?" I mimic the face Juniper

makes when she's pouting. That girl has an A+ pout.

My phone rings. "Oh, good, it's him! Will you take me?"

"Of course."

"Thanks—"

"With one condition."

So close.

"If Liam does ask, just say *yes*." And this time, she doesn't say it in a pushy way. She says it like she's offering me the last donut in the box. Like, here, take this, you clearly need it.

"Fine," I say, and grab the phone before it stops ringing.

I set up an interview in an hour and tell Sofia I'll meet her at her car.

I lift the winter formal flyer from my desk. Part of me is glad Sofia pushed the issue. It's the part of me that now secretly hopes Liam does ask me, so I can be selfish and seventeen and say yes.

Under the dance flyer is another bright pink slip. It's the township essay contest. I feel like this damn flyer is everywhere I turn, mocking me. I tried to write the essay after the last Friday night football game. I couldn't do it.

Auburn Proud, it demands.

But I'm not.

Chapter Twenty-Eight

ON MONDAY MORNING, I WAKE UP to the smell of coffee, and find Mom on the corner of my bed, two mugs in hand. It's still dark outside.

I sit up quickly, listening for some sound from the rest of the house, but it's quiet.

"Mom?"

She hands me a cup of coffee.

"Everything is fine," she says, and sips her coffee. She crosses my room to a little corkboard that hangs over my desk. She unpins one of the many college brochures and brings it back to the bed.

"So. This is the one?" she asks. New York University.

"How did you know?"

"I know everything," she says, and shoves her shoulder gently against mine.

We sip coffee quietly for a few more minutes. I know what Dad has always expected of me. He said I can't rely on any kind of talent to get me a scholarship for school, and to work really hard and get the grades. And I have. I've developed both a perfect GPA and absolutely no desire to go to the school he thinks is best. And a rather strong desire to go somewhere else out of sheer spite.

And somehow Mom knows.

"I applied last week," I tell her. "For early admission. I'll hear back this winter."

"How did you pay for it? Applications are expensive."

"Um, a fee waiver. Mrs. Riley helped me."

Mom is quiet for a moment, and I'm dying to know how she feels.

"Well, that makes our plans for today even more time sensitive," she says. "So, get dressed. Comfy shoes. Downstairs in ten?"

I make it downstairs in three minutes, hair in its typically messy bun at the nape of my neck, jeans pulled hastily on, and an old oversized sweater pulled over the tank top I slept in.

"You are going to regret some of those choices," Campbell says from the kitchen table, where she's eating a bowl of cereal. Juniper laughs, dripping milk onto the table.

No one rushes to clean up the mess.

I feel like I've woken up in an alternate reality.

"No time to change," Mom says. "Let's go."

And just like that, the girls are leaving their empty bowls in the sink and rushing me out to Mom's car, which is already turned on and warmed against the autumn chill.

We get in and buckle, and I finally ask.

"What is going on?"

"We are going—"

"Wait!" Mom says. "Wait. Let's surprise her."

"She hates surprises," Campbell says.

"I hate surprises," I repeat.

"You'll like this one," Mom insists. "Okay, music. Juniper gets first choice."

Campbell and I groan, and I reach for the travel mug of coffee I managed to grab in lieu of breakfast.

About ten minutes later we pull into the diner.

"Fun," I say. "But why did the girls eat breakfast at home?"

"We aren't here for breakfast," Mom says. "We are here for that."

She points to the far end of the parking lot, where a bus is idling.

"We are . . . going on an adventure," she whispers.

"TO NEW YORK CITY!" Juniper yells, so loud I almost drop my coffee.

"Seriously?" I ask Mom, disbelief thrumming through me. We haven't done anything like this in a really long time. "What about school?"

"Not going today. We decided that if you really want to live in New York, you at least have to spend a day there first, make sure you like it."

"Fair enough," I say. But I know I'll like it. It's the opposite of Auburn. What's not to like?

"The bus takes us into the city and brings us home at five, so we have to fill the whole day," Mom says. She makes sure Juniper has gloves and a scarf, and gives Campbell her own cozy hat. It's windy today; we can hear it whistling outside.

"We haven't had an Apple Day in so long," Campbell says.

"What's an Apple Day?" Juniper asks. Her smile is big and toothy.

Mom sips at her coffee, a gentle lift of her lips at Juniper's question, and I think of the memories it brings.

"We used to miss a day of school and work every autumn," I tell her. "And we'd all go to the orchards a town over, and we'd spend the entire morning picking apples, until—"

"Until the basket was so heavy that Dad was the only one who could lift it," Campbell says.

"Dad went, too?" Juniper asks. Her confusion is a testament to how much things have changed. Of course he went, I want to say. But that was another lifetime ago, wasn't it?

Campbell ignores Junie's question altogether, keeps talking.

"And we'd also eat them the whole time we were picking them, so—"

"By the time we got home we were sick from them, so many apples!" Mom says. "But there were still so many left. So we'd bake for the rest of the day. Apple pies covering every surface of the kitchen. But of course by then we could barely look at another apple, let alone take a bite—"

"So we'd give them away," I say. "We'd take two to Nana and Grandpa, and give them to the secretaries at school. We'd send a bunch to Dad's work for the crew."

"We'd keep one," Mom says, "and get some vanilla ice cream, and eat it for dinner."

"An Apple Day," Campbell says.

"Mm," Juniper says. "Apple Days sound delicious. Hey! Why don't we have any Apple Days now?"

I can't think of an answer to give her, and Campbell sits back into her seat again.

"We should," Mom says. "It's just hard since Nana is so far now, and without Grandpa. He was one of our primary apple pie eaters, you know."

"Well, it's still an Apple Day," Juniper says.

"It is?" Mom asks.

"Yeah," Juniper says. "The Big Apple!"

And just like that, she makes us all laugh, even Campbell.

On the ride to New York, I sit with Mom. She opens her purse and pulls out a worn copy of *Pride and Prejudice*. It's her favorite book, and I couldn't even finish reading it.

I should try again.

"Mom, um, how can we afford this? I know money's been tight lately. I don't need this," I ask, my voice low so the girls won't overhear in the seats in front of us.

"Tip money," Mom says.

But that still isn't right, because he keeps everything she earns.

He tracks the money.

"Cash tips," she adds. "I just set some aside. We needed something special after all the penny-pinching."

So she hid the money. He's away on a construction job, so I wonder if he even knows about this at all. We can't hide it; Juniper will slip up.

"Leighton, stop. You are thinking too hard. This is fine. I can take my daughters on a little trip."

There is more to that sentence. She just couldn't say it out loud.

I can take my daughters on a little trip *without asking permission*.

But this is a morning to let it go. And when I see the city skyline, I stop caring about our secrets and their consequences.

We begin with a scheduled tour of NYU. We ride in a taxi, to the complete delight of Juniper. Then we visit the Met.

On our way into Central Park we grab some hot dogs and fruit to eat.

It is every single cliché I can think of, and it is perfect.

Mom and Campbell and Juniper make it perfect.

I start to feel a sense of loss even though it's nearly a year away. The idea of being away from *them* is terrifying. Especially if I won't know if they're safe.

I sit on a park bench with Campbell, and she offers me one of the apples we bought. Mom and Juniper are collecting Juniper's favorite bright leaves out of the fall foliage. I bite into the apple and gag, spitting the bite back out. It looked shiny and red on the outside, but it must have been dropped a lot, because the inside is bruised and soft.

"Ew, yuck," Campbell says, grabbing my apple and her own and throwing them into a garbage bin. "We'll find another apple treat later."

We stay in the park for a while longer. The day is cold, but the sun is warm, and it's peaceful here. I tilt my face up to the light, and catch a glimpse of black in the corner of my vision. High up in an oak tree, there are three crows perched on a branch.

They are high enough that I can't be certain.

And of course it isn't true, this far away from Auburn.

But then they rustle their feathers, one after the other, and I'm more sure of it.

One of the crows is gray.

Chapter Twenty-Nine

"AUBURN WOLVES CAN'T BE BEATEN."

The *Auburn Gazette*'s headlines haven't been this positive in a long time. Sofia is entirely caught up in covering the team lately, in this rare moment when sports are genuinely as newsworthy as this town always wants them to be. She asked if she could interview my father about the Wolves' last winning streak, and I've been pushing the interview back with one soft excuse after another. Tonight they played their last regular-season game—another win. An undefeated season, for the first time in almost two decades.

This time when I decide to go to the game, I join Liam's family. It's perfect timing, actually, because Mom is taking the girls to sleep over at Nana's apartment so Juniper can complete her Auburn history assignment. The ride to the away game is quiet. As soon as I get in, Fiona hands me one of her earbuds, and she plays music for us the entire ride.

But the ride home is different, because it's a *win*, and

Liam had a great game.

I'm still quiet, but I notice some things from the backseat.

I notice how Liam's dad has a version of loud that isn't angry.

I notice how he drives with one hand on the steering wheel and the other resting in between the seats, holding his wife's hand. It almost looks unintentional, like their hands come together automatically when they sit beside each other.

I realize that Liam does this when he drives me to school, but I was never aware of it in the way I am now.

Liam will drive himself home from the school once the team bus gets back, so Fiona and I grab snacks and head down to their basement on our own while we wait for him. It's already late, but my parents said midnight, and I'm going to steal every last minute I can here before I have to go home.

Their basement has a gigantic television on one end, and big sofas and chairs. And the whole other half of the basement is turned into a little dance studio for Fiona, complete with long mirrors and a barre. She moves to her half of the room, slipping her shoes off and stepping into movements she's done a million times. I bet she dreams dance.

"When did you start it?"

"Dance?" she asks. She makes eye contact with me in the mirror as she stretches. "When I was three."

She sits down on the floor and pulls her hair loose from the tight bun it was in.

"I know, it looks crazy," she says. Her hair is curly and big after she takes it out.

"It's really pretty, Fiona."

"Psh." She rolls her eyes. "Tell that to Dylan Carpin."

"Who?"

She sighs, leaning forward. "A kid in my grade."

"What did he say?"

"He said he liked me," she says. "He said he wanted to ask me to winter formal."

"Do you want to say yes?"

"I did . . . until he asked what I planned to do with my hair for the dance."

"What?"

"Yeah, he said it's really pretty when it doesn't look *too exotic*."

"Wow, Fiona. What a jerk."

Fiona laughs. "Yup."

She stands up and moves to the sofa, curling up next to me.

"I thought he was nice. He seemed nice otherwise."

"Yeah, but *nice otherwise* could excuse a lot of terrible stuff, couldn't it?"

Fiona looks at me. "You're right. It could. Whatever. My friends and I are going as a group. We don't need dates."

"I've never gone with a date to a dance, and I always have fun with my best friend."

"Yeah? Good, decision made. Friends only. Well, for *me*.

Maybe *you* can finally go with someone . . ."

I pull a pillow to my chest. "Don't even say it, Fiona."

". . . like Liam?"

"You said it!"

Fiona tugs the pillow away from me. "You can't hide from it; I know you want to go with him. You two are dumb together. It's great to see a couple of smarty-pants be dumb together."

"Thanks, Fiona," I say, laughing.

"Just promise you'll say yes if he asks," she says.

What is it with everyone making me promise this?

Fiona gasps. "Or better yet, you should ask Liam!"

"Ask me what?" says a voice in the stairwell.

I glare at Fiona and shake my head *no*.

She just smiles, and looks exactly like her brother when she does.

"Congratulations," I tell Liam when he sits down on the opposite couch. He must've jumped right into a shower before coming down here, because his hair is all wet and he does not smell like he just played a football game. It's that same earthy shower wash again. The kind he used the first night we kissed. The memory makes me flush with warmth. Maybe Fiona is right. Maybe I am a *little* dumb with Liam. And maybe that's okay. To get out of my head and trust my feelings.

But it's nice to know that it's even. That I make him a little dumb, too.

"Thanks," Liam says. "But we aren't here to talk about football."

"We aren't?"

"We are supposed to work on art."

"Let's not," I say, pushing my backpack behind me.

"It can't be that bad," Liam says, reaching for it.

He tugs the bag from me and pulls out my art portfolio. He takes out my latest catastrophe, which I'm fondly calling *Portrait of an Old Crow.*

It's a drawing of Joe, but wearing a bow tie and a monocle. I've told Liam about the real Joe, but I think he didn't know how seriously to take me. *Guardian bird* is probably a weird concept to accept outright. It took Campbell, Juniper, and me a while, too.

But now he's just Joe. Always outside our house. Taking the crackers Juniper leaves him, and giving her marbles in return.

Liam takes the drawing over to the light, and he smiles at it.

"He's cute," he says.

"He's *dignified*," I correct.

"May I?" He gestures with his pencil, and I nod. Liam changes the shape of the eyes a bit with his pencil. The change is subtle—intuitive, for him—but the effect is real. It's like the eyes have come to life a little more on the page.

"Why is he gray?" Liam asks.

"Because the real Joe is gray. Turns out it's not just an

abnormality. My bird guy thinks Joe is an entirely different crow species, called a hooded crow."

"The most alarming part of this conversation so far is that you have a bird guy," Liam says.

"An ornithologist, if we want to get technical."

"Nerd," he says, and his shoulder rocks into mine. I roll my shoulder against him in return.

"The weird thing is that hooded crows are mostly found in Europe. How do you think Joe came to be here?"

"That's a little existential for a bird, don't you think?"

"You two are big geeks, you know," Fiona says, climbing off the couch. "It's Friday night, let loose a bit."

"Maybe we could 'let loose' if I didn't have an annoying, hovering sister around all the time," Liam says.

Fiona laughs, immune to his teasing.

"You love me," she says.

"God help me," he answers.

I smile and slip my drawing back into my bag. *Portrait of an Old Crow* can wait.

"How about a movie?" Liam asks. "I've got a great collection."

"Oh, no, here we go," Fiona says. "Here it is, Leighton. We've arrived. The moment you dump this boy. Liam *only* watches superhero movies."

"Well, that doesn't sound bad. Everyone loves superhero movies."

Fiona sits up. "It's not bad until you are on the third

Spiderman movie *in a row*, debating different director visions and deciding which iteration or decade of comic book portrayals best supports that vision." She collapses back into the couch. "He doesn't just watch superhero movies. He *dissects* them."

"Thanks, Fiona. You could ease her in a bit."

"To what a top-level geek you secretly are? There's no hiding it, Liam," Fiona says. She turns to me. "Ask him how many times he saw *Into the Spiderverse* in the movie theater. Hint: more than five."

"C'mon, Fi. A Black superhero origin story—and my favorite superhero, at that—with absolutely *out of this world* animation. And if I recall, you went with me to the movies three of those times."

"Whatever, nerd. I'm going upstairs. Mom is probably watching a home makeover show."

Fiona hops off the couch and starts to head upstairs.

"You know those are, like, crazy staged, right, Fi?" Liam calls. "Like, how can a preschool teacher and a community garden organizer afford an $800,000 house?"

Fiona leans over the steps at the last second, stretching out her arm and pretending to shoot a web at Liam before disappearing upstairs.

"So . . . *have* you seen *Into the Spiderverse*?" Liam asks, turning to me.

"Umm . . . honestly, it's a lot of *My Little Pony* and Disney channel in my house. I haven't seen any superhero movies in years."

"That's tragic, Barnes. Time to fall in love with a kick-ass film."

"*Film*," I tease. "Isn't this a cartoon?"

Liam pauses in his task but doesn't look up. "Not a *cartoon*. An Academy Award–winning animated feature."

I smile at this geeky side of Liam. I think of the glasses, and the shelves upon shelves of comic books in his room. There's something kind of vulnerable about loving something this much, and it makes me feel like I'm seeing a whole other version of him.

"You could have picked something you haven't watched a lot already," I say.

"And miss a golden opportunity to get Fiona to leave us alone for a bit?" he asks.

Well played, Liam McNamara. He joins me on the couch.

He isn't wrong, though. It's a great movie. Film.

"Ready to admit it, Barnes?"

"Admit what?"

"I have great taste."

"Well, clearly." I shrug.

"I meant movies."

"I know. But you're fishing for a compliment, and I'm not giving you the satisfaction. The movie's fine."

"Barnes, you're killing me."

"Of course it's great," I laugh. "Everything you do is great. I'd rather see some flaws at this point. No one is this perfect."

"I'm not perfect, Barnes."

"I know. You just want everyone to think you are."

Well, shit. If I could go back in time thirty seconds and bite my own tongue, I would. I tried to say it with some levity, but it fell terribly flat.

I mean it, and he knows I mean it. Liam reaches for the remote and pauses the movie.

He shifts so he's facing me. "It's not like it's an act. I just feel like I can't afford to make mistakes."

"I can understand that, Liam. But maybe . . . with me?"

"Let the guard down?"

"Not a lot. Just a smidge."

"Okay, okay. My greatest flaw is—"

"I didn't mean right this minute, Liam."

"I cannot sing."

I deflate. "That's not really what I meant."

"Sure, but I can't just not sing—I am spectacularly bad at it. Cannot find a note to save my life."

He knows I didn't mean singing. No one can sing. But I'll hold him to it anyway.

"Prove it."

Liam doesn't even hesitate. He pulls up a music app on his phone and chooses a song from the movie's soundtrack. He starts to sing. And, oh my God, he's *right*. He is spectacularly bad.

On the other couch, their cat lifts his head at the noise Liam is making.

I refuse to laugh, because this is such a cheating flaw and I was hoping for something a little more real, but he's making it hard.

I hold it together until he launches into falsetto. But when he sings the last high note, his cat runs out of the room, and I'm lost. I laugh until I'm crying.

He ends as loudly and terribly as he began. And he bows deeply even though he lost fifty percent of his audience during his performance.

"Baxter doesn't like your singing, but I do," I say when I can breathe again.

"You liked that?" He collapses onto the couch, and I half fall onto him.

"I loved that, Liam. If all of your flaws are this incredible, you should really share them with the world. You are depriving people of some very wonderful and very human flaws."

"Totally worth it. Gotta remember this."

"Remember what?"

"How great your laugh is. I could definitely get used to hearing that," Liam says, grinning. He reaches over and wipes a tear off my cheek. I cry a lot when I laugh. I cry when I'm sad and when I'm scared, and definitely when I'm angry, but also when I laugh. Especially when I laugh so hard it hurts my ribs.

Spoiler alert: Leighton Barnes cries *all the time.*

But now I'm not laughing or crying, I'm just curled up on a couch with a really sweet guy's arm wrapped around me. I'm not sure how I came to be in Liam McNamara's basement, snuggled up on the couch, seeing this side of him that I never imagined existed. I'd say it's like I've arrived on an alien planet, but Liam and his family are clearly the normal ones in this scenario. I guess that makes me the lost, out-of-place alien. Don't mind me, I'm just here to take some space alien notes on what a happy family looks like.

Liam pulls my legs onto his lap. "Leighton, I've been really wanting to ask you something. And I've honestly never asked this question before not knowing what the answer will be. And before you call me on it, yes, I know that sounds super arrogant. I just want you to know I'm feeling vulnerable here, too. Like a little baby kitten. So if you have to say no, be gentle, okay?"

"Okay, okay. I'm not *this* mean, am I?"

"I dunno." He smiles. "Let's see."

He's built this up so much that I'm genuinely nervous.

"Leighton, will you be my girlfriend?"

Oh.

I don't answer him right away. If he wasn't sure what my answer would be, neither am I.

I should say no, because. Reasons. I know that I should say no. It's selfish not to. But I've felt so trapped the last two years, and with Liam, I just feel like myself. Like how I could be all the time if things were different.

Besides, Liam McNamara just called himself a baby kitten.

"Do we have to date? I'm really just in it for the sex."

I've won a date night bonus round, and the prize is Liam's deep, booming laugh.

"Seriously, Leighton."

"Seriously, Liam?" I ask. I kiss his cheek. "Yes. I'll be your girlfriend."

"Does this mean I have a date to the Snow Ball?"

"You know that's not its name, right?"

"Does this mean I have a date to the Winter Formal?"

"Yes," I say, and only once I say it do I remember the promise I made Sofia. Maybe I was wrong, and I always would have said yes to him.

"I really wanna kiss you," he whispers. "But I can't right now."

"Why not?" I whisper.

"Because then you will miss the best part."

I lean my head on his shoulder, and we watch. It feels natural, and comfortable, and a thousand other things I haven't felt in a long time, and they all begin and end with the feeling of safety.

For the moment, I am the happiest creature on earth.

Chapter Thirty

I ARRIVE HOME AFTER MY FATHER has fallen asleep, and leave before he wakes up.

Sofia and I go to the mall and try on the most ridiculous dresses we can find. Sofia looks amazing in all of them, no matter how awful the color looks on a mannequin. I feel pale and washed out in every color I try on, my undecided reddish-blonde hair somehow clashing either way. It seems like the most popular colors are all some variant of neon—which is perfect for Sofia and an eighties-themed dance, but not so great on me.

Then Sofia slips me something dark under the dressing room stall. The dress dips low in the front and lower in the back, and the skirt flares just the right amount. It has *pockets*. It is shiny and black and perfect. I feel a drumbeat of excitement. Normal things. Normal high school things like a dance, and a dress, and a date.

I check the price tag, and let out a long, low whistle.

"Let me see it!" Sofia yells from the other side of the door. "Don't you dare take it off until I've seen it."

I unlatch the door and let it swing wide.

Sofia raises her eyebrows at me. *"Girl."*

I purse my lips to the side. "I can't buy both, Sofia."

"Ugh, Leighton. This dress is *perfect* for you. And isn't there another way to—"

"Maybe, but maybe not. And she needs this now, Sof."

"Yeah, yeah, I hear you. Let's go."

Sofia can't choose and gets two dresses in two fantastic bright colors.

We walk back into the sporting goods store we entered the mall through, and there it is again. On special clearance because it's gonna be cold soon anyway. One gorgeous, Tiffany Blue girl's bike. My saved-up Christmas and birthday cash from Nana might have gotten me that dress, or a few textbooks next year—or it can get this bike. Some of the things I've missed out on in the last few years have been hard to let go of. And lately I can't seem to say no to the time I've been spending with Liam. But this choice isn't difficult at all.

When we pull up outside my house, Sofia helps me prop the bike up in the front yard.

"Well, go get her," she says.

I pull Campbell away from the TV and cover her eyes with my hands.

"Leighton . . ." she whines just the once, and lets me lead her outside.

When I move my hands, Campbell is silent.

I nudge her forward. "Well?"

She runs her fingers over the handlebars. She presses softly into the seat. Finally, she looks up.

"Thank you, Leighton."

She wraps her arms around me in a very un-Campbell-like show of affection.

"No problem, babe," I say. "Now go get a ride in. It's freezing out, so your days with this thing are numbered until spring."

I say bye to Sofia and head inside. When Campbell comes in an hour later, she finds me in the armoire. Not hiding, but searching. For a dress.

Everything is old and doesn't fit right.

Campbell holds out a bag, the dress store's name on the side.

"Sofia says that if you don't wear this to the dance, she can't be your best friend anymore."

Chapter Thirty-One

THE REST OF THE WEEKEND PASSES like a dream. Someone else's dream, because I should know better. I spend Saturday night curled on my bed with the girls. They read while I fight with *Portrait of an Old Crow* some more. A quiet calm has taken over the house, and I bask in the normalcy. When you live in chaos, boring is a retreat. The mundane is magnificent.

By Sunday, I'm a fool.

He gets home from a weekend construction job early, the work cut short by a downpour. We spend the gray afternoon in our rooms, but eventually we have to come down for dinner.

"I've got a great idea," Dad says as he puts Mom's lasagna in the center of the table. "Let's have a game night. We used to have game nights all the time."

That's true. We did. At our grandparents' house.

It was different.

But Campbell and I share a look, and she shrugs. It might just be the eye of the hurricane, but that doesn't mean we can't appreciate a glimpse of the sun. And there's always that voice in the back of my mind that says, *You never know.* It's been a good week. Maybe this time it will last.

I wish that there were a voice narrating my life, just so that every time I dared to think *All is well*, some booming voice would say, "All was not well." It would remind me, on nights like this, not to get complacent.

"Deal," I say. "Just no Monopoly."

Even happy families break over Monopoly.

When dinner is finished, he offers to go get some dessert for us to eat while we play. We spend a few minutes weighing the pros and cons of ice cream versus candy, and then he reaches for the top of the fridge. Wallet, keys, gun.

Only he hesitates.

"Where's my wallet?" he asks.

"What's wrong?" Mom says from the table, where she and Juniper are stacking board games.

"Where's my fucking wallet?" he says, louder. "I put it right here, like I always do."

"I'm sure it's here," Mom says, getting up from the table. I watch as she squeezes Juniper's hand before she leaves her. "Maybe it fell behind the fridge."

But they pull it away from the wall, and his wallet isn't there, either.

"Let's go check the truck," she suggests. His jaw clenches tight, but he nods.

Campbell and I check the rest of the house, digging into the sofa and searching the entertainment center. My eyes do that thing they always do now, which is to slip past the part of the wall that isn't broken anymore.

There's a picture frame on the floor already, and I lift it back to its nail. *Stay,* I beg it silently.

We don't find the wallet, and a moment later, the door slams.

He comes into the house angry, kicking his boots off so that they hit against the back door.

He finds us in the living room, elbow-deep in the sofa as we check it again.

"Anything?"

"We're still looking," I tell him, but he's already so far gone.

"I found it!" Juniper says from the doorway to the room, and we all turn at once.

She's holding his wallet in her outstretched hand.

"It was just near the front door," she says. "It must have fallen out of your jacket."

He moves across the room and grabs the wallet.

"Fucking ridiculous," he says, putting it on top of the fridge.

We return to the table, dessert forgotten, and quickly settle on Apples to Apples. Juniper is next to me, and I realize that her hair and clothes are damp. I didn't realize she went out to search the truck with them.

A green card is flipped: "colorful."

Campbell throws down an opportune choice of "rainbow" and easily wins the first round.

We settle into the game, but that feeling of hope I had earlier is gone. Now it feels like we are on one of those rickety little bridges with the wooden planks in all the action movies, crossing over a deep ravine. As we cross it, the planks start to fall off behind us, so we are forced to run if we want to make it to the other side.

Don't look down. Just keep moving.

When it's his turn to judge, he doesn't grab a card right away.

"Sorry," he says.

We all fall silent.

"The wallet had cash in it from the job this weekend. I just couldn't afford to lose it."

"We know," Mom says. The girls and I stay quiet. It's not like his apologies are rare. He actually says sorry to us almost every time. It's just usually a day or two later. It takes that long for him to come back together.

Maybe his quick remorse—and the fact that he stopped at all—is a good sign.

"Let's just enjoy game night," Mom says, sliding him a card. He glances at her, and he must find whatever he's looking for, because he smiles and nods and takes the card she offers. Sometimes I think they only see some past version of each other. Like she loves who he used to be. I wonder if it feels like loving a ghost. I wonder if it feels like mourning.

We start the next round of the game, and my parents miss the way Juniper never fully settles back into her chair. She's ready to bolt upstairs if things escalate again. They miss the way Campbell grips the cards in her hands so tight they are bending, the fierce flat line of her mouth, the way her eyes stay on the cards no matter what.

My father reaches for a card. There are circles of lighter skin on his forearm. They've been there forever, but it took me years to put it all together.

He says his father was even more strict than him, but it's code. He means his father was meaner. The circles are cigarette burns.

There are other scars, too. And Mom has hinted enough for me to know that my grandfather didn't just scream and threaten like Dad does. He hurt them. He hurt them *so much* that my father is still angry, turning more so every day. And the only outlet he knows is to pass it on again.

My grandfather fought in a war and came back broken. My father grew up in a house that held anger like a stone in its palm. Like it was something worth keeping. And that became the shape of our family tree. When the legacy is anger, the inheritance is fear.

Chapter Thirty-Two

I DREAM OF LIGHTNING SPLITTING THE tree in our front yard wide open, and I wake up to the crack of my door hitting the wall.

Light from the hall spills in, framing the silhouette of a man.

"Get up. Get the fuck up. We have to go through this every fucking time. So I'm going to show you how to do it right."

Then he's gone, back into the hall, and I leap out of bed. He's walking to the girls' room.

"Leave them alone," I say. "It's the middle of the night."

"Well, you all should have thought of that sooner, and done the fucking chores right the first fucking time."

Another swinging door, spilling light on to wide-eyed faces. The girls are curled up in the same bed, as instantly alert as I was a moment ago.

Mom is standing on the stairs near me, but her eyes find mine. She mouths the words, *I'm sorry.*

I know. I know. I know. My heart races in time with the words I want to tell her. *I know, but it's so late and we should be asleep.*

I know, but in the morning you'll have forgotten that thing made of fear in your chest. That ache I feel every day and every night.

I move toward the girls.

"Listen, just let the girls go back to sleep. Show me what we did wrong."

"So you can all fuck it up again next time? No. Everyone up. Downstairs."

I shove past him and pick up Junie, then let Campbell follow me past him and down to our living room. Every lamp is on, in this room and the next, and in the laundry room, too. Even the porch light is on. My eyes shift along the wall to the clock. 2:37 a.m.

I have an exam in Honors Calculus in less than eight hours.

We plop onto the couch and await orders.

He comes downstairs with all of our carefully folded towels from earlier that night and throws them onto the floor in front of us.

"Show me how to fold a towel," he says.

I reach for the closest one.

"No," he says. "Juniper. Let's see if the youngest of you can grasp what the older two cannot."

Juniper is ready to cry, and I feel something sharp deep

inside of me when she reaches for the towel. She stands up, and the towel is longer than her body, but she still tries, folding it in half so it's a length she can manage, then in half again.

"No," he says, tearing the towel out of her hand and passing it to Campbell. "Your turn."

Campbell folds the towel lengthwise to start, then begins to fold it down.

"No." He pulls the towel from her hands and holds it out for me.

"If we knew how you wanted it folded, we wouldn't be awake right now. Why don't you just show us so we can go back to bed?"

I shouldn't have said it. I knew it before my mouth opened. But he doesn't scream. He doesn't even make me take the towel and fail at folding it correctly. He just looks at me with eyes that are wide and empty and, in that moment, remind me distinctly of a dead fish. His lips twist into a snarl and he still doesn't yell, he just says it with so much hatred.

"Stupid cunt."

He reaches for a vase on the coffee table, grabbing it and hurling it across the room. It hits the window, and ceramic and glass shatter together.

"Now everyone has a *good reason* to be awake. Since the towels weren't a good enough reason for Leighton."

Tears of anger fill my eyes, and I will them away with

everything I've got. He doesn't get to see it hurt.

He shakes out the towel.

Not a single tear falls down my cheek, but at a cost. My nails are dug into my palms and I'm biting my tongue so hard I taste blood.

"You fold it in thirds lengthwise," he says, demonstrating with the towel, "and then in quarters. Then the towels will actually fit on the goddamn towel holder in the bathroom and not look like shit."

He looks at us on the couch. "Do you understand now?"

We nod, silent.

"Good. Girls, go to bed. Leighton, fold the towels. And then clean up that fucking mess."

"I'll help her and then come up," Mom says, moving forward.

"Don't even think about it. If she folds them all, maybe she won't forget how to do it in the future."

They all file upstairs, but it's not until his door is shut that I let out a long, shuddering breath of air. I refuse to cry. I fold twelve towels, by threes and then fours, double-checking every crease and carefully lining up corners, all the time refusing to cry. I carry them up to the bathroom in three trips, and align them against the edge of the shelves. Straight lines, perfect folds, no mistakes.

It takes much longer to clean up the broken pieces of glass. There's still a barrier to outside—a storm window—so

I don't have to tape plastic over it tonight. I take my time with a broom and pan, brushing up the small shards. I pick up the larger pieces by hand, and break the jagged edges out of the window frame so that the girls don't forget and put their hands there and cut themselves.

I walk around the house, turning off every light. On my path upstairs, I hang the pictures on the walls. This house and its slippery nails.

When I go to turn off the bathroom light, I stare in the mirror. The far wall has shelves for the towels, and it is empty. I turn quickly and see all of the towels on the floor in disarray. I don't know how or why, but tonight I don't spend time on the strange things this house does. I'm too tired.

I fold the towels again.

By the time I get back to bed, it is almost five. For the next thirty minutes, I lie awake in the dark imagining how badly this night could have gone.

I throw off my blanket and reach for my light. If I'm not going to sleep, I should study for my calc exam. I sink into my desk chair and turn on my calculator. This is what I need to do: focus on school. Get into college. Move far, far away and . . . then what? Leave Campbell and Juniper to fend for themselves? I try to focus on the workbook in front of me.

In the figure below, AB and CD are perpendicular to BC, and the size of angle ACB is 31 degrees. *Find the length of segment BD.*

My eyes blur, and the problem rewrites itself on the page.

In the figure below, Leighton Barnes is perpendicular to freedom, and the size of angle ACB is irrelevant because she can never, ever leave. Find the greatest distance she can go before feeling she's abandoned her sisters.

I stare at the clock. Minutes sink into hours. I watch the sky lighten, layers of gray and then yellow. At dawn, I still don't have a better answer. Time's almost up.

AUBURN, PENNSYLVANIA
NOVEMBER 4

CROW POPULATION:
42,387

Chapter Thirty-Three

WHAT IS THE WEIGHT OF A WORD? Maybe it's measured in ink and paper. Maybe it's measured by the harm it causes. Especially the ones said out loud, in anger.

Some of them sink like stones inside of you. They tug you down from the inside, like an invisible tether. *Ice queen* always felt like that.

Brat rolls of my back. A drop of water. I ignore it like rainfall.

Bitch is a sliver of wood in my side—sharp. Thick enough to hurt. But I can hold my breath and pull it out. I can keep moving.

Cunt is different. Like a festering disease that settles in my gut. It lives there for months, and I can feel it there, always. Heavy enough to remind me of when he said it the first time, last year, and I felt that same thing that I feel now. Because it wasn't hatred in his voice, but victory. *I've got it*, it said. A tone of near pride. He knew he'd found a word that

I couldn't ignore, wouldn't forget. A word cruel enough to affect my sixteen-year-old self, who had never been called a name like that before, but had heard it directed at her mother enough times to know how it should hurt.

A word that reduces me to an assembly of parts, less than human.

A word that makes me nothing but the object of his hatred, which means I'm nothing at all.

Chapter Thirty-Four

IN THE MORNING WHEN I HURRY down the stairs, I want to ignore it. I want to let my eyes do that thing where they slip right past the window without seeing the wrongness. Without realizing the glass is back in the window frame, intact. And I do for a moment. I succeed in seeing only what I want to see, until I round the banister and see the coffee table, with the vase back in the center.

I grab it and run outside to the garbage bins. It's raining, but I don't care; I take my time and bury it deep, in the same bag where I swept its shards last night.

A crow caws in the tree in our front yard, and I look up.

I take a step back when I realize that the tree is full, like on the first day of school. Only now that all the leaves have fallen, there is nothing but black birds.

Joe caws from the lowest branch of the tree, and I walk over to him. I tug a slip of paper that is clenched to the branch under his claw and find Juniper's sprawling handwriting.

Dear Joe, please help us.

I back away from the branch, soaking wet and my eyes filling with tears. Joe flutters down to the ground beside me, then back to the tree. I ignore him, staring at Junie's latest note.

Joe flies back down again, nudges at something in the grass.

He lifts something shiny in his beak, and hops toward me, until he's just inches away from my freezing bare feet.

He drops the object.

I reach into the grass and pick up a wedding band. Our dad's wedding band. When he's working, he tucks it into the front pocket of his wallet.

I remember his lost wallet, and how Juniper was all wet from going out in the rain, and I realize that she didn't go out to search the truck at all. She went out to check for gifts.

And she returned with the wallet.

I stare at the ring in my palm.

I've been emailing back and forth with the ornithologist I interviewed, and I've learned a lot. Crows are actually exceptionally bright creatures. They can understand reciprocity, like leaving Juniper gifts in exchange for food. Like returning her leather cuff bracelet when she lost it.

They can also understand retribution. They hold grudges.

I wonder what the crows understand about this house. I

wonder what Joe understands.

Maybe the crows found the wallet where it was dropped, and somehow knew to return it to Juniper.

Or maybe the crows stole it in the first place.

Chapter Thirty-Five

I MAKE SURE THE GIRLS ARE safely on their way to school, and then I hurry across the street in the pouring rain to Liam's idling car. I hurl myself into the passenger seat and curl my arms around my backpack. It's a rock on the shore, and I'm clinging to it for dear life.

"Good morning, beautiful."

Beautiful.

I didn't cry at my father's ugly words last night, but for some reason, "beautiful" tips me right over the edge, and I can't stop the tears that spill down my cheeks.

"Leighton, hey, what's wrong?"

"Please drive." I try to rein it in, but I can't stop crying now any more than I can will the rain outside to stop. It won't rest until it's run its course.

My throat burns with everything I'm holding in. It takes immense effort to keep my crying silent and soft, instead of the sobbing, snotty mess it's likely to become if I try to speak.

I'm distracted by this internal struggle, attempting to keep some semblance of control, and I don't realize he's driven past the school until we are pulling into a small gravel lot. It is where we parked on the first night we went out together. Hidden behind a wall of trees, the car probably isn't visible from the main road anymore. It feels detached from Auburn, detached from reality. It feels like another planet.

"Liam, we have to go—" I sputter, but he's shaking his head.

"Leighton, you're scaring me. Please tell me what's wrong."

More tears, more burning.

His finger hooks under my chin and his hand—all gentleness—tilts my face up to his, tears and runny nose and all.

"Please, Leighton."

"I folded the towels wrong." It's the stupidest thing I could possibly say, but I have no idea how else to start.

But Liam doesn't look at me like I'm stupid, and that's all it takes for me to come undone.

It hits like a wave. First, more tears. *Loads* more tears. A world-crushing flood of tears. Liam's arms are around me, anchoring me, but I'm still breaking into pieces. I can't keep it in any longer.

I cry all the time, in small doses, but I rarely lose control, and never in front of someone.

This is different. This feels like those summer storms where the black clouds roll in fast, and the storm is relentless and violent, but you know that it will end as fast as it began. Summer will resume as if the storm never happened, and everything is just left wet.

Kind of like Liam's shirt at this point.

It feels better to cry with Liam holding me. Less lonely. And when the tears finally end, I find the words. Not as many words as there were tears, but enough for Liam to fill in the empty spaces, and understand.

"How long has it been like this?" he asks.

"Forever, I think. It wasn't always this bad. The last two years have been the worst."

"Why don't you guys get out of there?"

I sit back, uncomfortable with the question when I don't have an adequate answer.

"We have, a few times. When my grandparents were nearby, we stayed with them all the time. We just always went back.

"There's always some excuse for it. Money. The house. Forgiveness. He's changed. *Really* this time. But I don't know. It's like she can't even see he's a monster because she loves him. He isn't bad all the time, and he tries so hard."

It's hard to take my deepest, darkest fears of him seriously in the light of day. He does love us, I think, but it blurs the line, makes me doubt my own fear.

Liam is silent for a few minutes, staring through the windshield. Our parking spot is being transformed into a pond as we sit here.

"I think we should move. We're going to get stuck."

"In a minute," he says. He's thinking so hard. I'm sure he's imagining that he can come up with some way to make

Chapter Thirty-Seven

❧

AT 6:45 A.M. THE NEXT SATURDAY morning, I find myself parked next to an icy, wet field, preparing to interview men who are dressed in camouflage and carrying loaded weapons. It is 34 degrees outside, and I'm wondering precisely what life choices I've made that led me here.

My crow column can't leave out the first crow hunt. I sent an email to Dr. Cornell, my bird expert, earlier this week, asking about another town that had a crow problem. They used a series of crow hunts, but it looks like they weren't very effective. I wanted to ask what chance Auburn has of handling the crows on its own.

Dr. Cornell said that it might make people feel better to do something about it, but with the crows in such high numbers—his latest estimate was nearing fifty thousand birds—a crow shoot or two won't have any discernible impact on the population or their migration habits.

So, a pointless crow hunt.

this better. He can't. But it makes my heart pound in a hard, grateful way to know that he wants to.

"Does he hit you?" he asks, not looking at me. A few more *thank you* thuds for that.

"No," I say quietly, and now he does look up, like he doesn't believe me. "He hasn't."

"Hurt you? Or Campbell or Junie?" he asks, the pitch of his voice falling, like it is being pulled down by the gravity of the conversation.

"No. Um. He's thrown things at me. He mostly yells. Breaks the house. Threatens a lot. He calls me—" I stop myself. I've revealed enough already.

"Leighton, you've gotta get away from that. You don't deserve that."

"I'm working on it."

I am.

His hand drops down on mine, closing over the back of it and holding it tight, like I might run away. The dull thuds are not so dull now. They start to really hurt when I hear the conviction in his voice. He makes it sound so simple. So obvious.

But even when we left all the time, the return was inevitable. She'd tell us to get our things, we're going home.

Home.

As long as it is home to her, that's where we will be.

"I'm feeling better. Thank you. We should get to school."

"Let's go after first period," Liam says.

He doesn't have to suggest it more than once.

"Okay." I lean over until my head rests on his shoulder, and we watch the world around us as it becomes something else in the rain. Something soft and vulnerable, exposed like a wound only halfway healed. Just the thinnest layer of skin protecting it.

"Look at that," Liam says, pointing across the lot as the rain lets up. In one of the trees in front of us, crows line a branch. As we watch, one of the crows swings down, talons still wrapped around the branch now overhead. He hangs for a moment, upside down, then lets go. He glides, flaps, lands up above again. This time another bird tilts forward and hangs for a moment, bouncing on the branch before letting go.

We watch as they take turns on the wet, slippery branch.

We watch as they play.

When we finally arrive at school, second period has started. We offer the receptionist some excuse about the car. When we get to our lockers, I remember my calculus exam has probably started, and I slam my locker and sprint. I swear under my breath as I try to remember what I studied at five a.m.

As I walk into the classroom, a flyer catches my eye, and I pause at the door.

There is a crow hunt this weekend. No Limit on Birds per Shooter.

I'm not the only one running out of time.

Chapter Thirty-Six

CAMPBELL ASKS ME TO STOP TALKING BACK. Especially when he's angry. I can always find that sharp thorn of a comment that takes him from casually pissed off to losing his shit. If only she knew how much I'm holding back. All the words that I don't say. Instead, I swallow the words whole, and the letters are pointy on their corners and sharp on their edges and they hurt going down. They stay there inside of me and make my stomach ache. Sometimes I think that if someone cut me open, the words would really be there. Like a whale that consumed too much garbage, and now her body is nothing but a time capsule for all the things humans throw away.

In my research, I found another crow town that didn't try hunts or traps or flares or noise to drive the crows out of their town. Instead, when they realized the crows kept coming back year after year, they started a new town tradition: the festival of crows.

They turned their little town into a tourist attraction, selling visitors on the festival and the wonderment of a hundred thousand birds choosing the town as their temporary home.

"You know my dad wanted me to do this hunt with him?" Liam asks from beside me. He has football practice early today and offered to drop me off here for interviews. But right now his head is tilted to the side, watching the trucks pull in and neon-vested hunters climb out. He's studying them the way I've studied the crows. Like I'm trying to decode some great mystery.

"Really? I didn't know he hunts."

"Not often. He's too busy with the practice. But he used to hunt with his dad, and it's *really* not my thing. Sometimes I think he expected us to have the same experience he did growing up here. Which just wasn't gonna happen."

"Is he pushy about it?"

"Nah, nothing like that. He's just trying to, like, *bond*. And he totally understands and supports the things I am passionate about. He cares so much. But yeah, I have no interest in shooting crows out of the sky. I think I even like them."

"Me too." I say, my stomach dropping at the thought of

the crows being shot. I think of Joe. Juniper was so worried about him.

"So who are you going to interview?" Liam asks.

"Whoever wants to talk crows," I say. There are a bunch of hunters gathered outside now, walking around their trucks, guns bent in half awaiting shells.

"Leighton," Liam says, and whistles, passing his hand in front of my face. "You in there?"

"Sorry." I turn to him, trying to shake the feeling.

"Hey, wait. What's going on?" Liam goes from lighthearted to serious in an instant, reading my body language, or maybe the look on my face, I don't know.

But he knows. His hand moves to my arm, a soft gesture. A comforting one.

I force a smile.

"I'm great. I'm going to be . . ." I cannot make the word *fine* leave my lips. I keep thinking about Joe, and hoping he didn't follow me here like he did to visit my grandmother.

"It's nothing. Really. I just, uh, don't like guns."

"Wait." He leans back, then pauses as my words fall into place. "Does he have—"

"You should go," I say, pulling my arm from under the soft weight of his hand. "We'll talk about it later."

Liam stares at me for a moment, then shakes his head. It's not the time to get into it. We both have places to be.

"Be careful," he says. "Stay with the trucks."

"Of course," I say, and lean over to kiss his cheek.

Most of the hunters are happy to answer a few questions. None of them seem to actually care much about the crows invading Auburn, and none of them are fooled that this bird hunt will have an impact. They just enjoy it.

I lean against one of the trucks, reading my notes at first, but when the gunshots start, I'm too on edge. I end up just listening to the hunt, thinking about how much better a festival of crows would be. *Auburn born, Auburn proud.* But the crows weren't born here, and they're too good for this place. And I was born here, and I'm not proud.

Right now I wish I could fold the entire town into one of Juniper's notes and leave it for the crows to take.

I wonder what gift they'd give me in exchange for that.

Chapter Thirty-Eight

MY BOOTS ARE SPECKLED WITH MUD and blood and ice. The air is cold enough to hurt my lungs with each breath. There are dead crows everywhere. Obviously, a crow hunt would lead to dead crows, but it is different with them laid out like this. Frozen in their final standoff with mortality.

There are so many of them.

They've arranged the birds into the number they killed. The number 32 is shaped from the bodies of thirty-two bird carcasses. Feathers resting at odd angles, eyes now void of that shimmer of intelligence that I feel on me everywhere I go in town. Sometimes it feels like the crows aren't thousands of individual birds but a single being somehow living in a thousand bodies.

I read the numbers as I pass them.

57.

82.

154.

I imagine the aerial view. From above, the field of dead birds would be laid out like a page of a child's math homework. Exactly the view the live crows have now. I feel dumb as I imagine it. The crows don't care. But then I think of Joe and his gifts, and I remember that Dr. Cornell said crows mourn, and I wonder if maybe they do care.

I wonder if they'll remember this transgression.

I didn't think the hunt would bother me this much, but it's their little bodies, shaped into numbers, that gets me. It's almost perverse. A parody of death. And even though they're only birds on the field in front of me, it's girls in a crawl space that I see in my mind.

Chapter Thirty-Nine

IN LIT CLASS, WE BEGIN TO study women in literature. We read excerpts from Jane Austen and Alice Walker, poetry by Angelou and Plath. On Tuesday, we spend half of class discussing *A Vindication of the Rights of Woman* by Wollstonecraft, and then we move on to her daughter and *Frankenstein*.

Maybe it's true that men like Thomas Hardy write women well, as victims or survivors, wives or daughters, mistresses, or even soldiers.

But women write women as people.

And Mary Shelley wrote men as monsters, and I love her for it.

"Beware; for I am fearless," Mary Shelley wrote, "and therefore powerful."

I wonder if that's true.

When class ends, Mrs. Riley asks me to stay behind for a moment.

As soon as the room empties, Mrs. Riley slides a familiar pink sheet across her desk.

"Why haven't you applied for this?"

I sigh and drop into the chair beside her desk. "I tried. A few times. I just can't write to the prompt."

"So try again. Think about what's holding those words back. Push through it. If you become a journalist, you are going to get a lot of assignments you don't like. You've got to find your own angle. And the cash prize doesn't hurt."

"No, it doesn't."

I'm working on my next crow column now, and it's about crows in ancient folklore. There's a fable about a crow that is dying of thirst, but the water in the pitcher in front of him is too low for his beak to reach. So he collects pebbles and drops them in one at a time. The pebbles make the water rise, bit by bit, until he can take a drink. The moral of the fable is that necessity is the mother of invention.

This essay for Auburn Township won't be enough for me to get into NYU, let alone actually go there. But it could be a pebble. Right now it feels so far out of reach, but maybe, if I try, it'll get closer, pebble by pebble, until I can take a sip.

"I did have one idea. But I already know it isn't something the Auburn Township Council will want to read."

Mrs. Riley laughs. "Then it's probably something they *should* read."

I give her a half smile. "Maybe it is."

"If it's controversial, it might not win, Leighton. But you should trust your writing, and your voice. At the very least, you'll force six middle-aged, privileged white men to read something that matters to a seventeen-year-old girl. Maybe it'll plant a seed. And if you do win, you'll get your first byline."

"What?"

"The winning essay gets printed in the *Auburn Gazette*. You'll have your first real publishing credential."

The prospect is terrifying.

And tempting.

But I know what kind of men are on the council. Men who look the other way. Police officers, teachers, and old family friends.

Last year in trigonometry class, my teacher kept mocking a woman who'd been on TV all week testifying about a senator's history of harassment. He said, "If everyone is a victim, then it's like no one is," and I felt shame like scalding water on my spine, and stopped raising my hand in class.

And in the diner, when I sometimes catch the end of Mom's shift, I hear the way the men flirt with her, how she tolerates their rudeness. If she didn't, she'd lose tips. Or a job.

Auburn born, Auburn proud. But there's only one acceptable way to live here, and when you deviate from that narrow path, then you are the threat. Like your voice will crumble their entire world.

Maybe it's true.

Maybe it would break this town to know that the best athlete to ever come out of Auburn, who carried his team to a state championship and *would've gone pro*, has fallen, and he's taking his family with him.

But some things *should* fall apart. They should burn themselves out, like a candle that's run its wick to the bottom. It's dangerous to wish for such a thing, though, because some flames are too selfish to extinguish themselves.

There are flames that would set the whole world on fire if it were the only way to keep burning.

Chapter Forty

AT THE END OF THE DAY, I fill my backpack while dread settles into my stomach. My mom is taking the girls to dentist appointments, so if I get on the bus and go right home, I'll just be there alone with him. Normally, I would hide in the newspaper office for a few hours, but Mrs. Riley is already gone and the office is locked for the night.

Liam joins me at our lockers and kisses my cheek.

"I have something for you," Liam says. "But it's kind of a private gift and I don't want to explain it here."

A junior next to us looks over but doesn't say anything. I raise my eyebrows as a gentle reminder that she can mind her own business, and she hurries away.

"Okay. Well. My bus is leaving soon," I say.

"Yeah, but your sisters have dentist appointments. You can't go home."

I'm surprised that Liam even remembered that from when we talked on the phone last night. It was just casually mentioned. I'm more surprised that he has taken it a step further and understands the implications of no one else being home after school.

"Office is closed for the paper, and I don't have a ride," I explain.

"We have weights and game tape viewing until five. Is that too late?"

"No, that's fine; are you sure you don't mind?"

"Yeah. I'll be in the weight room, but the gym will be open. You can hang out and read or whatever."

We start walking toward the gym as we talk, and I know I've already made up my mind.

"Thanks," I say.

Liam pauses outside the gym.

"You can't be late—Coach will kill you. Or make you run sprints, which in my book is the same thing."

Liam laughs. He looks nervous. Oh, right, the thing. He has something for me.

"What is it?"

He reaches into his backpack and pulls out a phone.

"It's an older model. It's actually my old one. But it works perfectly fine."

Everything clicks into place at once. He got me a phone. A lifeline.

To use in an emergency.

I sniffle and try to ignore the gigantic frog in my throat.

"That's really thoughtful, Liam. I can't even tell you . . . thank you."

"If you keep it charged, it can at least call 911, until next week, and then it will work for normal phone calls and texting, too."

"How?" I ask.

"Don't worry about it," he says. But this is a smartphone, which means it needs an actual plan. And data. And the truth is, I could swallow my pride enough to ask for help like this, if I knew it was safe.

But it isn't.

I look at the phone in my hand.

And then I give it back.

"I can't," I say. Tears now threaten everything. I suck in a deep breath and steel myself.

"What?"

"I can't take this, Liam." A tear spills over, and then another. Dammit.

"Leighton, it could—" I hear the ghost of the sentence even though he doesn't finish.

Save your life.

And he's right, it could.

Or it could get us killed.

"He's weird about phones. And police. If he found this, Liam . . ."

"So hide it really well."

"There's nowhere that's safe, Liam. I—I appreciate the offer."

"You really aren't gonna take it?"

I don't answer, but I make myself meet his gaze. And I know that, tears and all, he sees my resolve.

He shoves the cell phone into his backpack.

"I'm late for practice," he says, and walks around me.

"Liam—"

"I get it. I do. I'm not upset with you, it's just—"

It's *a lot*. It's a lot to ask him to *know* and not do anything.

"I'll see ya after." He's gone through the doors to the gymnasium and turning right into the guys' locker room.

That went well.

In the gym I sit at the end of the bleachers. I pull out our lit textbook and work through review questions.

For most of Liam's practice, I study. There is some constant white noise coming from the closed weight room—the clanging of weights and the easy, low talk of the players. I finish my homework too soon, and pass the last half hour trying—and still failing—to write the Auburn scholarship essay. It's frustrating. I've never really struggled to find the words before, but this one essay is defeating me.

I pack up my backpack and climb off the bleachers. I trade my bag for a basketball sitting in a bin on the side of the court and start to shoot at the net. I miss nine of ten shots, but it feels good to move my body when my mind gets stuck, so I think about Auburn and I throw the basketball, again and again. Then the doors to the weight room burst open, and a group of guys emerges. I walk all the way across the court before I realize it isn't the football team, but wrestling.

I make eye contact with Brody as he comes out. I turn away, but not soon enough.

"Hey, did you guys hear that the ice queen is finally dating someone? I guess she isn't as frigid as we thought after all."

A few chuckles. Mostly not. I guess even Brody's own teammates think he's a jerk.

"Or maybe she just doesn't like white guys," Brody says.

"Shut the hell up, Brody." I turn back as I say it, and realize he's followed me across the court.

"Maybe when you're done with Liam, you can give me another shot? Now that you're a little thawed out by McNamara." Brody reaches out, probably just to make some stupid comment about my skin not being ice cold, but I step backward.

I throw the basketball as I move, and it hits Brody in the center of his face.

Really hard.

A waterfall of blood starts to pour out of his nose.

And that's when the football team comes out of the locker rooms.

"What the *fuck*, Leighton?" Brody yells.

The football coach joins us, shouting for someone to get

some paper towels for the blood.

"What the hell is going on here?" Coach Tenley asks.

"That bitch broke my nose!"

"Hey, hey!" Coach holds up his hand. "Language."

The sight of Brody being scolded for cursing in front of a teacher while bleeding profusely might actually be worth the trouble I'm in.

Liam is at my side. "Leighton?"

"He was . . . he was being a jerk. He was going to touch me."

"Did he touch you?" Coach asks.

I shake my head no.

"Did you think he was going to hurt you?" he asks.

Again, no.

I just reacted.

"Detention tomorrow," he says to me, then turns back to Brody. "Go get cleaned up. Your nose isn't broken."

Coach walks away, shaking his head as he goes.

Liam picks up the forgotten basketball and gives Brody a cold look.

"Leave Leighton alone. Enough is enough."

"I can't believe you're defending her. She's totally unstable."

"Or maybe you just shouldn't touch girls if they didn't say you could."

"Whatever, man." Brody spits blood on the floor. "Enjoy fucking an ice queen."

Liam lifts the basketball so it's level with Brody's face.

"Think fast!" he yells, shooting his arms out but releasing the ball as he does it, catching it with his forearms.

Brody throws his body backward before he realizes Liam never threw the ball, and the other guys laugh at him.

"Just leave her the fuck alone, Brody."

Liam and I leave, grabbing our things and hurrying out into the cold. The car ride to my house is silent, but it's the loudest kind—where every breath and turn-signal click and scratch of gravel under a tire is a reminder of the fact that we haven't said a single word to each other. I'm embarrassed by what I did. I never respond to people like that. And I didn't think I had that kind of violence in me. I wasn't even angry in the moment. I just reacted on fear, or instinct.

Liam parks just before Mrs. Stieg's house, because I asked him to. He's the kind of guy who would insist on walking me to my door every night, if my door were the kind where that would be okay. My dad knows I have a boyfriend, but hardly any other details. I'm trying desperately to keep those worlds from colliding.

"I'm not like him," I say. My voice is tight with the threat of tears.

"Like Brody? God, I know."

"No, like *him*." I shrug toward my house.

A few beats of silence pass between us.

"I know that, too," he says, softer this time. "Brody's always been an asshole to you. Part of me is surprised you didn't throw something at him sooner."

I laugh through the tears now falling down my face.

"I have detention."

"Yeah. It's okay. You are long overdue for some rebellion, Leighton."

A few more beats in the quiet car. Leave it to Liam to have me laughing not twenty minutes after that whole thing.

"You really won't take the phone?" he asks.

I turn to him in the dark, and I can see just the outline of his face, stark against the porch light on at Mrs. Stieg's house behind him. I don't want to tell him no again, but it's the only answer I have.

"It's dangerous, Liam. The last thing was over towels, and I'm not taking unnecessary risks with my mom and sisters there."

"Just unnecessary risks for yourself, then."

"Liam . . ."

He sighs and runs his hand over the top of his head. "I'm sorry. I'm being an ass. I'll get over it by tomorrow."

"You're not an ass. It's a really nice gesture."

He laughs without a trace of humor.

"I hate that you don't feel safe, Leighton."

"Me too, Liam. I'm working on a plan. I promise." I kiss him goodbye and climb out of the car. Liam always waits until I get into the house before driving away. It's such a weird protective quirk when we both know I'm probably better off outside.

I stand in the front yard a moment longer, staring at the house. Most haunted houses are plagued by the dead, not the living.

Except this one. This one is possessed by all of us, even when we aren't here. Like it's taking little parts of us, storing us in its foundation and nails and the wood where it's gone soft.

Run. I pause on the step.

Run, something deep down inside of me screams. It shakes the bars on its cage and tells me to turn around. No, not just *something.* I know what's locked in there. What shouts my darkest worries at me as I'm trying to fall asleep. The thing that freezes when I talk back to him. And it's still there on days when things are all right and the sun shines on my face; even when I'm safe, there's a part of me always wondering when it's going to start again. And it's there in my chest—that thing.

It's fear.

And I've locked it away, like the dangerous creature it is. Because fear makes me act stupid. It makes me weak. *I'd run,* I want to tell the fluttering thing inside of me, *if there were anywhere to go.* There's no place. *Noplaceintheworldtorun.*

My chest is tight in the cold air, and my breath catches every time I breathe. It's already too full, with that creature in there. Too full to make room for oxygen, for life.

I step into the house.

Chapter Forty-One

MY SISTERS AND I ARE WRAPPED in a cocoon of blankets on my bed. We made it through Thanksgiving without anything happening, and he is going away for another out-of-town job this weekend, so we are up late planning our two perfect days. Our long hair hangs in triple waterfalls off the edge of the mattress.

"We need a movie marathon tomorrow," Campbell says, snuggled beside me. "It's the perfect time of year for it. Cozy blankets. Lots of junk food."

"Great idea," I tell her. "What'll it be?"

Juniper starts suggesting movies, her voice muffled by the blanket half covering her face.

It's freezing in here. Money has been tight again the last few weeks, and we see the evidence in less frequent grocery trips and the fact that the heat is off. I'm tempted to use the lantern, but I resist. It generates a good amount of heat for its size, but the oil won't last forever, and we should save it for a night less peaceful than this one. It's getting too cold for construction, and between being trapped in the house and being low on income, it's going to be a stressful winter.

So we are enjoying this weekend while we have it.

"Oh, I've got it," Cam says. "Lord of the Rings: *Fellowship, Towers, Return of the King.* We can fit them all in if we start in the afternoon."

"Snacks?" I prompt now that movies are determined, and the girls begin a list that is perfectly balanced in that it has an equal ratio of salty treats to sweet ones.

I'm dozing off to the sound of their happy little voices when I hear a familiar name.

"What was that?"

"I asked if Liam can come for our movie day," Campbell says.

"Oh, well." I am stumbling, trying to think of a good reason to not invite Liam. "Our movie-thons are kind of sacred. We can't have any boys there."

"A *boooooy,*" Junie sings next to me.

I tickle her until she threatens to pee on my bed.

"I want to meet him," Cam insists a few minutes later. "You know we have to hang out with him eventually. If we don't like him, what's the point?"

The girls giggle more, but Campbell isn't wrong. If my mom or sisters don't like him—or if Liam can't look past the bad things here and see how much love we have coiled up inside—then I probably am wasting my time with him.

"Okay, okay, I'll ask Mom," I tell them.

If I do invite Liam over, it will mean my worlds collid-ing. It's a terrifying thought, but it is a good weekend for it. Quiet, with him away at work.

I fall asleep to the sound of Campbell and Juniper whis-pering, and I don't think of the crawl space once.

Chapter Forty-Two

IT SNOWS OVERNIGHT. I WAKE UP to a room glowing with sunlight bouncing off the snow outside. I am still snuggled in bed with Campbell and Juniper, all of us tucked under the dragonfly quilt. I carefully extract myself, not ready to wake the girls and disturb the strange and welcome quiet in the house. It's freezing, so I pull a throw blanket off my chair and wrap it around my body. My breath comes in puffs of air.

My window is foggy, and I use the blanket to wipe away the condensation. The snow outside is crisp and clean. It's almost as though the crows recognize its perfection, because they haven't touched the yard.

But then I look around and realize that the crows aren't filling the yard or the tree like I've gotten used to. I tilt my head and look up at the roof. Empty.

Across the street, crows cover the snowy outlines of Mrs. Stieg's rosebushes. They line her gutters and have demolished her yard with feathers and droppings.

Then again, the clock is ticking on our pristine yard. A force of nature known as Juniper Mae will see to it shortly.

I sneak out of the room, squeezing my body through the narrow opening of the door so that I don't make it creak and wake the girls. This stupid door causes me more trouble than a door ever should. I've tried putting grease on the hinges, but nothing stops that creak.

Mom is in the kitchen holding a cup of tea, standing at the sink. Steam rises off the mug and forms a little cloud around and above her. She looks calm and collected, and the moment I see her, I know it's going to be a good day. Mom is here. Really here.

I steal some of the hot water from the kettle on the stove and join her at the counter. She smiles in greeting, but we stand together quietly. An unspoken agreement to savor the moment. It doesn't last long. *Creak.* Footsteps on the staircase. Two sleepy faces come around the banister.

"Morning," Mom says. "Did you see the snow?" Juniper's eyes are wide with delight as she nods. Campbell yawns.

"Still tired?" I ask her.

"Junie woke me up," she says. Campbell has never been a morning person.

"She's good like that," Mom says, sitting at the kitchen table and pulling Juniper onto her lap.

"Breakfast?" I ask them. Juniper shakes her head.

"Snow?" She nods emphatically, and I laugh. "Okay. I'll go find snow pants."

There is a pull-down ladder to get into our attic, and I climb into the coldest part of the house. I'm just glad our winter things aren't stored in the basement.

It takes a little while to find the right box. The attic flooring is patchy, and some parts are just soft insulation, so I step carefully. Finally, I see the word *winter* and reach, tugging a cardboard box down.

But when I open it, it's not snow stuff. It's Mom's stuff from high school.

I sit down on the dusty attic floor, letting the dingy lightbulb swing overhead. Yearbooks and letters, mostly. I dig a little deeper.

The next book has a soft cover and is decorated in a collage of art and drawings. *Amethyst*. It's Auburn High School's literary magazine, but from twenty years ago. I open it to the credits page. Editor in Chief: Erin Davis. Mom.

There's a note from her in the beginning, and when I flip through the pages, I find so many of her poems. I knew she loved poetry because she still reads it sometimes, but I didn't know she used to write it.

I put the rest of the box back the way I found it, but I keep the magazine. I finally find the winter clothes and tug the box downstairs with me. From my room, I grab an extra notebook I have and a sticky note off my desk.

These are amazing. You should write more. —L

I stick the note to the magazine and tuck it into the notebook.

I walk into a kitchen filled with laughter. I set the winter box on the floor, and Juniper springs from her chair, digging for extra hats and matching mittens.

I set the notebook and magazine next to Mom's tea mug, so she's sure to see it.

"Hey, Mom?"

"Yeah, Leighton?"

"Do you mind if Liam comes over today?"

She looks up from the table. "Yeah, sure. Tell him to drive safe. Roads aren't all plowed."

She turns back to Campbell, just like that. Like everything is normal. And it kind of is, without him here. No eggshells in sight.

Liam answers his cell after half a ring.

"Meeting your family?" Liam says. "Big step, Barnes."

"It's time."

"Past time," he tells me. "I'll be over in a bit."

"Drive safe," I tell him, and Mom nods. "Bring gloves."

"Gloves?"

"It is officially snowball fight season, McNamara. Be prepared."

"Me versus the Barnes sisters? Give a guy a chance."

His automatic inclusion of my little sisters makes me smile, and I can't think of a good response that acknowledges how sweet it is without sounding smitten.

"You're smiling, aren't you, Barnes? I can hear it."

"No, you can't." I frown in response to his correct guess.

"Totally can. I have special powers. Someday I'll reveal them to you. Maybe. No promises. Aaaand, you're smiling again, aren't you?"

"Like I'd give you the satisfaction of saying yes. Maybe I'll tell you later. No promises." I use his own words against him. But he was right: I was smiling again. And I still am when I hang up the phone.

The truth is that I like that he can hear it in my voice: my happiness. I like that he's the kind of person that cares to listen for it.

Chapter Forty-Three

WHEN LIAM ARRIVES, I WATCH FROM the porch as he parks as best as he can on the snow-filled street. The plows haven't come around yet. His car is at least a foot from the curb, but so few cars are out on the roads, it doesn't matter. I greet him at the driver-side door and catch his smile when he sees me standing there. My stomach is weighted with nervous excitement. When he steps out, I turn my face up to him, and I'm blinded by the brightness of the winter sun, and I'm dumbfounded by the thought that this good day belongs to me. I catch my breath on the notion that it could all go wrong.

The girls are already out back, so I lead Liam past the front door and around the side of the house. We stand in the backyard for a moment, suddenly unsure of ourselves. And each other. The snow is only calf-deep, but Campbell and Juniper are practically diving into it. It dawns on me that Liam might have thought I was joking about playing in the snow, and that the scene unfolding in front of him might not be at the top of every seventeen-year-old guy's checklist. I turn to ask Liam if he would rather—

A snowball hits my sweatshirt, disintegrating on impact.

"Not the best packing snow," Liam says, shaking his head. "Way too soft to really sting."

"I'm feeling a sudden kinship with Fiona."

"Ha," Liam says. "Okay, we need shelter, and we need teams."

Campbell and Juniper scream in delight as they join us.

"Captain!" Liam yells, and looks around fiercely, like he's daring anyone to challenge him. Even Cam cracks a smile. "And who will be my mortal enemy?"

"Oh, that's me," Campbell says, and I laugh. She is taking her role as protective little sister to heart.

"Okay . . . my first choice . . ." Liam looks back and forth from Juniper to me. He looks really torn.

"Juniper!"

"Seriously?" I ask. "I'm last pick?"

"It's okay, Leighton, we're gonna do great," Campbell says, scoping the yard. She's clearly working out a strategy here.

Liam leans down and whispers something in Juniper's ear. She giggles and shakes her head. He whispers again. Nudges her.

"You're going down!" Junie yells, and then lets out a shriek so loud Liam covers his ears.

"It ain't over till it's over," I tell her. It's the best smack talk I've got. Liam grins.

"Be careful, you don't want to unleash Juniper 'the Beast' Barnes," he says.

In twenty minutes, we've made walls in the snow and a tiny but impressive hoard of snowballs.

I peek over the wall.

"Hey, uh. What's the objective?"

"Destroy the enemy's fort!" Liam calls from a much-sturdier-looking wall. There's some mumbling behind it.

"Take no prisoners!" Juniper yells. Oh man, what is he teaching her over there?

Twenty minutes of prep is followed by four minutes of action. Liam's strategy is to hit Cam and me with as many snowballs as possible to cover Junie "the Beast" as she runs straight at our wall. She is like a nine-year-old-shaped missile, and we don't stand a chance. Campbell and I realize our mistake too late and run back to protect our wall, but it's a lost cause. By the time we get there, Juniper is laughing, making a snow angel in the heap of snow that was our fortress. Campbell and I shrug: we got beat. Campbell laughs and plops down in the snow beside June Bug. Two angels.

"Gonna join them?" Liam asks.

"Nah, I'm already frozen," I say. I've had enough days like this with the girls to be able to picture my own face right now: cherry-red nose and cheeks. Tears in my eyes from the cold. I mentally add "cold" to the unending list of things that make me cry.

"I'll warm you up," Liam says, and he leans over and kisses me. His lips are shockingly warm for having been outside this long.

"Leighton and Liam, sitting in a—" Junie starts, but Cam shushes her.

"Don't tease them, Junie, we like him," she whispers, but we hear her.

I grin and press my face into Liam's shoulder to hide it.

"This way," I tell him, and lead him past the girls, still giggling in the snow, to the pine tree out back. When I turn to Liam, I'm facing our garage—an old, dilapidated thing that we don't really trust enough to spend any time inside. But a single crow flies over, lands on the roof. The crow steps onto the slope of the roof, and begins to slide, down, down, until he reaches the edge and flutters back to the top.

He does it again. Slides down, flutters back up. And again.

He's doing it on purpose.

Just like the birds hanging off that tree in the rain.

He's playing.

"You okay?" Liam asks.

I shake my head. "Just overthinking things."

"Well, that's a fun change from your usual."

"Thanks for playing with them," I say, changing the subject, and distract him with a kiss.

Liam catches my face in his gloved hands and leans down for another.

And then one more.

"Hey, lovebirds!" Campbell yells, a beacon of annoying little sister if there ever was one. "Hot chocolate time!"

"It's hot chocolate time," I whisper against his lips.

"Then we should go," he says, and straightens. "I don't want to be on Campbell's hit list."

"Pff, join the club. There are so many members."

"Hey, what's that?" Liam's eyes go to the branch just past my ear, and he reaches a hand out. There is an envelope tucked into the pine needles. It has a few drops of wetness on it. The front says in simple, nine-year-old scrawl: JOE.

"Look," I tell Liam, and open it up. A handful of peanuts fall into the snow, and I stoop to collect them again.

"'Dear Joe,'" Liam reads aloud. "'I'm so sorry for the hunt. I hope none of your friends got hurt. Please stay close to the house so you are safe. Here are some peanuts. Thank you for the new marbles, I love them. Love, Juniper Barnes, age 9.'"

Liam reads it again, silently this time, and then holds it up like it's a precious ancient artifact. "Are you kidding me? Juniper writes letters to Joe?"

"Yes. And he brings her presents."

"Presents?"

"Feathers, marbles, an old button. She has a pile on her dresser." I don't mention the wallet, or the bracelet, or the ring. For some reason they feel beyond the reach of this conversation. Beyond cute and whimsical. More like strange and absurd. Impossible.

"That is the most adorable thing I've ever heard."

"Right?" I return my focus to the conversation. "My bird guy said crows have been recorded doing this kind of thing before. They are smart enough for reciprocity. So yeah, Juniper feeds them—and writes notes—and they leave gifts."

We return the note to its safe hiding place in the tree, peanuts and all, and head inside.

As we sip hot cocoa, I nudge Liam under the kitchen table.

"This is the most normal day I've had in ages. Thank you for coming over."

"Normal with bird letters and presents?"

"Normal for us," I clarify.

"Well said," Liam tells me. He kisses me over our cups just as my mom walks into the kitchen, but she pretends not to notice. On her way back out of the room, she winks at me.

Hello, Mom. I see you in there.

She burns so much brighter when he's not here.

And just like that, the spell breaks. I hear a car rumbling outside. When I step to the window, I pray for a plow, which is the only vehicle I can think would find our road under inches of snow.

It's not a plow.

He's home early.

Mom moves past me, stepping onto the front porch to

greet him with a kiss and a cup of cocoa. He accepts both with a smile. Then he gestures at Liam's car.

"Back early?" I ask when he enters the house. His smile falters for just a moment, and then it's back.

We have company.

On cue, Liam comes into the kitchen.

"Oh, hello . . . sir."

Even as an afterthought, my dad seems to appreciate the show of respect. He steps forward and extends his hand. "Liam, right?"

Liam nods.

"Nice to finally meet you. Leighton's told us so much about you."

Liar. I've only told Mom, and she told you.

"You like trucks, Liam?" he asks, pointing to his *pride and joy* out front. "Mind giving me a hand cleaning out the snow?"

"Sure, yeah," Liam says, and they move outside. I want to hold Liam back, but I have no good excuse for doing so, and it would just make everything more tense and awkward.

"He's back really early," I say to Mom.

"Didn't want to get snowed in away from home," she says knowingly. "Especially since it's a holiday weekend." She expected him.

"You could have told me," I say.

"So you could tell Liam to leave?" she says, her words sharp.

Of course, I want to snap back at her. *Of course I didn't want them to meet.*

Less than fifteen minutes later, they come back in from the cold, shaking their shoes off in the mudroom. We are starting dinner, spaghetti boiling on the stove while Campbell and Juniper set the table.

I catch the tail end of their conversation about college.

"Those are excellent schools," my dad says. "You must have, what, a perfect GPA? And you play ball?"

"It's pretty good," Liam says. I can't read his face, and I want to know everything that was said outside. "But I think Leighton's GPA is just a *little* higher than mine."

"Our girl is smart," Dad says. "She's gonna do great at main campus next year."

"What, like state school? But Leighton wants—" I shake my head from behind my dad, and Liam stops short.

They start talking about the football season, and how well the Wolves are doing. I keep listening, not for the words, but the tone. Football is a hard subject in this house. This calm moment could shift with no provocation, or at least, nothing I've been able to identify. Sometimes all it takes is one word out of place, an imagined slight, and it's like the whole room changes, a string pulled tight across it. And after that, even the smallest motion can snap it, and unleash whatever he's pent up for weeks.

There's nothing out of place at all, but the creature in my chest shifts and tugs at my insides, waiting, pacing. It's inevitable that this house will break again.

But when?

Liam is still standing in the mudroom in his wet boots, and when my eyes meet his, he gestures outside.

"I should go before sunset. This is gonna turn icy."

"Yeah, of course," I say, relief making me answer too fast.

"Sure you don't want dinner?" my dad asks.

Is there an edge to his voice? Did I hear that?

"The roads could get dangerous," I say, and look to Mom for help.

"Why don't you walk Liam out? But hurry back to help with dinner."

I tug on boots and open the front door and pull Liam along with me until we are crunching through the snow on the front lawn.

"You could've grabbed your coat," Liam says at his car door. But then he rubs up and down my arms with his hands to warm me, and I'm glad I left the coat.

I glance at the house. Picture-perfect from out here: a family cooking dinner together. Juniper laughs. Campbell smiles, always despite herself.

I smile at Cam's smile and will the thing in my chest to quiet. Everything is fine tonight. Nothing jagged or sharp to cut that taut string.

Not yet, warns the creature inside of me.

"Today was fun. Impressive snowball-packing skills, Barnes."

I smile at him and wonder if my smiles all look as forced as Campbell's smiles do.

Liam begins to lean in to kiss me—I step back, my boot landing on a patch of ice, and I scramble to catch my balance. Liam's hand finds my elbow, steadies me. "What's up, Leighton? You're all over the place."

"Sorry. Just. Not when he can see." I nod at the house. I've never really dated before, and I don't know what kind of reaction to expect after Liam leaves. And I want the space back between these things, enough space that I can enjoy hanging out with Liam and not have it associated with the tension I've been holding on to all afternoon.

"Shit, sorry."

"Not your fault."

"Not that kind of sorry. Just. I'm sorry you have to worry about every little thing."

We say goodbye, and I run back to the house, my arms frozen without Liam's warm hands on them. The scene in our dining room is calm, normal . . . terrifying. I'm safe right now, but I'm about to fall. I know it, because the thing inside of me knows it, as sure as anything.

It quakes in my chest, scared of nothing, because that's all that happened today: nothing. But every good day here ends with the phrase that's been thrumming through my chest all afternoon.

Not yet.

Chapter Forty-Four

NOT YET LASTS FIVE DAYS, AND then Mom's cry wakes me in the middle of the night.

Seconds later, the girls burst into my room. The door flies on its hinges, smashing against my wall. I am with them in a moment, noting how pale they are, how wide their terrified eyes.

"What happened?" I ask, pulling them into the room. It's 3:47 a.m. Witching hour.

"I don't know," Cammy says, her voice cracking as she starts to cry. "It's bad. I think he's hurting her."

Juniper cries, too.

"Okay, it's going to be all right."

I shepherd them straight to the armoire. Part of me wishes it still locked just for some added layer of protection, but our grandfather was always terrified we'd get ourselves trapped inside someday, so he took the key away long ago.

"Go in with Campbell, June Bug. Campbell, close the door. No lantern. Stay in there, no matter what. Do you understand?" Campbell nods.

I'm nauseated at the idea of leaving the girls hiding alone in the dark. But then I hear her, again. Not a sharp cry this time, but a whimper.

"We are fine, Leighton," Cammy says, pulling June in tight. "Please help Mom. Please."

I run down the stairs, but then when I hit the bottom step, I freeze. I wait. I listen.

They are in the kitchen, but when I look around the banister, they are out of sight.

"Please, stop," Mom says, her voice a strained whisper. "Let me go."

The willpower it takes to not go to her is unprecedented. I pretend my feet are now a part of the stairs themselves and I couldn't possibly lift them. I'm nothing but the carpet, the wall, the stair. Less than that. A hair on the carpet. A spot on the wall. A nail in the stair. I'm not even here at all.

Because I can't just go to her. If he is hurting her, my sudden presence could escalate everything.

So I wait, and I sit on our narrow staircase.

I press my feet against the cold wall, hard. It is fine. She is fine. It's going to be fine. I repeat the mantra, with my eyes shut. I feel something give under the heel of my foot. A crack appears in the wall where I was pushing on it. It splinters up, past my toes. Past the nails on the wall where the pictures are no longer hanging. They litter the staircase like birds that just suddenly fell from the sky for no reason. The line on the wall continues to grow, even though I've stopped applying pressure. I stand to watch as it reaches the ceiling, and doesn't stop. It turns outward, breaking the ceiling. The tiniest fracture line, but it's splitting the whole room in half. Like the house was just waiting for the slightest provocation to fall apart.

I'm still watching the line when they come into the living room.

Mom isn't crying, but I can tell that she was. Her face is puffy and red, and when she sees me standing on the stairs, she shakes her head. She doesn't have to say a word to convey a message. She wants me to go upstairs, but I'm rooted in my spot. He catches the subtle movement, though. There. The glimmer of silver. Not the dull gray of his gun.

He's holding a kitchen knife.

I think of the crawl space. The stupid crawl space. I feel like I'm already in it, walls closing in. Which is stupid, because if you are dead you can't feel claustrophobic.

"Let's go back in the kitchen," Mom says. Her voice is light, like there's nothing wrong. But this isn't her pretending everything is okay. This is her trying to convince him. He looks at me and sneers. His nose is running and his eyes look wild. Mom takes his hand, leads him into the kitchen. He places the knife on the counter.

I step off the stairs. I follow. I'm so dumb, but I want to

take her with me. I cannot leave her down here with him.

"Let's go to bed, Mom, it's late," I say.

"She'll go to bed when I fucking tell her to, Leighton. Get out of here."

I don't listen. Instead, I grab Mom's hand, and I try to pull her along.

He charges at me.

I am shoved against the kitchen countertop. The force of the impact knocks the wind out of me. When I turn around, he towers over me. Eyes bloodshot. How can he hate me this much?

He spits in my face.

Mom screams at him, pushes him away from me.

Mom is crying, lifting me to my feet.

"Go, Leighton," Mom says, leaning in to brush my hair behind my ear and wipe off my face.

She pulls me in tight. Whispers in my ear that everything is fine.

I let go of her. I run away from the kitchen with its too-bright lights, where Mom is crying and the knife is on the counter and the gun is on the fridge. I run until I'm safe, tucked into the armoire with the girls, breathing harshly and choking on tears.

A few minutes later, I hear the front door slam, and I burst from our hiding spot and down the stairs. I hear the engine rev on his truck a few times before he pulls away.

He's gone.

AUBURN, PENNSYLVANIA
DECEMBER 6

CROW POPULATION:
56,221

Chapter Forty-Five

WHERE DOES IT HURT? MOM WOULD ASK.

When I was four and I stepped on a piece of scrap metal in the yard and sliced the bottom of my foot open. When I was seven and woke up in the middle of the night, on fire with a fever. When I was eleven and couldn't stop sobbing when I got my period the first time and thought that I was dying.

This time it is Mom who fell down. Mom who is hurt. Sick, maybe.

Confused.

"Where does it hurt?" I ask her, searching.

"Everywhere," she says. She is hunched over, curled in upon herself, facing the kitchen floor. Her tears don't even touch her cheeks: they fall straight from her eyes, into air, onto the linoleum. I can hear the crows on top of the house. On the mailbox. On the street.

Cawing.

Like a chant.

I want to help her, to comfort her. I lean in closer, to remind her that she's safe now, he's gone.

But she already knows, because those are the words she is whispering.

He's gone. He's gone. Why is he gone?

And then I realize that she doesn't hurt everywhere because of him grabbing her face, calling her ugly names, holding a knife against her throat, telling her she's better off dead than without him, telling her that he'll take her to hell himself.

She hurts because he left.

She hurts because she wants him to come back.

Where does it hurt? I ask myself this time.

Everywhere.

Chapter Forty-Six

I WAKE UP WITH A STOMACHACHE. Mom and my sisters are all in bed with me, Campbell stretched across the foot of the bed. We are like Tetris pieces, fitting together just right. I untangle myself and go to the window, steeling myself for the image of his truck parked outside.

It isn't there. I guess he stayed at the office again, which is nothing more than a trailer in a lot, surrounded by the few work vehicles that Barnes Construction still owns. It must have been freezing.

The thing in my chest is unusually quiet. No pounding heart. No flutters of fear. Just an aching sadness that I can't quite place.

I hear the bed groan behind me, and Mom climbs out, settling Juniper back to sleep with a murmur and a soft kiss.

"Coffee?" she asks, dark circles under her eyes. She borrows a brush off my nightstand and tugs her hair into a messy French braid that curls down the side of her neck, her breasts, her ribs.

"Yeah," I say, and we sneak out of the room together.

I watch her as she brews it, and pours it, and as she sits at the table across from me, pushing the milk over to my side. I don't know what I'm looking for—some kind of sign that this is it. The morning after when she says enough.

I don't see any sign.

"Remember malaphors?" I ask.

She's silent a moment, and I wonder if she heard me, or if she's too buried in her thoughts. But then she shifts, sips her coffee, and looks up, bright blue eyes as clear as ever.

"Let's burn that bridge when we get to it," she says.

"Don't judge a book by another man's treasure," I counter.

"A bird in the hand is worth two birds with one stone."

I smile. It was a game we played when I was younger. We'd try to find the best nonsensical combination of idioms and metaphors. Mom was always brilliant at it. And Dad liked to lose to her. He liked how clever she was. Now our cleverness irritates him. It's like he thinks we are mocking him, all the time. Like the town. Like his father.

"Scaredy-cat got your tongue," I say.

"Sleep with the fish out of water."

"Home is where the crow flies," I say. Home. It feels like I've sworn in front of her.

"Mom . . ." I start. "You need a restraining order. We need a restraining order."

"Leighton, don't start."

"Mom—" My hands are shaking. Hot coffee drips all over my fingers.

"I know last night was scary, but he's been under a lot of pressure. You know construction work slows and stops in winter, and we have a lot of bills. We could lose the house, Leighton."

"You could make him leave."

"This is *his* home. He grew up here. Let's go stay with Nana for the weekend. We'll let things blow over."

"Forget things blowing over. Things have blown up." I stand and start to walk away. I've never been this mad at her before.

"I'm gonna take the girls to see Nana. What are you going to do?"

I ignore her and stare out the window at the snowy lawn.

"Leighton, I don't want to make any rash decisions. This is my marriage."

"You sound ridiculous."

"I'm still your mom. This isn't your decision. It's not your job to take care of the girls, either."

"Well, somebody has to do it."

These words have teeth, and we fall silent after I say them. Mom turns away, but not before I see the hurt on her face. I feel shame like a splinter inside of me, embedded in my skin, and I hate that I feel guilty for causing her any pain, when she overlooks mine so easily.

"I need time, Leighton," she says. "I need to think about it."

It isn't much, but it's all she's offering.

"Then I need time, too. I'm not coming to Nana's. I'll stay with Sofia this weekend. I'll see you Sunday."

"We could use the time as a family this weekend."

Family.

"My art show is this weekend. We are required to attend. For credit."

Checkmate.

There is a long moment of silence strung between us. We've run out of any semi-decent words to say to each other. All that's left is yelling, and it's like we both know it.

"I'll see you at home Sunday night, Leighton."

She goes upstairs, and I hear her moving around, waking the girls. Getting them packed. Like it's for fun. Like we aren't running in fear. I slip into my room to pack a weekend bag, too.

Campbell sneaks in as I'm finishing up.

"What happened?"

"We argued."

"She's not leaving him." It's not a question. Campbell seems to have already known what the outcome of last night would be: nothing.

"I need a break from her. Will you two be all right?"

"Sure," Cam says. "We like it at Nana's, and we get to miss school."

"Okay," I sigh. "I'm gonna figure this out."

Campbell turns and looks up at me.

"I know, Leighton," she says. I know the tone of her voice when she tells half-truths.

She doesn't believe me.

I'm not sure I do, either.

Mom and the girls leave for Nana's place, but Liam still hasn't arrived to drive me to school. I take my bags and leave the house. I don't want to be here whenever he decides to come back. I walk in the general direction of Liam's house. There are snow-covered fields on either side of the road, stretching for acres. Dotted with crows. Hundreds and hundreds of crows. Within five minutes, I spy a car coming down the road, and the thing in my chest stirs at the sight. Not a muscle car. An old Ford. Liam. He pulls off to the side and leans over, pushing open the passenger door.

"What the hell, Leighton?"

"Bad night," I say.

"Are you guys—" His hands are tight on the steering wheel.

"Fine. It's fine. I'll tell you all about it later, promise. You're late today."

"Yeah, I told you I would be—airport, remember? I had to drive my parents and Fiona over. It's her dance competition."

"Shit, I'm sorry, I completely spaced."

"It's fine."

We drive to school, and I let the old car warm me up. After a few minutes, Liam reaches over and takes my hand.

He doesn't say anything else on the ride, just keeps it there, my hand tucked into his. When we park, he looks up. "Wanna tell me now?"

"I want to, but I have to find Sofia. My mom took the girls to my grandmother's place and I didn't want to go, so I need to crash at her house this weekend."

"Or not."

"What?"

"My parents and Fiona are gone until Sunday for her dance competition. There's plenty of space—guest room is all yours, so don't worry about that, and . . ."

"What?"

"It'd be really nice to just know for sure that you are safe for a few nights."

"Oh. Um."

"Or not. It's totally up to you. We can go find Sofia instead."

"No, I'd like that, Liam. I'll stay with you."

We skip half of first period right there in the school parking lot while I tell Liam an abbreviated version of last night's events. He swears softly a few times, but doesn't interject otherwise. Until I tell him she isn't getting a protection order.

"She isn't even gonna try?"

"Nope. She said she has a lot to think about."

"What the hell does that even mean?"

"That we are going back there. Sunday."

"I don't understand how you are so calm about this, Leighton."

This song and dance might be age-old to me now, but he hasn't dealt with this. The terror, the relief, and the realization that nothing has changed. Again. It's a turning record for me, but Liam has never even heard the song before.

"I'm sorry, I suck."

"You don't, Leighton. Just don't shut me out now, okay?"

"Yeah, I'll stop. I'm sorry. Defense mechanism."

He leans over. "It's gonna be okay. We'll figure something out."

"Yeah, okay. Let's just get through the school day."

"Okay," he says, and releases my hand. I want to reach for his again, but stop myself. We won't figure something out. This isn't his mess. I will figure something out.

Later I skip lunch and slip into the newsroom. I need a few minutes of quiet—and privacy—to do some research. I type "protection orders Pennsylvania" into the search bar and hit enter. For thirty minutes, I scroll. I read sample protection orders. Words like *hospitalized* and *lacerations* filter across the screen. The images are horrifying. Bodies that are more bruised than not. And I feel it creep in, like it always does when I get this far: doubt.

Whenever these things come up on the news, the almost immediate reaction is to downplay the situation. To find the inconsistencies. To wonder how men will be impacted if we just all start believing women when they say they've been hurt or afraid. And I'm terrified that if I say anything, they'll do the same thing to me. They'll ask how I could dare to ruin his reputation over just a few minor infractions. They might say it isn't that bad. I'm overreacting.

Or maybe it's simpler than that. Maybe they just expect me to accept that this is how things are.

Maybe fear is the toll women pay to exist in this world at all.

Chapter Forty-Seven

OUR FRIDAY EVENING IS MUNDANE, AND I'm grateful for it.

Liam shows me how to use his shower. I forgot to pack a shirt to sleep in, so he leaves me one of his. An old football shirt that falls midway down my thighs. When I pass through the upstairs hallway, I run my fingers over the picture frames. I marvel at how the walls in this house hold on to things.

Liam offers to make dinner, and while he does, I slip down to their basement to choose from his collection of superhero movies again.

We meet back upstairs in their family room. On the coffee table is a huge tray filled with peanut butter sandwiches.

"We've got our classic pb and j here." He gestures. "Some Nutella options over here. And for dessert, peanut butter and marshmallow fluff."

I laugh at the elaborate display.

"It's perfect. Thank you. Here, I grabbed all the superhero

movies with women on the front."

"So . . . two."

"Yeah . . ."

"Well, what we lack in quantity for women-led superhero movies, we make up for in badassery. Pick whichever one you want."

"Okay. *Wonder Woman*. She looks like she could kill me with her pinkie finger."

We curl up on the sofa and eat from the tray of sandwiches.

"I feel like such a rebel," Liam says as he bites into a sandwich.

"Why? Because I'm staying here?" I ask.

"No, eating on the couch. My mom would flip out if she knew I was doing this."

"Liam?"

"Yeah?"

"Don't you think she might also object to the whole sleepover thing?"

"Nah, they'd understand. Mitigating circumstances."

When we finish eating, Liam puts the plate down and then pulls my legs over his lap. We sit, entangled and content, as we watch the movie. At one point, I think he's leaning in to kiss me, but he just reaches for a blanket that he throws over our legs, and continues watching the movie. Finally, he must feel my stare, because he turns.

"You okay, Leighton?"

"Yep," I say. "Just wondering if we were ever gonna fool around again."

Liam laughs and pulls me farther onto his lap. I have to turn a bit to kiss him, and it would take just the slightest shift for my legs to be on either side of his hips. We've been here before, but it was in the cramped front seat of a car.

Not an empty house.

Liam's hand moves under the edge of my shirt. Or rather, his shirt that I'm wearing. His hand drifts up slowly across my belly and ribs. His movements are as unrushed as ever. I never bothered to put my bra back on, so when his cool hand brushes my breast, we both gasp. He pulls away immediately, hand out of my shirt, and lifts me off him.

"Liam, what's wrong?" I ask, a little disoriented by the sudden departure from our unspoken plan to make out for the rest of the evening.

Liam pulls up his legs and faces me on the couch. He looks dead serious, and I feel my stomach sink a bit. Something is wrong.

"Look, Leighton, I'm enjoying the hell out of this, but I'm afraid of what it is gonna lead to."

"Oh?"

"Yeah, I mean, don't get me wrong, I'm definitely very interested in that, with you, but I really don't think we can do anything tonight without me feeling like I'm taking advantage of you somehow."

I feel a wave of anger. Because my dad doesn't get to have a part in this. He doesn't get to make me feel like a stranger in my home and terrify the girls and hurt Mom *and* have any kind of influence on what happens with me and Liam. That's not fair. It's too much. This is mine. Mine and Liam's.

"Liam. Stop. You can't associate this good thing with that bad thing, or I'll never forgive you. I swear you've never pressured me. And if we do anything, ever, it will be because we both want to."

He looks unconvinced.

I get up and find my purse, digging around it in ruthlessly. Dammit. I'm fighting angry tears and can't see into the dark bag, so I dump its contents on the floor instead. There. I grab a small plastic case and hand it to Liam.

"What is this?" he asks.

"Open it," I say.

He opens it and examines it for several seconds.

"We did take the exact same health classes, didn't we?" I ask.

"Shit, yes. Sorry. So . . . you're on the pill?"

"Yeah. Have been for a little while now. See? No rushed, emotional decisions on my part. I've been thinking about it, and planning for it, and that doesn't mean I'm ready tonight or anything, but if we did, it wouldn't be because I'm stressed or scared or anything. It's because I like you, and because I want to."

"Okay, I hear you. I'm sorry."

"Thank you."

"I honestly had no idea you were seriously considering it. We really can take all the time in the world."

"We still can. My original time line has us waiting until July, but after the car incident on our very first date, I wasn't sure we'd make it that long."

Liam laughs. "Of course you have a time line. Why July?"

"Nine months since we started dating. It seemed logical to me that we shouldn't be having sex if we can't even make a relationship work as long as a pregnancy would last."

"Wow. That is logical."

"Too logical?"

"Just a bit," Liam says, but he softens it with a kiss. "But it's cool."

"Yeah?"

"Honestly, it's totally fine. That stuff is fun, but so is everything we've been doing together. I like you a lot, Barnes."

"Yeah, yeah. I bet you say that to all the girls, Liam McNamara."

Liam turns on the couch, pulls his leg up under him, faces me.

"I don't. Listen, I know I've dated a lot, but that's because it's what we do—don't roll your eyes, just let me finish. The girls I dated were my friends, and it was all about social status. We never really liked each other. It was . . . superficial. But that's not how I feel with you."

"Oh," I say. It's all I've got, because I have no idea where he's going with this.

"Yeah. Pretty sure I'm in love with you, Barnes."

"*Oh.*"

Of all the things I expected could happen this weekend, Liam McNamara saying he loved me might have been number 167 on the list. It's not something I was looking for. And considering everything, I don't know how I feel about it. Love is complicated.

But then I think of a different definition of love. Like the kind between friends, or sisters. I think of how much I love Junie and Cam, and I realize that it isn't all about expectations or promises. There's just loving someone without reason or time frames or endings in mind. Maybe it's okay to love in the moment, and it doesn't have to be with intentions and goals. We don't have to want to grow up and marry each other to enjoy this now.

But I'm not ready.

"Liam, listen—"

"No, wait. Listen, this is totally the same as me moving too fast with the physical stuff after a stressful week. So, don't say anything back now."

"Are you sure? I just—it's a lot to process."

"Say no more. Should I say it again? I have this theory that if something is awkward, you should just go with it. Awkward to the tenth degree. It can't sustain itself. Here, watch: I love you, Leighton."

"That *was* weird. You didn't call me Barnes."

Liam laughs, and the tension snaps like a broken spell. He was right. Exponent-level awkward works. I lean in and kiss him. He turns and catches my head, my neck. His thumb brushes the side of my face when I pull back.

"I think I do, too," I say when we break free. It's the closest I can come to saying it. For now. "But no promises, okay?"

"What do you mean?"

"I mean, let's not pretend we are going to be together forever, and then break each other into pieces when we aren't, and have all of those unrealistic expectations to live happily ever after."

"Oh, agreed. I'm only in it for the sex."

"Liam!" I swat at his arm.

"I really like being with you, though," I add, to soften my non-love declaration.

"Also agreed."

"Even if you are an arrogant jock," I say.

"Even if you are a nerd," he counters.

"So . . ."

"No promises."

"No promises," I repeat.

We finish watching our movie, but my mind is anywhere else. It makes twenty-four hours of complete emotional upheaval a little better, though. To end on such a high note.

Chapter Forty-Eight

I WAKE UP LONG BEFORE DAWN to the sound of soft rain hitting the window. For a moment, my mind is a perfectly blank slate, awake, but not yet aware. I am nothing but a breathing thing in the pitch-black. Nameless and floating. A lone bird in the night sky, weightless and free. But a few moments pass, and I feel my weight in the mattress, pulling me back to earth. I realize that the window I'm looking at isn't my own, and gravity—reality—finds me again, grounds me. I'm aware of the bare arm wrapped around my ribs. A larger hand wrapped around my own. Liam's warm breath is on the back of my neck. Oh, right. We're sleeping together. Nothing happened, we just wanted to be near each other.

I haven't slept this soundly in ages. No nightmares. No creaks or noises to wake me up, to make me wonder if this is the night something really bad happens. I lie in Liam's bed, studying the shadows of his room, trying to remember what they were in the light. Now sleep is the winged thing, just out of reach.

We aren't alone.

I slip out of Liam's hold and step to the window, barefoot on the cool hardwood floor. Joe sits in the tree outside Liam's window. He is facing the street and looks almost like a statue of a bird instead of the real thing. I wonder if he has been there all night. I wonder if he's been there for a hundred years, watching. He looks frozen in time. But just as I think it, his head tilts, and I can see his black eye, his gray feathers, his scissor-sharp beak highlighted by the street lamp's light.

"Good night, Joe," I whisper, and let the shade fall into place.

Chapter Forty-Nine

PEOPLE THINK CROWS ARE HARBINGERS OF war and death.

But my research has taught me that this is untrue.

Crows more fundamentally symbolize change. New beginnings. Sometimes that could mean a death, but usually in literature and history, the bird's arrival just signifies some great awakening. An upheaval of the status quo.

Liam is already out of bed when I wake up. I rouse quickly, hypersensitive to the idea that I just slept in a guy's bed. I check Liam's bedroom window. No Joe this morning, but there is a collection of little oddities on the windowsill outside. I slide the window open and pull the gifts inside: a screw and a book of matches. I look over them carefully, remembering that some of Joe's earlier gifts were our own things returned to us, but these seem random. I drop them into my pocket so that Juniper can add them to the collection she's laid out carefully on her dresser at home. Before I go downstairs, I grab Mr. Jelly from Liam's desk and put him back in his place of honor on the center of the bed.

I find Liam in the kitchen. He's already showered and is dressed for the cold weather.

"Oh." I'm surprised. "Do you have plans?"

"We have plans," he says. "We're going for a hike."

"But . . . it's cold."

"Yes. It will feel good. Invigorating."

I frown. He is clearly a morning person. And he likes hiking.

"Liam, this might not actually work out between us."

He laughs and hands me a scarf. "Here, I have extra cozy things you can borrow. You'll be warm once we start moving."

Liam opens the pantry.

"Cinnamon apple? Maple and brown sugar?"

"Maple."

He pulls out instant oatmeal and prepares it for us. It's not until it's done and cooling that he tries a different tactic.

"Hiking is not like running. It's leisurely. We can birdwatch. Call it crow research."

"You can't use my column against me like that." I point my spoon at him.

"I'm pretty sure I just did."

I open my mouth again, but I've got nothing. The art show isn't until tonight, and the fresh air might feel good.

"Okay, fine. I'm in."

"Great. We're meeting the others in thirty minutes."

"What others?"

"Amelia and Sofia are going."

"When did you even coordinate—you know what, never mind. I don't want to know how much you and Sofia are plotting together."

"That's probably for the best. Let's go."

And with that, he shoves a travel mug into my hands and we are out the door, driving toward the hiking trails closest to school. We pull into a familiar parking lot, and Amelia and Sofia are already there, waving to us.

"Hey, this is my favorite parking lot in Auburn," I say.

"What a crazy coincidence, mine too," Liam says.

I take a sip from the mug he gave me earlier. "Wait, this is hot cocoa."

"Mmhmm. It's delicious."

"Coffee is delicious, and it has caffeine."

"Coffee is *not delicious*, you heathen. And you know I don't drink coffee."

"What do you have against coffee anyway?"

"Uhh . . ." Liam rubs his hands over his head, which I've realized he always does when he isn't sure what to say. A little spacer to give him time to collect his thoughts. "You know how I can get really stuck in my head about stuff? I worry a lot. Caffeine just kind of amplifies those thoughts."

I think of the school pamphlets on his desk and his thing

with glasses and his perfectionism in just about every area of his life, and it all clicks.

"That makes sense. I'm sorry I was nosy."

"No worries." He dismisses the uncomfortable topic, and then gives me his winning smile. "You ready?"

Our hike is quick and breathless in the cold air. Sofia and Amelia are laughing ahead of us.

"Hey, I forgot to ask which pieces of yours are in the show tonight," I say. We turned in our portfolios a few days ago and decided with our art teacher which ones should be displayed.

"Oh, I'm not actually sure. I really wanted him to pick my moonscapes, but Mr. Taylor liked another set better. What about you?"

"*Portrait of an Old Crow.*"

"Good, I like that one."

I think of Joe and my pocket full of gifts, and I smile.

I like it, too.

We reach one of the lookout peaks and find a perfect view of Auburn. It looks so small from up here.

Amelia and Liam start chatting about student council, and I sit next to Sofia, who reaches for the travel mug in my hands.

"Mmm, hot chocolate," she says after taking a sip. "Good, you drink too much caffeine."

"I drink the exact right amount, thank you very much," I say.

"So," Sofia says, and I can guess what's coming. "How was last night?"

I look over my shoulder at Liam, but it doesn't seem like he can hear us. He and Amelia are looking up, and I follow their gazes. There are dozens of crows soaring just off the edge of the lookout.

"Um, fine. Very . . . uneventful."

"Oh yeah?" Sofia raises her eyebrows at me.

"Well, actually, there was something."

"Oh my God, I *knew* it."

"Not that. Liam said he loves me." I double-check that Liam isn't overhearing us.

"Whoa."

"Yeah."

"That's huge," Sofia says, passing me the hot chocolate again.

"Yep." The crows are now rising and diving, and it reminds me of the morning in the rain when Liam and I saw them playing. Today it's like they are surfing the wind.

"And you . . . ?"

"Oh, I panicked."

"Naturally," she says, laughing and putting her arm around me. "Take your time with it, Leighton. He's been smitten with you from, like, day one. And I think you have been, too. But that doesn't mean you have to say anything you aren't ready for."

"Yeah? I'm not being frigid?"

"Leighton, you have the biggest heart of anyone I know." Some of the crows descend and land in the trees below, and a new batch of crows rise like a dark cloud. Dr. Cornell sent me another update on the crows—some kind of thermal map that experts use to track bird migration habits, and that they've used on Auburn. It looked like one giant maroon mass to me, but Dr. Cornell explained in his notes that the birds are mostly drawn to the mountains and the water supplies. Auburn officials are trying to bring in falconers next. They'll release live hawks to torment the crow populations, encouraging them to leave with a natural enemy.

But crows are intelligent, resourceful. They can problem-solve. I don't think anything the town tries is going to work.

The crows will leave when they want to.

And when they do, I hope they know better than to come back.

Chapter Fifty

WE ARE REQUIRED TO ATTEND THE art show and stand by our drawings. I'm sure there are worse forms of high school humiliation, but not many.

I'm standing next to *Portrait of an Old Crow*. It's the best piece I've submitted all term, which isn't saying much. Liam thinks I should go right into Art II this spring with my last elective. He said I have "potential."

I told him that's what people say about ugly old houses that need a ton of work.

I try to pretend that tonight is like ripping off a bandage. One quick tug, then the pain is over. But the minutes I spend standing there, letting everyone stare at and comment on my drawing, are not quick. The town feels particularly small tonight.

I check the clock every ninety seconds.

As soon as the clock hits 7:30, I bolt from my station. I buzz through the small labyrinth of display walls that have been erected throughout the gym for the show. There is still one small crowd gathered, and I'm so pleased for him when I realize that it is Liam's spot. We make eye contact, and he frowns.

I slip through the people standing there, and I'm about to ask what's wrong, when I catch his art pieces. I stop hard. I'm just another onlooker now, staring at the drawing that Liam has displayed for the show. It's designed to look like the cover of a comic book.

In one corner, a little girl stands with her arm outstretched. A crow is perched on her forearm. The other side shows an older girl. She is turned partially away, and the drawing is of her upper body, her straight hair, her soft face. She has wings growing out of her back. Big, thick feathers sprouting right from her shoulder blades. The center drawing is a young woman. She is drawn kneeling on the ground, crying. She is surrounded by a sea of black feathers. She looks alone. She looks devastated.

She looks like me.

I try to unsee it, but I can't. The third girl is me. Not exactly, but there is a familiarity. The shape of her jaw. The part in her hair. My eyes scan the three drawings again, and then find the little tag that is taped below them, giving the title and artist.

"THESE BROKEN WINGS: AN ORIGIN STORY"
LIAM McNAMARA

Liam is looking right at me. For a moment, I don't remember that there is a small crowd beside me or that we are at school with our peers and teachers. All I see is him, looking at me.

"Is this how you see me?" I ask.

"Leighton," Liam says. He moves toward me, and I step back.

I'm hurt and embarrassed and trying to process too many emotions in too public a space.

I turn on my heel and make my way toward the girls' locker room. He's following me.

"Leighton, I'm your ride," he says.

I stop walking. How could I forget that? Not just my ride. I'm staying at his house.

"Please, Leighton, let's just drive and talk," he says.

He looks miserable. He isn't chasing after me now. Just leaning against the end of the bleachers, waiting for me to make a decision.

I nod.

It is freezing cold outside, and windy, and there is black ice everywhere. Liam offers me his arm while we cross the slippery parking lot, but I don't take it. I slip once, and pick myself up, silent.

The drive is quiet, in part because I'm still angry, and in part because the roads are dangerous, and I want Liam to focus. He pulls into the driveway at his house.

"I'm sorry," he says.

"I am not broken," I say, finally interrupting the silence.

"No. Leighton. I know that," Liam says. "I swear, it's a stupid piece for class. I didn't even mean for it to look like you. You're just on my mind a lot, and it . . . happened. And Mr. Taylor liked it a lot; I couldn't convince him to pick something else."

"You could have taken it out of your portfolio."

"It would have risked . . ."

He stops short.

"Your grade? You didn't want to risk the A."

He sighs and nods.

"I am not a broken thing you have to fix. I'm not your four-point-oh. Or your application to Harvard. I'm not a hobby or a project or a school assignment."

"I know that."

"You could have warned me," I add.

"Definitely, yes, I should have," he says.

I stop for a moment, collecting my thoughts, weighing my feelings. I realize I don't actually know how to argue and reach a resolution. I haven't ever seen that.

"I didn't mean to hurt you, Leighton. I'm really sorry."

"I know," I say. I saw that before I even saw the drawings— the regret on his face when I walked up.

"I know you're mad, but could I show you the rest of it?"

"The rest of what?"

"The comic. The ones at the show were just the cover."

I follow Liam into the house, shrugging off our heavy coats

and boots. In his room he reaches for a thick notebook on his bedside table and flips through it. The pages are divided up into a comic book layout—with thought bubbles and speech boxes. He gets to a few pages that are all filled in. It's the girl surrounded by crows, but in the next box, she rises. Her arms stretch out and birds land on them.

In Liam's drawings, this girl transforms until she is more feather than girl. One box focuses on her new wickedly sharp talons.

"She's a superhero. This is her origin story."

"Yeah," I say softly, running my fingers lightly over the page of drawings. "She looks so fearless."

"That was on purpose. Not broken."

I look up at Liam. "This is amazing."

"I made one for Fiona, too. Her hero alter ego can dance-fight people to death. And I was going to make one for Campbell next, but the only power I can think of for her is that she kills people with her brain."

I laugh.

"Campbell would *love* that," I tell him. Liam's fingers touch the back of my hand, almost like an accident. I turn my hand until our palms fit together.

I could have refused to see the rest of the drawings. Refused to even talk to him. It would have been so easy to stay mad, to dwell on it all night, but I've seen how that kind of relentless anger builds on itself. I get to decide for myself what things I'll carry, and anger isn't going to be one of them.

Chapter Fifty-One

ON SUNDAY, I HAVE TO GO HOME.

When I walk into the house, I find everyone in the living room. Dad sits with his head between his hands, and when he lifts his face at the sound of my entrance, there's real regret there. Real pain. There isn't even a crack on the wall or ceiling anymore, like once again the house is pretending it never happened.

"Leighton. Thank you for coming home." He says it like I had a choice in this.

I stand in the doorway, neither coming nor going, unsure of what I'm waiting for.

"I just want you girls to know that I'm really sorry, and I have no idea what came over me the other night. It's been a lot of pressure with the company, things I don't want to worry you guys with, and I think I was just bottling it all up."

Mom moves to sit beside him on the couch. "Your father and I talked *a lot* this weekend on the phone, about how terrible his behavior was, and what needs to change around here so we don't have a repeat of Thursday night. Starting with us keeping the house in really good shape so it doesn't stress him out after a long day at work. And we have to watch heat and energy use and keep the bills as low as we can."

Every word makes my jaw tighten more. Dad takes over, listing a few more things that are part of their grand strategy—but it's all focused on this house, and us. Like it was only our actions that led to his outburst.

Campbell meets my eyes and gives me the subtlest shake of her head. She is thinking the same thing.

And silently asking me not to say anything.

But this isn't a solution.

"And we are going to add some more fun stuff," he says. "We haven't been good at family time lately, being low on money and everything, but your amazing mom made a list of things we can do that aren't too expensive."

Now he looks to me, because Juniper is smiling and Campbell is nodding along, and Mom is holding his hand. We've all come back together, and he's waiting for me to join the moment. To commit to their plan.

"Please, Leighton," Mom says softly. "Can we just try?"

I bite the inside of my bottom lip, worrying it with my teeth.

"Okay," I say. And there are a lot of things I don't say.

"I'm sorry," he says again. It isn't a lie. He means it. He always means it.

Dad offers to make everyone dinner, and Campbell and

Juniper offer to help. I make myself some coffee and go sit on the front stoop.

"There are so many," Mom says as she joins me outside. The tree in our yard is full again.

I spy Joe near the top, his gray feathers giving him away.

I try to remember the estimate that came with the thermal image of them.

"Well over fifty thousand now," I tell her.

We sit in silence for a few minutes, sipping our coffee and watching the birds.

"He's not a monster, Leighton," she says. "He's just a person. A flawed person, who has a lot of demons."

"I know," I say. *But that's not an excuse*, I think.

"But that's not an excuse," she says, and I turn to her. Her eyes are still on the tree. "I know it's been really strained here lately. I just want to believe that those good things can prevail. I still see that side of him. I see him fighting for it. Fighting for us. He spent the weekend sleeping on a friend's couch, Leighton. He's humiliated."

"I don't care if he's humiliated."

In fact, I like it. Most of the time it seems like we are the ones who feel all of his shame. "Where did he stay?"

I guess the answer before she says it, hope that I'm wrong.

"With Bill," Mom says.

Officer DiMarco. Of course. It's the only option awful enough to be true. Instead of protecting us, the police harbor him.

"He feels out of control," I say. And it's the truth, or at least what I can understand about it. All those promising futures closed off, and now this business is failing, and even though I think he must've hated his own father and some part of him resents the business, I know how stressful it is to fail. His anger is not some great mystery.

Maybe I never took his football dream, but I left the cap off the toothpaste so that it dripped all over the counter. I didn't wreck his knee in that championship game, but I folded the towels wrong.

I didn't steal his wife on purpose, but she loves us most, and he knows it.

Our family is a solar system of planets rocked off their orbits a little farther with each incident like the other night. We are moving around each other in increasing chaos, haphazard and violent, all of us bracing for impact. And I don't know how to break away from it, because there's gravity here, in between us. There are good things that bind us to each other.

I take Mom's hand.

I see a fractured system, delicate and damaged, that could collapse right under our feet.

She sees home.

Chapter Fifty-Two

IN THE DARKNESS INSIDE THE ARMOIRE, we come home to each other. Things are quiet tonight, but it is not calm. It is disquiet. The house feels ill at ease with itself, the walls more shadowed than usual. The winter wind is blowing hard outside, and we can hear the bones of the house creaking from the force.

My job tonight is to reassure—to distract. Our lantern burns, and we play all our games. Anywhere But Here and Shadows. Juniper asks for a story, and I tell her about a girl made of flowers. She had big bluebells for eyes, and instead of hair, she grew sunflowers, heavy and swollen with seeds, and their faces would follow the sun as the girl walked. Her fingers were the fuzzy leaves of a violet.

The girl made of flowers was beloved. She was somehow both soft and strong, and girls like that always find admirers. Her honeysuckle scent drew them in like worker bees, and she never minded. She'd share her blooms, plucking a rose from her wrist and a dahlia from her slender neck.

One day, the flower girl fell in love with a man who was like an oak tree. Solid and strong. He offered her shade, protection from the harsher elements. Most important, he let her be still. She sunk her roots deep into the earth by his side. She flourished, blooming even larger and more beautiful petals. But then the oak tree started to lose its leaves, and the girl gave him her flowers in their place. She gave and she gave, and he took them all, not seeing the way she wilted without them. She loved the oak tree too much to leave him, but she could grow her flowers just fast enough for him to pluck them from her. She could no longer share her beauty with the world, so consumed was she with keeping him happy.

After the girls are asleep, I swing open the armoire door and lift them to my bed. Campbell is almost too big for this, but I manage it, barely. I push Campbell's books aside at the foot of my bed—collections of haunted house stories, her new obsession.

I reach for my backpack and pull out the latest *Auburn Gazette*. The football team has claimed another win, and another front page. *On to semi-finals. First time in nineteen years.* I turn the pages to the Help Wanted section and scan the listings. The library needs help. And they need a receptionist at the law firm on the corner. The diner is almost always hiring waitresses, but that's it. I circle the most promising ones, and then I turn to the housing page. There's one apartment building in all of Auburn, but some people rent out the spaces over their garages, or an extra room. There are a few options with rent that isn't too bad. I circle those, too. The next page is township news, and there's a box at the bottom advertising the essay contest. Right now, college feels impossible. Leaving them to this feels cruel.

I set aside the pages I marked and reach for Campbell's books. She always wants my copy of the *Gazette* when I'm done. But my movement disturbs Juniper, nestled in the middle of the bed, and she kicks Campbell's stack of books off the bed. It's muffled by the carpet, and they don't wake up.

I pick them up and find one of Campbell's notebooks splayed open. There are sections of newspaper cutouts pasted onto the pages, the words familiar.

It's my column.

I turn the pages of her notebook and find more of them. All of them. Each of my crow columns, carefully saved; her quiet support makes me smile.

But then I turn one more page, and stop. It isn't a column. It's a police blotter from the *Gazette*.

Every week, local police highlights get printed in our paper.

And Campbell has been cutting them out, saving them here. There are dozens of them.

"APD responded to a check-in request on an elderly woman on Pine Street. The woman was well, and said she isn't returning her son's calls because she is mad at him."

"APD responded with animal control when several callers reported a donkey walking down Main Street. Officers were able to harness the animal and locate the owner."

"APD officers responded to a reported break-in at 58 West Elm. No evidence of a break-in was found. A kitchen window was left open and several stray cats had wandered into the home."

I put the notebook back and turn to lie down.

Campbell's eyes are open.

"Hey," I say, and rest my head on the pillow. We can see each other over Juniper's head. "I'm sorry. It fell open; I shouldn't have read it."

"It's fine," she says.

I reach over her and turn off the light.

"Campbell?" I ask the darkness. "Why do you keep them? The police reports."

I know she's just a few inches away from me, but it's pitch-black in my room and she's silent for a moment, and we aren't touching. I reach out until the tips of my fingers graze her arm, to reassure myself that she's right there and not a million miles away from me like it feels.

"One day we'll be in there," she says, and all of the little hairs on my arms stand up. "And it will either mean something really good happened, like his arrest, and we're finally safe, or it'll mean something really, really bad happened."

There's a flash of the crawl space in my mind. It feels like a premonition, and it makes me sick. I imagine the little block newspaper letters that I love so much betraying me, writing my obituary.

"It'll be good, Campbell," I say.

Too late.

She's asleep.

Chapter Fifty-Three

FOR MY NEXT CROW-THEMED COLUMN, I'm covering the December town hall meeting. The crows have been brought up in other ones, I'm sure, but this month the entire meeting is dedicated to a sole purpose: deciding how to get the crows out of Auburn.

I don't have a ride. Liam is at practice, and it's Sofia's mom's birthday, so she couldn't leave. So I ask Campbell for help, and I bike. Three miles. In December. But it's a dry night, and it isn't terribly cold, and I couldn't bring myself to ask my parents for a ride. All of our recent wounds are too painful.

I arrive at the municipal building, hot under my sweater and winter coat from the exertion. I lean Campbell's bike against a tree and strip down to my T-shirt. A flash of black right next to me catches my eye, and I turn to face a single crow perched on the edge of the curb just inches away from me. He's the only one on the street.

A cigarette dangles from his beak.

"You should quit," I tell him as I walk past. "Those things will kill you."

When I get inside, the meeting has just started, so I slip into the back of the room and lean against the wall, pen and notepad poised.

"Last crow hunt was a complete failure, anyway," says a man in a uniform. The game warden.

"How many crows did we get at the first shoot?" asks a member of the town council from the front of the room.

"Ahh, that was . . . six hundred and thirty-three."

"And this last hunt?"

"None, sir."

"I'm sorry, did you say none?"

"No birds."

"How is that possible? We had, what, thirty hunters register for it, right?"

"Well, we got out into the fields and the crows flew too high. Like they knew how high we could fire. Like they remembered."

I make a note to ask my ornithologist about it. They probably did remember.

"Damnedest thing I've ever seen," the game warden concludes. I bet he'd love to hear about Joe's gifts.

The council member rubs the space between his eyes. I don't recognize him, but a few of the others are notable

Auburn residents. Bill DiMarco is up there, but as a citizen, not representing the police force. So is the principal of the elementary school. One of the school librarians. In a town this small, civil servants usually have to pull double duty or more to fill all the seats. These are the men who would be evaluating my scholarship essay.

"So, the hunts are useless. I don't see any other options left than to pay for wildlife experts to come in and use more extreme measures."

A murmur rustles through the crowd. The hundred or so residents who bothered to show up look like mourners, all dressed in their black winter coats.

"We have the option to contract out—these people have dealt with large bird concentrations before. They'll use flares, flashes, and noise. The idea is to try to overwhelm them so much that they leave. It will be expensive. It will be loud. And on that note, I open the floor to comments."

A woman near the front stands first.

"The crows are in the trash every day. On every street. The whole neighborhood smells. They've memorized the trash days."

Mr. DiMarco leans forward to his microphone. "I'm sorry, ma'am, but what do you mean, they've *memorized* the days?"

"I mean that our street has trash collection Monday, so the crows come Monday and wait for the garbage men to open the cans, and then they attack the bags in the truck and pull anything left in the garbage cans out. On Tuesday, the crows are waiting on Maple Street. On Wednesday—"

"I understand, thank you," Bill DiMarco says, shaking his head. I think he doesn't believe her. His facial expression is mirthful, like he'd laugh at her if it were appropriate to do so, or like he might laugh at her anyway.

His condescension makes me dislike him more.

A man just across from me stands next.

"The crows killed my cat," he says. "Cornered the poor thing near my garage. Pecked it to death."

Another murmur in the crowd.

"Did you see this?" a councilman asks.

"No. But I'm sure it was the birds."

"Let's try to stick to things we've seen, arguments in favor of or against releasing these funds."

A small woman stands, and I recognize our neighbor, Mrs. Stieg. I guess I could have asked her for a ride.

"Those birds have wreaked *havoc* on my roses," she says.

Oh no, not the precious roses.

"Did you see this?" a council member asks.

"I did. The first time was in September, when they'd just started arriving. I woke up at dawn and saw them tearing one of my prize-winning rosebushes into pieces, snapping the branches and plucking the petals off the blooms. I'd just almost lost another bush, and then this one was completely destroyed."

I remember the ruined bush that I saw when we walked to school, how I thought it must have been Campbell, angry and resentful about Mrs. Stieg's unkind words to us that weekend. I was so sure it was her, but I was wrong. It was the crows. But why would the crows ruin a rosebush?

"And then a few weeks later, one more bush! Gone! Do you have any idea how many years it takes to cultivate a rose garden like mine? The dedication to each plant? And those horrible birds have spent all autumn tearing down my plants."

"I'm very sorry to hear about . . . your flowers."

"Well, I say we bring in any experts we can find. Get rid of the damn nuisances once and for all," Mrs. Stieg says, and then she sits down. A few people clap for her.

"Okay, I think we've heard enough. On the table is Town Ordinance 4420, proposed on this date, the ninth of December, to approve a budget to contract out for crow eradication. All those against the ordinance say nay."

There is silence in the room.

"Nay!" I call out, and everyone turns to look. Then they turn back. One nay.

"All those in support say aye."

People yell their ayes. They stand and shout it. Some of them shuffle on the floor or raise their arms. One person climbs on his seat.

The ayes have it.

I bolt from the room, my sneakers squeaking on the

shiny tiles as I run. I burst through the door and suck in the cold night air. The street in front of me is filled with crows. A few hundred, at least. They are facing the door to the municipal building. Cawing, cawing. They are so loud, cawing over each other, yelling like the people inside, and suddenly I don't hear caws. I hear nays. "Nay!" scream the crows in their dark feathers outside. "Aye!" scream the people in their dark coats inside. Mirror images of each other.

If the crows could vote, the nays would've won.

Chapter Fifty-Four

I CLOSE THE DOOR AND LEAN against it for a minute, unwilling at first to move farther into the house. Everything is quiet except for the buzz of the television.

When I finally reach the living room, Campbell and Juniper are curled up on the chair, and my parents are on the couch. Mom is leaning into his side, and his arms are wrapped around her. The embrace is so normal, so gentle, but the sight makes my chest constrict.

"Leighton, how was your meeting?" she asks, patting the open space on the other side of her. I move into the room and sit down.

"Movie night?" I ask.

"We had to cancel the cable, so we're picking from our favorites that we own," Dad says, and the sentence is laced with guilt. He's always sorry for the wrong thing.

"Good choice," I say. "Anyone want some popcorn?"

Campbell and Juniper nod eagerly, and I head for the

kitchen. I know they asked for an effort, and I want to try. It's just hard.

Dad follows me into the kitchen.

"Here," he says. "The popcorn machine is out of your reach."

He gets it for me out of the cabinet over the refrigerator, carefully moving his wallet and keys and gun to the counter as he does so.

"One more game," he says out of nowhere. It takes me a minute to raise my eyes from the counter. From the gun.

"Hmm?" I ask.

"Liam must be excited. One more win and the Wolves go to states."

"Oh, yeah. I guess he's happy."

"Ah, yeah. I could barely sleep leading up to those last few games. The whole town was, well, you know. You see it now."

I know the right response here: "I hope we win," or maybe "It's really exciting." Even a simple "go Wolves" would suffice. But I look at him in the soft kitchen light, and I want to try harder.

"That must have been a lot of pressure."

He looks up from the popcorn machine. "Yeah, it really was. And people around here don't forget."

"No, I guess not," I say, handing him the container of kernels. "Do you want to go?"

"To the game?"

I nod.

"Yeah, why not? We can cheer on your boyfriend, show some town spirit."

Auburn proud.

"Okay. It's Friday."

"Sounds good, Leighton."

"How was work?" It might be the wrong thing to say, again, but if he wants us to try, then he has to try, too. He has to let us ask normal questions and not tiptoe around his temper.

"A mess," he says, his laugh a humorless bark. "Lost out on a job outside of Philly. Got underbid. Again."

He doesn't sound angry, though; just sad, disappointed.

"I'm sorry," I say.

"Thanks," he says, and his hand falls to my shoulder for a moment. Sometimes I really wish he were just mean through and through. Evil is easy to hate, but broken . . . broken can love and be loved.

The kitchen is noisy with the popcorn now, and I feel like the air has been sucked out of the room.

"I'm gonna go work on my column for a bit; I'll be back down."

"Okay. Study hard."

As soon as I step into my room, something cracks against the window. It's Joe on my windowsill.

This time I don't open the window slowly, waiting for him to leave. I throw it open to the cold December air. He still doesn't fly away, just shuffles his feet in irritation. I reach for my backpack and pull out the few packets of crackers I stashed for him. I squeeze the packet until the crackers break and the bag bursts. A little cloud of salt dust is released, and I can taste it in the air.

Joe waits patiently for my offering, and when I sprinkle the crackers onto the outer sill, he bows his head and drops something. It lands softly on my carpet, and glimmers in the moonlight.

A rusted little key. I drop it onto my nightstand, next to the screw and matchbook he left me at Liam's house. I keep forgetting to give them to Juniper, but then again, her own collection has grown so much. Nearly a dozen marbles, twice as many feathers. Buttons and coins.

When I return to the window, Joe is gone, and I close it against the cold.

My window faces our front yard: the street, the truck, the tree. But it's dark outside and bright in here, so all I see is my own reflection. Window Leighton looks kind of tired, dark circles under her eyes. I can't see them right now, but I can feel the crows on the other side of the glass.

They are not polite guests who clear their dishes from the sink or remake their beds every morning. They aren't visitors.

They are Vikings.

They've conquered this town. They now flood the sky in droves, darken Auburn like there's a storm rolling in. They caw day and night, until the noise is part of us. Until we can't remember what it's like to not hear them.

And yet.

I like them.

I like the crows because they can't be shut behind a door, or hidden behind blinds. People can't turn away and shake their heads and say, "It isn't our problem."

I like the crows because they refuse to be ignored.

Chapter Fifty-Five

I'VE MADE A HUGE MISTAKE.

I promised Liam I would be at his game, but now that we are here, I regret it. We are out of town, and I feel the loss of the crows' presence more than I thought I would.

The noise is layers deep. The low, constant murmur of people talking in their seats. The shrill whistles from the referees, and the heavy, meaty sound of so many bodies colliding on the field. The cheerleaders are right below us, in perfect unison. But something is off tonight. The clanging cowbells feel like a warning.

It is strange to have my whole family here, sitting on the bleachers in a row. Around us, it looks like the entire town showed up: the familiar faces of my teachers, and the game warden from the township meeting. Bill DiMarco is sitting two rows behind us, and he chats with my dad for a while before we take our seats at the start of the game. I spy the Auburn fire chief, who has worked with my dad to evaluate fire-damaged structures before the construction team moves in. The few times I met him, he always struck me as the most serious person I'd ever seen, even in third grade when he taught us to stop, drop, and roll and how to call 911 in an emergency.

The first quarter ends, and the bleachers feel like they could collapse under all the people jumping up and down. The Wolves are winning.

But the fire chief doesn't look worried tonight, about the structure of the bleachers or anything else. He's even smiling and waving a maroon-and-silver pom-pom around while he stomps his feet with the rest of the crowd.

"Huge night for Auburn's Wolves. They haven't gone this far in almost twenty years. Maybe this time they'll go all the way!" This comes over the loudspeaker.

Mom nudges me. "Leighton, let's go get some hot cider with the girls." Her voice holds tension that is such a contrast with the mood of everyone around us. She noticed it, too. I saw it when we were all getting ready, when for a moment he thought he'd misplaced his keys, but they'd just slid to the back of the fridge, and Mom found them quickly. And on the drive here, how angry he got when someone didn't let him merge in time, and we missed the exit.

The collective, silent relief that rippled through us when we arrived and safely parked.

"You okay?" I ask her, and she shakes her head. She isn't

saying no. She's saying not here. I glance over her shoulder to my father. Something shifted in the last few minutes.

"C'mon, let's go get cider," I say. I don't know what I missed.

"Erin, we're leaving. This was a mistake," Dad says suddenly. Whatever was building is at its tipping point, and I don't even know what set him off this time.

Mom sits down.

The line of his jaw is tight. It's an expression so familiar to me that a chill runs from the nape of my neck down my spine, and I tug my sweatshirt tighter around me. I don't know what to expect in such a public place.

He reaches down. It's a subtle movement, but I'm watching now, and I see the pressure in the grip of his fingers on her forearm. "I told you we're leaving," he says.

She shakes her head.

The cowbells grow louder as the team returns to the field. An alarm ringing in my ears.

"Get the fuck up," he tells her, a little louder this time. A few heads turn in their direction. Mom looks around. People notice the commotion.

She smiles. A big, beautiful smile. You can't even tell it's broken from the outside, but there's a fault line underneath.

"Not yet, Jesse," she says, shaking her arm, pulling it from his grasp. She turns back to the field, tugging Juniper into her lap, and people closest to us avert their gazes.

My eyes are on him. If she's a fault line buried beneath

the surface, then he's a volcano, about to—

"You make this so much more goddamn difficult than it needs to be," he says. He seizes her arm again, and this time many people look over. His grip is like iron, and even though she has a jacket on, you can see where fingers are pressing into her. I want to scream at him. I want to throw up.

"Fuck it," he says. "Suit yourself." He releases her arm. It's going to leave a bruise.

He pushes past me and climbs down the bleachers quickly.

"He's gonna take the truck. Dammit. Stay with the girls." Mom moves after him.

When I turn back to Campbell and Juniper, Bill DiMarco is watching us. It looks like he saw the entire thing. I'm sure he was close enough to hear it.

He looks back to his wife and small daughter, and then joins the crowd when they cheer. Wolves have the ball.

"This fucking town," I mutter.

"That's a bad word," Juniper scolds me.

"Sorry, Junie. I have to go stop Mom."

"We're coming." Campbell isn't asking, and I'm not going to make her sit here alone.

We make our way down the bleachers, and Sofia is waiting at the bottom of the stairs. She ignores me, turns to Campbell.

"Campbell! Hey, girl. I've been trying to catch you all night. Can we *please* talk about this dance, because I know

Leighton is going to try to wear a cardigan over her dress and put her hair in a messy bun."

Despite everything, Campbell smiles. Rolls her eyes. "Leighton, you totally would try that."

"Can I keep them for a minute?" Sofia asks, meeting my eyes over the tops of Campbell's and Juniper's heads.

"Thank you," I mouth silently. And then I hear my name from the bleachers, and see Fiona barreling down the stairs toward us.

"Leighton!" She throws her arms around me. "Are these your sisters?"

She turns to Campbell and Juniper. "I'm Liam's little sister, Fiona. I've been dying to meet you guys. Leighton talks about you so much."

Juniper beams, and I almost burst into tears.

"I've gotta run if I'm gonna catch her," I say, and she nods.

Fiona has already tucked Juniper's little hand under her arm, and they're talking about getting cider.

I take off down the track after Mom.

Chapter Fifty-Six

BY THE TIME I GET TO where we parked earlier, in a field
for overflow cars, his truck is gone.

Shit.

My chest aches, and I sit down right there, on the cold
ground. I feel like I'm suffocating. I lean my head down to
my knees, hug them to me, and try to suck in enough air.
The thing in my chest is rattling its cage so hard it's stealing
my breath.

I hear footsteps approach, and then someone sits down
beside me in the grass.

I finally raise my head. It's Sofia, with her usual lopsided
smile and bouncy ponytail and spotless cheering uniform
now sitting in the mud with me.

"Hey," she says.

"Hi."

"Fiona has the girls; they're getting hot cider. Are you
okay?" She tucks the loose hair in my face back behind my ear.

"I don't feel good, Sof."

"Just breathe," Sofia says, rubbing small circles on my back.

We don't move for a few minutes. It starts to flurry outside, and the ground is freezing. I can hear when the game reaches halftime and the band starts to play. The cheerleaders usually perform at halftime. Sofia won't just be missed, she'll get in trouble with her coach. But she makes no move to leave.

When I can breathe normally, I sit up.

"Thanks, Sof. I'm fine now, really. You should get back to the field."

"Don't worry, it's just a stupid game."

"You'll get in trouble. And you're covering the game for the paper."

"Coach will get over it. I'm the best one she's got. And there are, like, a thousand people who can fill me in on the seven minutes of game time I'm missing."

Sofia doesn't budge, and I lean my head on her shoulder.

"Is it stuff at home?" she asks.

"Yeah."

"It's bad, isn't it?"

"I honestly wasn't even sure you knew."

"I've known you forever, Leighton. I know why you hardly ever want to hang out at your house. And you are never fully relaxed around him, even when his charm is turned way up." Sofia mimics turning a dial. "I'm not stupid. I knew.

I just didn't think you wanted me to know, so I pretended not to notice things."

"I didn't want you to know," I said. "Or maybe I did. But I didn't want to acknowledge it."

"I can understand that," she says. "Listen, if it gets scary and you need a place to run away to, I'll literally leave my bedroom window unlocked twenty-four seven. Just come right in. Bring Cam and June Bug. We'll have a slumber party."

I laugh and shake my head, suddenly sniffling, and not from the cold.

"Thanks, Sof."

"Ready to go back in there?"

"Yeah," I say. She jumps to her feet and pulls me up.

"Are you frozen, snowflake?" she asks.

"You're the one in a skirt," I point out, and she laughs.

Just inside the stadium, I find my mom.

I wrap my arms around her immediately, and Sofia slips past us, giving me a little wave before jogging away.

"I thought he made you go," I say, my voice a little muffled against her jacket.

"Without you guys? Never," she answers. "Sorry, Leighton."

"It's not yours to apologize for," I tell her.

"We have to figure out a ride."

"There's a bus that runs to Auburn. It passes right through this town, just a few streets over."

"Do I want to know why you know that?" she asks.

I look up at her. "It runs by Nana's place, too. If we want to go there tonight."

"I just want to go home," she says.

Home.

I let go of her.

"I'll go get the girls and meet you at the gate," Mom says.

She walks away, but I hesitate for a moment in the cold. I stick out my tongue and catch some snowflakes. They melt in an instant, and I wonder if that's how my life will look. Here for a fleeting second, and then gone. If I don't get through whatever this is, then that's all I will be. A memory in my classmates' minds. Their true-life crime story to tell at frat parties.

There has to be more.

I can be brave, like Campbell and Juniper think I am. Like I'm not just one little snowflake, about to disappear, but the whole storm. A force to be reckoned with.

I'll be an entire season, but my season is not the soft brown earth of spring or a blue-sky summer. I'm not drifting yellow leaves or crisp white snow.

My season is inconvenient, messy, loud.

The season of the crows. The color of mourning.

Nothing about Auburn feels like home anymore.

But if Auburn can have its miracle, however dark and strange and feathered it might be, then maybe I can have one, too.

Chapter Fifty-Seven

WE TAKE THE BUS BACK TO Auburn and arrive late. We use the phone at the diner to call the house, and it takes another hour before he comes to pick us up.

He doesn't apologize this time.

We can hear the stereo from the front yard, and he starts yelling as soon as we are inside the house.

"How could you embarrass me like that, Erin?"

The coat closet is torn off its hinges. Our shoes are everywhere. One of his steel-toed work boots rests against the sliding back door, and there is a cobweb fracture at the base of the glass where he must have struck it.

In the living room, nothing is on the walls, and the frames on the floor are all broken, the glass inside splintered.

There is a dent in the wall where one of the frames was thrown. I bend down and pick it up. It's the homecoming picture, but the two faces in the photo aren't visible through the shattered glass. I set it back down gently.

I gesture for Campbell and Juniper to go to my room.

"You *left* us there," Mom says. And there's something there I haven't seen before. Her own anger.

"I hate this town," he says. "I can't get work. The business is done, Erin. Done. And we try to get away from it all for one night—one *goddamn* night—and all anyone can talk about is my other major failure, even though it was twenty years ago. Enough!"

On the last word, he kicks the living room chair over, and it cracks against the wall. Dust and plaster fall to the carpet.

"It is enough," Mom says. "You have to go."

"What?" He stops, turns on her. "What did you say to me?"

"You need to leave."

"This is my house."

"Fine, then we'll leave." Mom heads for the stairs, but he cuts her off, one hand going to either side of her, so she's trapped against the wall.

"Go upstairs, Leighton," he says.

"Mom," I start.

But he turns to me, lifts the vase from our coffee table, and hurls it into the wall next to me.

I run upstairs, but I don't go to my room. I sit on the top step and peer through the bars of the railing.

"You aren't going anywhere," he says, and he walks into the kitchen, takes Mom's car keys off the counter, and pockets them. "You want your keys, come get them."

Mom stands in the living room.

"Get them!" he screams. When she doesn't move, he laughs.

"That's what I thought."

He goes into the living room and turns off his music. He turns the television on and starts flipping through the channels.

I slip into my bedroom before Mom comes upstairs.

None of us says a word when she climbs into bed next to Campbell, Juniper, and me.

AUBURN, PENNSYLVANIA
DECEMBER 14

CROW POPULATION:
64,759

Chapter Fifty-Eight

WHEN WE WAKE UP, EVERYTHING THAT was broken last night is not broken anymore. But this time I know Mom sees it, because when we come downstairs, she runs her hand over the glass that is once again smooth in the picture frames, and the part of the wall where he smashed the vase near my head.

It is a quiet, long weekend.

He never gives her keys back.

He doesn't let us leave the house.

He keeps the phone with him.

This time, I don't feel like challenging him. This time, I don't feel fearless. I feel powerless.

On Sunday afternoon, I'm working on my final crow column in my room. It's about the town hall meeting and the last bit of crow folklore—the Morrigan. In Celtic mythology, she was the shape-shifting goddess of war, fate, and death. She was most often depicted as a crow flying over battlefields and crying out for the dead. Sometimes she was seen as a predictor of death, landing on the shoulders of those who would soon meet their fate.

I'm proofreading when a shadow crosses my desk. My room stays dark, and when I look outside, I see why—there are crows filling the sky. Dark like storm clouds, so thick they're blocking out the sun.

I open my window and watch them fly.

Auburn Township voted to allocate thousands of dollars to bring in experts to help drive the birds away. They begin their work as soon as the new year starts, so the crows have just a few weeks left here.

The wind picks up, hitting a pile of papers on my desk, and pages start to fly everywhere. I slam the window closed and turn to clean up the mess.

A familiar pink flyer lies on the floor in front of me. The scholarship contest. The deadline is tomorrow at midnight. *Auburn born, Auburn proud.*

This is what I know of *pride*. I know that it keeps the secrets of cruel men. I know that it holds us in the shadows, because we are too proud to admit we need help. I know that pride values a man's reputation over a woman's life. It calls her selfish for speaking up, even when she speaks the truth. *Especially* then.

This is what I know of Auburn. I know about frantic knocking that goes ignored in the middle of the night. I know about men who look away when their friend is the problem. I know exactly how easy it is for people here to avert their gaze at a football game, comforting themselves with a hollow sentiment: *It's none of our business.*

Because this is a town where people see only what they want to see.

This is a town where they see nothing at all.

So I begin with the thesis statement, the truest sentence that I know, and every word thereafter must support my claim.

It is not the crows that make Auburn ugly.

Chapter Fifty-Nine

LIAM IS A WRECK WHEN HE picks me up Monday morning.

"I wasn't sure what happened. Fiona and Sofia filled me in, and I called all weekend—"

"Yeah, he took the phone."

"Leighton," he says. "I was so worried. I didn't know if I should call the police. This isn't normal. You need help."

"I know," I say. "Sorry I missed the end of your big game."

"You know I don't care about that."

"I'm sorry you lost."

"Doesn't matter. Honestly, it's kind of a relief. Who needs the pressure of a championship game?"

Who, indeed.

I'm not sure if what I'm planning is right. There's so much unknown. And maybe it's awful at home, but at least that fear is *known*. Familiar.

The drive to school takes twice as long today. All the roads near my home are covered with crows. They're just *everywhere* now, covering every surface. Liam drives slowly, waiting for them to shuffle and fly away rather than risk hitting them. It takes ages to get there, and the whole time I think about how my silence benefits only one person.

When I get into school, I don't even pretend I'm going to class. I head straight to the newspaper offices and crash into my desk.

Sofia stands up at hers, startling me. I didn't realize anyone else was here. She immediately leans forward in her chair, as though she's coming for me, and I hold up a hand.

"I'm fine. I promise. I'm just angry. And right now, I really need to write. My column is due, and I'm submitting this essay today before I lose my nerve."

My voice is clear and confident, and there isn't even the hint of tears today. I just need to get the words down while I have them.

"I'll guard the door," she says. She springs from her desk, shuts the door, and turns off the lights. She sits down next to it in case anyone disturbs us.

"Thanks, Sof."

"Write!" she says.

I boot up my ancient public-school desktop. My dinosaur computer that I secretly love. I want to win this scholarship. But it's more than that.

There's another reason I want to submit *this* essay to *them*. There is a part of me that feels like bruised flesh. That just wants to force them to read it. I struggled so much to write about Auburn, and now I know that it's because I wasn't seeing Auburn in its entirety.

This town isn't just my grandfather's buildings and my dad's anger. It isn't just people ignoring the thing right in front of them.

This town is also Sofia being there when I need her, and Fiona noticing something that grown adults didn't see and helping my sisters. And Liam being so stoic and so soft and so good.

This town is Juniper's notes to Joe and Campbell's righteous rage and the unending depths of our mother's courage anytime his anger shifts to us instead of her.

And it's me. I'm part of Auburn, too, even when I criticize it. Even when I hate it.

Once I figure out what it was missing, the essay is easy to write.

It was missing *me*.

Chapter Sixty

LIAM AND I DRIVE TO THE same spot we went to that morning we skipped first period together.

Lately it's been too cold to leave the car, but tonight isn't so bad. Liam pulls a thick blanket out of his trunk, and again we sit on the hood of his car that is still warm from the engine. When we lean back and look up, the treetops form a circle around a patch of star-spotted night sky. The trees look like giant sentinels, steadfastly guarding this little patch of earth.

Or maybe it is us they are guarding.

I'm glad we came out here tonight. It was like we both just wanted to be alone.

Turns out we can be alone together.

It's now been several days of strange silence in my house. Days since Auburn lost their semi-final game, and the town retreated from its football fervor.

I lean toward Liam and press my lips against his cheek.

I snuggle a little deeper into the crook of his arm. With my ear pressed against his ribs, all I can hear is his heart. When he asks me something, I miss it, and have to pull away from him and ask him to say it again.

"Why journalism?"

"I just think I would like to use writing to tell people things they ought to know about. To tell the truth."

"That sounds perfect for you," he says.

I think so.

"Liam, I have to tell you something."

He turns on his side. "Yeah?"

"I submitted an essay to the township council."

"The scholarship contest?"

"Yeah. I wrote about home."

"Oh."

"There's something else. If I win—which I won't, because I basically called out the whole town—they're going to print it in the *Gazette*. I had to agree to that when I submitted it."

I watch him carefully, trying to catch the expression on his face, but it's too dark outside.

"So the essay is about him?"

"It's about Auburn mostly, but yeah, it's about him."

He falls silent, and I wonder what he's thinking. He curls his finger and hooks his knuckle under my chin, tilting my face up to his and kissing me softly.

"I just want you safe," he says.

"I know," I say. "Me too. Part of me hopes I don't win. But I'm also tired of hiding in the shadows here, ya know?"

"Yeah, I get that," he says.

"Do you like growing up here?" I ask. I've wondered for a while, and writing about Auburn made those questions resurface in my mind.

"Ah, yeah, sure," he says with a soft laugh.

"What does that mean?" I ask.

"It's complicated. I do well here. But I do well because I work really hard."

"Too hard," I correct.

"And I know people like me," he says.

"Everyone adores you, Liam."

"But sometimes I feel like they love me like I'm an exception. Like if I let down my guard, if I'm ever *not* perfect, they'll all turn on me in an instant. It's mostly little things, certain comments, assumptions—but I'm aware of it all the time. I have to be. Like they love when I score a touchdown for the team, right? But they'd act a lot differently if I was kneeling before the game. This town only takes the parts of my identity it likes, ignores the rest. It's exhausting."

"I'm sorry, Liam. I can't imagine how that feels," I say.

"I just hope all the work pays off. Gets me where I want to go."

"It will." I don't know what it's like to feel that way every time I step outside my home. To have to wonder if the people around me are hiding some ugly prejudice that could surface when I least expect it. My worry is the inverse of Liam's—my guard is up when I step into my home, not out of it.

"I am tired of it," I say. "Not physically tired. It's hard to explain. Some days I feel like I'm a hundred years old. Like being afraid has always been my life and it's always going to be my life."

"Hypervigilance takes a toll," he says. "But Auburn isn't the center of the world. We can leave. We *will* leave." Liam slides off the car, pulling me with him. He faces me, wraps the blanket around both of us. "Besides, you are tough. You've got this."

"Liam, I literally cry, like, all the time," I say.

"You don't give in to any of it. And I don't have to be there to know you don't ever cry in front of Campbell and Juniper. You are the bravest person I know."

"You really don't have to—"

"Still not flattery, Barnes. Seriously, it was what drew me to you in the first place," Liam says.

"No, it isn't, you didn't even know me."

"Okay, fine," he admits, raising his hands to confess. "I first noticed you because you're cute as hell."

"You are ridiculous."

"I couldn't ignore you. I tried. You've always been quiet, but it's like you think loud. And even though I could kind of tell you were just trying to blend in and be unseen, I couldn't not see you, Leighton. And then at our lockers . . ."

"What happened at our lockers?"

"You smiled. I don't think I had ever seen you smile before. And then all I could think was that I wanted to make you smile again."

"Liam McNamara, you are . . . a damn romantic," I say. I'm smiling now. "But I was right, it wasn't about my personality after all."

"Not until English class. I mean, you barely even talk in school, ever, and then all of a sudden you were flipping out on Brody over a book."

"Wait a second. You wanted to date me because I went on an angry feminist rant in front of the entire class?"

"God, yes. It was so kick-ass. It confirmed what I was already starting to guess about you."

"Which was what?"

"That you are *brave*, Barnes. I like being surprised by people, and you definitely surprised me."

"Yeah, I've got lots of fun surprises," I say. "Am I more than you bargained for yet?"

I ask like it's a joke. But I've wondered about this for real. There's no way he would have consciously chosen to be with me if he'd known everything. It's too much for anyone. Even me.

"Leighton, if you think that asshole is gonna scare me away from loving you, you are bat-shit crazy."

I laugh in spite of myself. It isn't supposed to be funny.

But I'm learning to steal my joy wherever I can find it.

Chapter Sixty-One

THE DAY BEFORE WINTER BREAK, Mrs. Riley calls me out of art class to come to the newsroom. She smiles when I walk in, but immediately gestures for me to close the door behind me, and I'm nervous before she even starts talking.

"So here's the situation," she dives in without preamble. "The council is choosing your essay."

"What, that's—" Huge. Amazing. That's five thousand dollars. That's a big pebble.

"Wait." Mrs. Riley holds up her hand. "It's not that simple. They're giving you the scholarship, but they're refusing to print your essay in the *Auburn Gazette*."

I sit down in the chair in front of her desk.

"But why would they do that?"

"They seem to really believe you deserve the scholarship money. They were impressed by the essay and the topic. So was I, by the way, when they forwarded me a copy, Leighton. But they don't want to print it. They called it a liability."

"A liability for who?"

"Well, they implied that printing it could be dangerous to you . . . your family. But, Leighton, we both know it's a liability for the town, too."

I look out the window and find Joe sitting right outside, not five feet away. One big black eye is fixed on me, like he knows. Like he's waiting to see what I do. He shuffles on the window ledge, plucks at the gray plumage on his side.

His beak opens, but the wind carries the sound. He's yelling, but no one can hear.

He might as well be silent.

I turn back to Mrs. Riley.

"Tell them to publish it anonymously."

She leans back in her chair. "I don't know . . ."

"Then it's not a liability to me. Only to them. And if they still refuse, at least we know it wasn't just about protecting me. At least then I tried everything."

"But this is yours, Leighton, you deserve the credit for it."

"I'll . . . I don't know, I'll send it to the rest of my college applications. I'll see if NYU will let me submit an updated personal essay. I'll use it in another way. I still think it should get published without my name here. I wrote it for Auburn."

"Okay, I'll ask them," she says.

"Thank you."

When I turn back to the window, Joe is gone.

Chapter Sixty-Two

WE HAVE ALWAYS LIVED IN THIS house.

And our father's father lived here before us.

And before that? I guess it was just timber and nails. Nothing evil, I don't think.

My father's father wasn't evil, either.

But he also wasn't good.

And maybe when he built this house, he corrupted it.

Maybe all the things we create have some piece of us, something we impart, or something we just leave behind. And perhaps if my grandfather was so angry, then maybe he left it here. Built it right into the foundation and the walls, the practiced hammering of nails. Maybe he built it into this whole damn town.

Magic, Campbell called it once—but maybe she's closer to the truth now with her haunted house books.

Whatever it is, I used to wish it were here for us. So we could believe that there was something more potent in this home than fear—maybe even something watching over us. But I was wrong.

It's always been protecting him.

I wonder what that would feel like, to behave however you'd like, and wake up day after day never having to face the consequences of it. I think it would make you feel like maybe you never did anything wrong at all.

Like maybe it's not so bad if you do it again.

Chapter Sixty-Three

THE HOUSE QUAKES WITH HIS MUSIC.

I turn over in my bed, reaching for my alarm clock. It is a quarter past three in the morning, Christmas Day.

For a moment I stay there, wondering if maybe for the rest of my life the sound of Axl Rose's voice will make me feel like throwing up. But then I hear the raised voices from downstairs, and I climb out of my warm blankets.

I sneak into the girls' room. They are awake, huddled in the corner of Juniper's bed, pillows lined in front of them like a shield.

"C'mon," I say, and lead them back to my room. In the hallway I can hear that he's yelling about his cell phone. It's lost again. He's been losing things a lot the last few weeks, and we always seem to face the consequences for it.

I hesitate at the door, trying to turn the lock. He broke it last year, the last time I tried to lock him out. I flick on my light and look closer. It just needs a new screw to secure the piece on the door. I run over to my desk and dump out my pencil holder. I'm sure it's here. I swipe aside a matchbook, and there it is. The screw Joe left on Liam's windowsill. I didn't end up giving those things to Juniper—matches and hardware don't really fit with her collection of marbles and feathers, anyway.

Back at the door, I line up the screw. It fits. I twist it in as far as I can with my bare hands. It isn't great, but it's better than nothing. It makes me feel better when I shut the light off and join my sisters in the center of my bed. I hear his footsteps on the stairs, and we stiffen in unison when a shadow appears in the line of hall light under my door.

The door rattles on its hinges, but the lock holds.

Mumbled, angry sounds.

"Stop, don't—" Mom says.

CRACK!

The door splits along its edge, one long, splintered piece holding the lock flying off into the room, and the rest of it sagging on its hinges where it's bent and broken. There is a flood of light, and the silhouette of a man who isn't evil, but sometimes forgets.

"Get up," he says.

We crawl out from behind the pillow. The girls follow me, and I follow Mom. We step carefully over the pieces of my door and the picture frames that litter the floor. We make our way into the kitchen. He holds up a copy of the *Auburn Gazette*. It's turned to the page that has township news, police blotters.

The winning essay of the Auburn scholarship contest.

"You wanna tell me what the fuck this is." He doesn't yell this time, and somehow, that's worse. My head throbs from the music, the adrenaline, the fear.

His eyes are wide. He throws the paper down onto the counter and reaches for a pack of cigarettes. Mom walks to the counter, lifts the paper.

My essay.

My first real publishing credential, even if my name isn't on it.

And it might get us killed.

It is not the crows that make Auburn ugly.

It's the complicity.

Anyone who has looked the other way.

This essay isn't an accusation, though. It's a love letter. For Mom. Campbell and Juniper. *This* is worth saving. We can do this together, if we call it by its name.

If we say, *Enough*.

"There's no writer on it."

"Fuck that. That's you," he says, lighting his cigarette right in the kitchen and pointing at the paper. "I know because someone on the council told someone they know, and that someone told me. There are no secrets in this town. Everyone'll know in a few days."

Good, I think. I want them to know.

And it's true, there are no secrets in this town.

His anger wasn't a secret, but somehow me talking about it is the embarrassment.

He's opening and slamming kitchen cabinets, knocking things over.

"And you know what they'll do next? Never hire Barnes Construction again. So congratu-fucking-lations, Leighton, you've ruined the family business. And where is my goddamn cell phone?" he says. "And why is it so hot in here?" He reaches for the thermostat, shutting the heat off, and starts moving around the kitchen, opening every window. Mom sets the paper down on the counter and walks over to us. She puts her arm around me.

"We're going to bed," she tells him.

"Not until I say you can," he says, still moving through the living room, opening more windows.

"Go to hell," she says, pushing us toward the stairs.

He stops what he's doing. His eyes are dark. They scare me. It's like he's not even in there.

"Don't push me tonight." He moves upstairs, I presume to make sure the second floor is freezing, too. Mom follows, closing the windows behind him as she goes.

Barely a moment passes, and we hear a strangled cry from upstairs.

I run, hurling myself around the banister. He has her at the top of the stairs, bent over the railing backward, his hands on her throat. I'm on him in moments, shoving into him as hard as I can to get him off her. I push him into the bathroom door, and he swears at me. He charges at me, and shoves, and I slam into the banister. I hear something crack, and for a moment I'm not sure if it's something in me.

The wood beneath me splinters, and shards stick up at every angle, jagged and broken. I try to suck in air, but the wind's been knocked out of me, and it *hurts*.

A moment passes. Two. Three.

I gasp a breath.

Campbell runs across the hallway and swings her fist. It connects with the side of his head. There's no way it hurt him much, but it doesn't matter. He's out of control, and he turns on her next. He reaches for her, and I scream. It's a noise I've never made before in my life, and I'm on him like a wild thing, scratching anything I can reach. He releases Campbell, and I grab her and a sobbing Juniper, pulling them into my bedroom. I usher them into the armoire, and hear the sound of him pulling Mom back downstairs, and all I can think is how he's taking her closer to his gun, it's right there on the fridge, it would only take a moment, one second, and he could destroy our entire world.

Tap. Tap. Tap.

Tap.

A cracking noise from the other side of my room, at the window, and when I get to it, there's the flash of feathers in the dark as a crow flies away.

And something else.

A gift dropped onto my windowsill outside. I push open my window and reach for it, confused. Grateful.

It's Dad's cell phone.

AUBURN, PENNSYLVANIA
DECEMBER 25

CROW POPULATION:
78,460

Chapter Sixty-Four

RED AND BLUE LIGHTS FLASH ON the worn, once-white siding of the house. Red, blue, and gray.

A different kind of American dream.

It's cold outside, and each of my hands is wrapped around a smaller one. Our flannel pajamas aren't holding up against the wind.

Officer Bill DiMarco is the first to arrive. When I see him, I feel that thing trapped in my chest panicking. Will he just let him go again?

But he doesn't. He puts him in handcuffs. He acts like he doesn't even know him.

Another officer arrives and calls a judge at home, waking him to request an emergency protection order.

The second officer pulls Mom aside, but I can hear them. He explains that because of the holidays, a real hearing will take some time, but we can extend the temporary order until we get into a courtroom, probably after the new year.

If he's released before that, the order bars him from the house and any of us.

And according to the order, he has twenty-four hours upon release to surrender his firearm.

Officer DiMarco walks over after putting our father in the back of his car. I wonder if they said anything to each other.

He shifts back and forth on his feet. He looks so uncomfortable. I imagine he'd rather be anywhere else but here responding to this call tonight.

"I read the essay, Leighton. I'm sorry. I, uh—I'm just sorry. That was really hard to read."

"It was really hard to live in." I'm exhausted. And freezing. I'm not in the mood for any more of the halfhearted atonements of grown men.

Officer DiMarco just nods once and turns to Mom, promising her that he'll personally deliver a physical copy of the temporary protection order later in the day.

Mom never wavers.

I don't think about tomorrow. I don't think about the possibility that she could change her mind again. Tonight, for the first time in a long time, I feel like we've been heard. I feel like maybe we are safe.

And it feels so damn good.

AUBURN, PENNSYLVANIA
DECEMBER 31

CROW POPULATION:
84,784

Chapter Sixty-Five

WE GET READY AT MY HOUSE, for once. Sofia has been here before, but rarely. We stand in my room, each tugging on an extra layer of tights because it's freezing outside. The black dress is as fantastic as it was the first time I tried it on. Sleek and shiny. The black satin makes the reddishness of my hair stand out. More like Mom's.

"How's it look?" I ask Sofia, putting my hands in the pockets and spinning around. The skirt flares in response.

"You know you look amazing. Like a melding of Audrey Hepburn and Strawberry Shortcake."

"Wait, is that a compliment?" I ask, facing the mirror. Sofia comes to stand next to me. She's three inches shorter, but she almost makes up the height difference with her teased hair. Add the cobalt-blue heels she picked out, and she'll be taller.

"Of course it's a compliment," she says. "Strawberry Shortcake is a *babe*."

There's a knock at my door.

I open it to Campbell, and her eyes go wide.

"What d'ya think?" I ask, pursing my hot-pink lips at her.

"Very eighties," she says. "And gorgeous."

"Thanks," I say. "Okay, we've gotta go."

"Don't want to keep Liam waiting," Campbell says, but she smiles and helps me zip up the side of my dress.

The day after Christmas, I found two newspaper clippings on my desk. The first was my essay, framed. The second was another police blotter.

"APD responded to a domestic dispute. 36-year-old male arrested, pending charges of terroristic threat, false imprisonment, and assault."

And a note stuck on top of the newspaper clipping that said, "You were right. It was good. —C."

"Oh God," Mom says when we step into the kitchen.

"What?" I ask.

"Nothing. Just my entire childhood hitting me in one flash," she says. "Have fun, girls. Drive safe."

In Sofia's car, the heat runs full blast. It's a bitterly cold New Year's Eve. A dry cold. No snowstorms coming in to cover up the crows.

There's no hiding them anymore. Every tree on the highway is filled. Every parking lot and field. They now outnumber humans more than ten to one. It seems that every few minutes another group of them is startled and rises into the sky over us. Instead of trees, we have crows. Instead of fields, we have crows. Instead of clouds . . .

They run this town now.

Auburn's plans for driving them out of town begin tomorrow.

I know that it is only the year ending, but in this moment it feels like it is the world. The sun is low and heavy on the mountain. The sky isn't pink like summer or orange like autumn, but dark red fading fast into black. With the billowing dark clouds circling around, it almost looks as though a nuclear bomb has gone off.

"It's like the apocalypse out there," Sofia says, reading my mind. We pull up to the school. She chose a bright blue taffeta dress that really does look like something she traveled through time for and pulled off a rack in the 1980s. "Here," she says, "you didn't tease your hair enough."

She pulls me closer and tugs a comb through my hair, pushing the curls out, out, until they are practically a separate entity from me. "Really, Sofia?" I ask, my voice muffled by the mountain of hair between us.

"You look hot," she says, and tugs again.

"If I hadn't grown up with two sisters, this would hurt like hell," I tell her.

"Fortunately, your scalp has been numb for years," she says.

Liam whistles low as we walk up to the gymnasium doors.

"Wow," he says as Sofia and I stop and strike poses on

the sidewalk. "I'm way out of my league."

"Eat your heart out, McNamara," Sofia says, laughing, as she pulls open the door and marches her three-inch heels inside. I look down at my flats. Glamorous.

"Perfect," Liam says. He steps close, lifts my hand, and spins me around. He's wearing what should be a ridiculous all-white tux, but he looks amazing as usual. He has aviator sunglasses tucked in the front pocket of his jacket, and I reach for them. "Nah-ah," he says, capturing my hand over the pocket. "Wrong ones."

"What do you mean?"

Liam reaches into another pocket and pulls out his glasses case. He puts on his real glasses instead.

"Okay, now I'm ready."

"What? You aren't embarrassed?" I ask.

"Nah, fuck 'em," Liam says. I laugh.

"What changed your mind?"

"Uh, this cute girl I know. She says I look good in them."

"Oh, well, she's right. You should listen to her more often," I whisper, just before his lips reach mine, and I feel the smile on them when we kiss. He pulls back abruptly.

"Check this out."

He unbuttons the top few buttons of his button-down shirt and opens it. Under his pristine tux, he's wearing a Superman T-shirt. I laugh.

"That's perfect."

"Thanks. Not too geeky?"

"Oh, very geeky. But that's a good thing."

"Hey, so, I got my first acceptance," Liam says. I like how he says *first*, like he knows there will be more.

He's right. There will be. No question.

"Congratulations! Where?"

"An art program, actually. The art director got in touch and said he really loved my portfolio, and graphic novels aren't usually their thing, but my *'exceptional talent'* convinced them I belonged there. So if I go, I can actually pursue the comic book thing, for real. They have all these design classes, and storytelling, and the faculty is diverse and incredible."

"That's really cool, Liam."

"You know what else is cool? Calling out an entire town in *their own damn paper*."

Liam wraps his arms around me, pulls me in close. It's freezing, but I don't care. I hear the sound of rustling paper and turn slightly, not letting go of him. Liam is holding up the *Gazette*, folded in half on page five.

He reads:

"'The charm of this town is lost on its victims, and perfect is just a fairy tale. We have to stop pretending we'd be great again if only the crows were gone, and work on the parts of this town that were broken long before the birds arrived.' That's my favorite part."

"Yeah?"

"And the part about the walls. And complicity. And bird migration habits as a metaphor for intergenerational violence."

"That bit was tricky."

"It worked," Liam says. "It's good, Leighton."

"Thanks."

"Leighton!" I am practically side-tackled in a hug.

"Hi, Fiona." I twist so I can wrap my arm around her. "Hey, I never got to thank you for helping at the game with my sisters. That was really nice."

"Psh," Fiona says. "It was nothing. They're adorable. Well, Juniper is adorable. Campbell is *intense*."

"No kidding," I say. "You look so pretty."

"Thanks, Leighton. We're having so much fun. Glad to see *you* changed your no-date rule, though. Go be dummies together."

Liam leads me into the gym, and we skip the punch bowls and photo line. He tugs me right onto the dance floor. It's a slow song, and the music isn't so loud. Liam's hand finds my hip and pulls me in until I'm tucked right under his chin. I imagine this kind of thing happens every single day, but sometimes things are ordinary and incredible all at once.

One day last year, the girls and I got off our bus and it was pouring rain. We were soaked straight through our clothes in seconds, and still had to walk all the way down our road. But about a minute into our wet walk, the rain stopped, just like that. In one instant, it went from torrential downpour to nothing. The cloud had passed over us. We could see it raining in the field across the road, but not on us. And it must happen a million times a day—the weather shifts, changes direction. The rain cloud moves or the wind dies. We usually miss that split-second transition, though, so seeing it happen that afternoon, we felt like we were the only witnesses to something special. It's how I feel right now in Liam's arms. Like, sure, this happens a million times a day all over the world.

But I get to be here tonight for this one perfect moment.

Chapter Sixty-Six

"I HEARD YOUR DAD TRIED TO kill your mom."

And there goes that perfect moment.

Liam and I turn to face Brody, who is grinning at me.

The police blotter.

Liam takes a step toward him, and I grab his arm. "Let's go," I say.

"Leighton." Liam's arm is tight and tense under my fingers.

"Let's just leave."

"But they haven't even announced the Winter Formal Ice King and Queen," Brody says. "I hear you two are the favorites."

"Jesus, Brody, how much of a jackass can you be?" Liam asks.

"Ignore him," I say. "C'mon."

"Brody, you have to leave," says a voice behind me. It's Amelia. Perfect hair, perfect dress . . . perfectly cold glare in her eyes as she faces Brody. "As student council president,

I'm telling you to leave the dance."

"Whatever," he says. "Lame-ass dance anyway."

"Go," she says again. Just like at the football game, I'm surprised by how forceful her voice is for someone so small.

Brody flips her off before turning away, but he does leave the gym.

"Thank you, Amelia." My hand falls onto her arm. I'm so grateful, I don't even know how to say it.

"Don't let him ruin your night," Amelia says. "Oh, damn, someone's putting the basketball nets down. They're going to wreck my balloon arch. I've gotta go."

She waves goodbye.

Sofia is on the other side of the gym, already yelling at the kid who is lowering the basketball nets and gesturing wildly at the balloons. I laugh, but when I turn back to Liam, he's still angry.

"Wanna get out of here?" I ask.

"Really? Where do you want to go?"

"New York City," I say. "California. The moon."

Finally, he laughs.

"First, the newsroom. I need to check my email."

"Lead the way," he says.

The newsroom is pitch-black, and we stumble our way through it, unwilling to turn on lights and attract a teacher's attention.

"It's gonna take a little while to warm up," I whisper,

turning on my dinosaur computer.

"*Mmmhmm.* Did you bring me here under false pretenses, Barnes?" Liam asks, his hands finding me in the dark.

"Maybe," I giggle. The computer starts up, and I click on the email icon.

"You know, this takes a while to open, too," I tell him.

He turns me in his arms and lifts me up onto my desk. He kisses me slowly, his hands tangling in the teased curls of my eighties-styled hair. I laugh when he fails for the fourth time to move my hair. "What exactly are you trying to do?" I ask, my eyes on the ceiling.

"Kiss your neck. It's like a lion's mane."

"I am woman," I say. "Hear me roar."

He laughs, and then he is kissing me again. I can feel his smile against my lips, and there's no place in the world I'd rather be than in the school newsroom, making out with Liam McNamara.

The rustle of my dress sends a chill across my skin. I'm glad we are alone. This feels like how really well-written words make me feel. Not like an article for the paper or an essay for lit class. More like a sonnet. My legs are parentheses around his waist. When I sigh against his neck, it's an apostrophe—in the possessive. And every word of it is familiar already—I've been memorizing them for months. Liam's arms come around me and pull me in tighter, he kisses me deeper, and I wonder where this is going—

My email dings.

He pulls back, tilts his head. "Probably not the place."

"Definitely not the place."

I hop off the desk and turn to check my email. I scroll through the dozens of junk emails and college emails that have cluttered my inbox in the last week. And then one catches my eyes: Early Admission Application Update.

"It's from NYU," I say.

"You don't think?"

"I don't know," I whisper, and we both turn to look at the screen.

"Oh, look. This one's from my ornithologist."

I click on that email first.

"Wimp," Liam whispers, his hands trying in vain to gather up my wild hair so he can look over my shoulder. I read the first email out loud.

"'As promised, I've enclosed the second thermal-imaging map of the crow roosting habits in Auburn, Pennsylvania . . .'" I trail off and open the attachment. Like the first thermal map he sent me a few weeks ago, another brilliantly colored map fills the screen. Yellow and orange on the outskirts of town, where there are fewer crows. Red and maroon where their concentration is higher. But this map looks different from the first. There's a lot more dark red, and now there is one patch of black—the highest concentration—and the entire thing is shaped like a storm, with an epicenter where the most crows have gathered.

I look at the street outlines on the map, and my breath catches. The black spot falls almost perfectly over my home.

"Liam . . ." I click to enlarge the map. "What the hell do you think that means?"

"Leighton."

"It's strange, right?"

"Leighton," he says again. "You opened the other one."

He's right. I clicked the wrong button. Instead of enlarging the map, I closed it.

And opened the email from NYU.

"Lay-TON!" Liam shouts. He lifts me up in my shiny black dress and spins me around.

I got in.

AUBURN, PENNSYLVANIA
DECEMBER 31

CROW POPULATION:
93,270

Chapter Sixty-Seven

I ASK LIAM TO TAKE ME home early, even before the fire-works. Holidays have always been hard for us, so Campbell and Juniper and I made up our own traditions. Every New Year's Eve, we sit on the roof outside my window and watch the fireworks over Auburn together. I'm not going to miss this one.

We park at the end of my road, near the mailboxes.

Liam gets out of the car and opens my door.

"Beautiful," he says.

So I kiss him. My face and neck are cold, but Liam's lips are warm.

Like all of the trees in Auburn, the ones around us are home to crows, and I hear them moving on their branches. They're very unsettled tonight, shifting and cawing and fluttering off the branches and back again. Above them, the sky feels like a magnifying glass, focusing on us standing here. The night is so clear, and the stars are a river.

For a moment, it's like nothing exists at all beyond us. It's just me and Liam and the trees and the night sky.

The world revolves around us.

And the words rise in me of their own accord, fast, effortless, like air, racing unseen past that thing in my chest before it can catch them, and tumbling out into the cold air before I can think: "I love you."

It feels good. And right. Liam's arm tightens around me. He doesn't miss a beat.

"Tell me something I don't know," he says, and he steals one, two, three more kisses, as warm as sunshine.

"No promises, though," I add.

"Whatever you say, Barnes," Liam says, pulling me in close. The stars alone bear witness to the huge smile on my face.

Well, the stars and the crows.

"No promises," I repeat.

AUBURN, PENNSYLVANIA
DECEMBER 31

CROW POPULATION:
97,361 AND COUNTING

Chapter Sixty-Eight

I STAND ON THE EDGE OF the sidewalk that ends too soon and watch as Liam drives away. The red taillights blur and then fade into the night, and I still don't go inside. Instead, for once, I let myself imagine the future. I imagine a future in which we don't say "No promises," but promise each other everything. I imagine coming home to Liam, and the thought makes me smile.

Boom! I startle, and look up. An arch of red light streaks across the sky. The fireworks are starting. I head toward the house, suddenly aware of how dark it is. Why aren't any lights on? It isn't even that late.

And it's New Year's.

It isn't until I get to the front step that I realize all of the windows are open. It isn't until I'm standing there, inches away from him, that I realize I'm not alone. He doesn't turn on the light in the foyer, but I can see his outline in the dark. I get the distinct feeling he's been waiting for me, and the thought turns my stomach sour. What have I come home to? When did they release him?

I step to the door and try to recall that good feeling that I had just a second ago, but his presence has scared the happy thought. It is hiding somewhere in the shadows of my memory. Because he's broken the protection order. He's here. And I could try to run away, but the girls are probably terrified. Or hurt.

The house is too dark.

I open the door, and he is a six-foot shadow in the dark.

And then I remember the thought I just held a moment ago, the one time I let myself imagine a bright future.

I wonder what it would feel like to come home and not be afraid of what's waiting inside.

Chapter Sixty-Nine

THE LIGHTS AREN'T JUST OFF IN the house: the power is out. No lights. No heat. He's shut it all off as punishment.

I'm in my room with the girls, in the dark. It's quiet downstairs, and tonight I almost wish for the music. Something to break the tension. The thing in my chest is panicking, flapping its wings and railing against the bars of its cage. My heart is cracking my chest, a hammer against my ribs.

We stay upstairs. We stay quiet. We stay hidden.

I need to call the cops. Where is the cell phone?

And then another thought.

Where is the gun?

Crack!

A red light streaks across the sky. More fireworks.

"Can we use the lantern?" Juniper asks. "I'm scared."

"In a bit," I say. I'm holding her, but I'm distracted by my own fear.

I hear voices rise from downstairs. An argument. It is

brief and muted. I wish that were all of it, but the feeling that this will get worse before it gets better won't go away.

I think of the crawl space in the basement.

We need to get out.

"Girls, I have to get Mom," I say. I don't know what I'm doing, I just know I need to move. It's always the waiting that gets to me.

"Please, Leighton," Campbell says, and her voice cracks. I don't think any of us could explain it. We just know how bad this might get.

Boom!

I walk over to the window as another firework goes off, and I jump at the noise. It shoots into the night and breaks across the sky. Brilliant streams of red and yellow spill down toward earth. The outline of crows shimmers in the bright light. They are moving.

I send the girls to the armoire, and kiss them.

"I've got to get Mom, and then we are leaving," I tell them, hoping my voice sounds assured and confident.

I make my way downstairs. They are in the dark living room, sitting on the couch.

"Mom?" I ask. She looks up. I can't tell anything at all about her expression. But I feel the hairs at the nape of my neck prickle to attention. He stands, and I see it in the dark. His gun.

I retreat, slowly, one step at a time. Mom rises from the

couch, too. Follows him as he comes closer to me.

"Is this what you guys wanted? Is this what you fucking wanted?" he asks. I stop moving.

I'm silent, staring at him. Anything I say right now would be the wrong thing to say. I don't blink. I don't move.

And then I hear that telltale creak of my bedroom door. This house that has healed itself a hundred times over, but not that creak, and thank God, because it's how I know the girls are in danger. Campbell and Juniper are at the top of the stairs. Every curse word I've ever heard streams through my brain as I try to think of a way to get them to go back into that room.

I don't think they can see him from where they are, and even if they could, they wouldn't see the gun, which hangs limp in his hand. Now I've stopped breathing, too, and it's like I'm already practicing for death.

Campbell must know something is deeply wrong. Maybe it is the rigidity of my body. My unwillingness to face her. It is my *unmovement* that turns her away. Whatever it is, it works. Their dark shapes at the top of the stairs retreat back into the room. I hear the faintest creak of the door as it closes.

I breathe.

I blink.

I'm still here.

"Come talk to me in the kitchen," Mom says.

She moves, the smallest, most calculated of movements.

Then she takes a step. I know what she is trying to do, how she is moving tiny degrees at a time. Until she is between me and the gun.

My heart shrinks, withers, dries up inside of me. The fear in my chest isn't rattling in its cage anymore. It sits quiet, beaten into submission. It knows that I cannot afford to listen to it.

Mom is in between us now. She reaches over, puts her hand on my arm.

"Go upstairs, Leighton," she says. Her eyes never leave the gun. "I'll be right up."

No, you won't.

I know I should go. He would probably let me right now. But my feet won't listen. They weigh a thousand pounds each, held down by every memory of my mother holding me and kissing my forehead and making everything better when I was sick or hurt. My mother staying in my bed when I couldn't sleep, reading her book by the dim hall light for hours and showing by example that books give comfort when all else fails. Even when homes feel broken and treacherous. My mother putting her body between me and the gun. My mother, the most beautiful creature in the world, telling me she loves me, she loves me. She is gravity and I'm the world, and you can't just make it stop. It's physics. It is a force unto itself.

She loves me. She loves me. She loves me.

There.

These words have meaning.

I know that I can move now, so I do. I move, but it's still like gravity, and I can't control what pulls me.

I can't control it, but I can recognize that it is very, very stupid.

I reach for her.

Chapter Seventy

THE FIRST THING I NOTICE IS the smell of smoke. Which doesn't make any sense. Guns don't start fires.

Boom! A firework.

Crack! A gun goes off.

In a town already so loud that no one could possibly notice.

I'm pushed back against the stairs, with Mom over me.

"Leighton, are you hurt? Oh my God, Leighton," Mom says, running her hands over me.

"No," I say, turning. It's just the house again.

The wall next to me is the wounded one. It's been shot, and it's bleeding.

Someone needs to help it.

"Shit," he says. "Shit."

He backs away from the stairs. He doesn't even check the wall.

"Keys. Where are the keys?"

And then there is a familiar sound, feathers on air.

Joe flies into the living room through one of the open windows, landing on his shoulder.

I think of the Morrigan, predicting the fates of men.

"What the—" But before he can react, the crow moves, crossing to the coffee table, knocking the vase down, and it shatters against the floor. There are little blue marbles rolling everywhere. There are pennies and paper clips. The gifts left for Juniper. And in the middle of them, the keys to the truck, shining in the moonlight. Juniper must have hidden them inside. Another firework flares in the distance, and for a moment, everything is bright and clear and illuminated.

And then Joe's claws close over the keys, and he takes off again through the open window.

Chapter Seventy-One

SOME OTHER LEIGHTON BARNES DOES NOT survive this night. In a parallel universe, it is the end of the night, and the end of the year, and the end of her. I feel the truth of it in my chest, where the wild, caged thing is still living. It's been spared, when a bullet should have found it.

Another creature in another world wouldn't be so lucky.

But here, tonight, this bullet doesn't split my skin or crack the bones of my chest or nick the small, soft wall of an artery. It just skims across my ribs, so close that I feel its heat, and buries itself in the wall of this house. This house that hides his violence.

This time I watch it happen.

It's like the sliver of broken glass in my bedroom window. The vase on the table and the frames on the wall. The plaster where he struck the walls in anger. The black crack in the wall where I pressed the heels of my feet too hard because I was scared, opening the house and revealing its dark insides.

This house built by anger.

The kind of rage that pulses like a living thing and was poured into the concrete, nailed into the wooden beams that form the foundation—down deep in its guts. A house haunted by the things it refuses to let go of.

The wall is moving. A gleam of black metal as the bullet falls out. The plaster shifts, dust like an imploding cloud coming back into place. The shattered pieces come together. And it's this—the house fixing his violence again—that makes me realize we still aren't safe. From him or this house or its strange, dark magic.

This night isn't over.

Chapter Seventy-Two

MOM LIFTS ME TO MY FEET and pushes me.

Why do I smell smoke?

"Leighton, go," Mom says.

He's still holding the gun, staring at it like he only just realized it was in his hand. His hand closes over the gleaming metal. Squeeze. Relax. Weighing it. Weighing something. Realizing he cannot run away. His keys are gone.

We have to go. But the only way to go is *up*. To the girls.

"Go, Leighton."

I crawl up the stairs, hand over hand. I'm not hurt, but I'm tired. Like a hundred years just passed in the blink of an eye. Forever can exist in a moment. In the crack of a firework. The pull of a trigger.

And then I don't just smell smoke. I see it, coming from my room, and I know it's the lantern, and I know it's the girls.

But how? I always hide the lighter. They don't know where I keep it.

Mom and I fall into my room, and she locks the door behind us.

I don't see Campbell or Juniper.

The lantern is spilled, burning. As I watch, it catches the curtains of my window, the edge of my quilt.

The book of matches that Joe left me is on my bedside table, open. Missing a few matches.

Smoke starts to fill the room, and the girls are—

I hear a muted scream. The armoire.

I run across the room and bang on it. It's locked. I hear Campbell coughing, Juniper sobbing.

I pry at the locked doors with my fingernails. Panic swells inside of me. The girls. The flames grow into a wall of heat beside me, and I'm coughing so hard I can't catch my breath. I scratch at the door until my fingers start to bleed. Why is it locked? My fingers slide over the keyhole, and it's burning hot.

The keyhole.

I run to my dresser while Mom takes over prying at the armoire's door. I grab the rusted key that Joe left. The key we thought was lost years ago, tucked into a safe place by a worried grandfather.

At the armoire, the key slides right in, and turns.

The doors swing open, and the girls fall out. Their skin is hot to the touch. Shiny tracks of tears mark their flushed cheeks.

Mom lifts Juniper into her arms.

"Leighton!" Cammy says between coughs. "Are you hurt?

We heard the gun."

"No one is hurt," I say. "You started a fire?"

"You're bleeding," Cammy says.

I look down at my hands. They are covered in blood, but I'm not hurt. The house is hurt. And now it's burning.

Something slams into my bedroom door. Shit.

Mom understands before I do. We are trapped.

"We can't put it out," she says, coughing through every word. "We have to go."

Another slam on the door, and the lock shifts.

We usher the girls to the window.

Boom! Fireworks light up the sky outside.

We make it onto the roof outside of my room, but it isn't far enough. I hear another slam of the door inside. Wood splinters but holds.

"Keep going," I tell them, and we shuffle along the roof until we are outside of Mom's bedroom. We are out of the smoke, for now.

Higher, something in me screams. The creature. Fear. It knows where I need to go, and I know to listen. No sooner does the thought cross my mind than something breaks inside the house. He's in my room. But at the same moment, I hear another sound—the front door. I look over my shoulder and see he's out of the burning house, but only for a moment.

A chaos of crows descend, and they drive him back.

They force him into the house.

And I see them at every window, cawing and diving.

Making it impossible for him to leave, even as smoke billows out, choking everything in its path.

I hear sirens in the distance, but they sound so far away. Too far.

The smoke thickens, but we can't go back, so instead we lift the girls, cupping our hands under their feet, pushing them onto the highest part of the house. Mom helps me next, and then I pull Mom up. Smoke streams out of the bedroom windows, burning our eyes.

I hear the glass of the window shatter, and outside of my room, something emerges—but it isn't him. It's a shadow, moving across the roof of the porch. It's some part of this house, breaking out, coming after us. A shadow in the shape of rage.

We've gone as far as we can. I hear a noise behind us and shift, careful to balance. At the far end of the roof, half hidden in smoke, the figure rises. It's on the roof with us. It is little more than a silhouette moving toward us. Still, it comes. It hurts to look at it—it pulses with anger. All the rage he ever felt, detached from him, unleashed on us. And here we perch, with nowhere to run.

I grip Campbell's hand on one side and Junie's on the other. Mom stands on the other side of Juniper. Soon they'll see the shadow emerging from the smoke.

But when I look from side to side, their eyes aren't on the figure in the smoke. All three are calm, looking straight ahead.

I follow their gaze.

The crows are coming.

Chapter Seventy-Three

I DID NOT SET THE FIRE, but I might as well have. I could tell you that I didn't mean for this to happen, but that would be a lie.

I didn't set the fire, but I willed it. I dreamed it. I harbored the ill wish deep inside of me. It was nestled in my stomach, feeding on all the fear that I've swallowed living here. *Burn, baby, burn.*

I did not set the fire.

But I wasn't about to put it out once it finally began.

Chapter Seventy-Four

FALLING IS LIKE THIS.

You take a leap of faith in the dark. The sky is on fire above you, and the house is on fire below. You feel the roof beneath you start to give, and there is nowhere to go but out, into the night. I know it's Joe out there. I know they will save us from this, even as an inferno opens under our feet.

So we jump.

And they are there—cawing, clawing, and covering us in feathers.

They catch us.

Off the burning home and away from the burning night, we are carried by the crows.

Chapter Seventy-Five

THEY SET US DOWN ON THE other side of the road.

Before even a moment passes, Campbell takes off toward the house.

Mom screams, reaching, her fingers barely catching at Campbell's shirt, but it's not enough. Campbell pulls free. And I realize she's going after him, in the burning house. She's going to save him from the fire she set, and I wish more than anything that I'd started that fire so the guilt would be mine, because I think I'd let him burn. I know I would.

But not Campbell.

I race toward the house. The crows don't guard the door anymore, and when I get inside, I see why—he's unconscious on the floor. Campbell is straining to pull his heavy weight toward the door.

My lungs are on fire, choking on the black smoke filling the room.

"Campbell." I gasp for air, but just cough harder. "Go. Go!"

She refuses, pulling, crying and sobbing and coughing violently. So I reach out and grab his shirt, pulling with her. It's the only way to get her out. Flames flicker up the doorway to the kitchen, and I feel them catch on the hem of my dress.

Campbell smacks at them, putting them out.

We pull, and once we are at the door, we roll him out, over into the yard. Mom and Juniper run forward and help us pull him across the street.

We hear a crunching sound. At first, I think I feel it underneath me, like the whole world is about to split open, but it's really the house, folding in upon itself.

It holds for a heartbeat. Two.

Shudders.

And then it collapses.

Chapter Seventy-Six

WE HUDDLE IN THE STREET, TOES numb and hearts unsure. The EMTs examine us while we answer the police officer's questions. Mrs. Stieg brings us blankets and brews coffee for Mom, the officers, and emergency responders.

An oxygen mask is placed over Campbell's face, and my dress is cut open over my ribs, showing a bloody track where the bullet grazed my side. I guess the blood was mine.

At some point, Bill DiMarco arrives, and begins to say words we've waited for—like *arrest warrant*. He tells us the violation of the order, the endangerment of children, the gun being fired, and the injuries we sustained will all make jail unavoidable.

But I step away from him and get as close to the remains of the house as the fire chief allows.

I think about that shadow that followed us. How close it came to claiming us. How easily we could have been consumed by whatever evil thing it was.

A legacy of anger. An inheritance of fear.

But this time, the house won't erase his violence.

Its ashes are as dark as a crow's wings.

Chapter Seventy-Seven

WHEN THE SUN BEGINS TO RISE, so do the crows in our yard.

The crows in the tree follow.

There's a flash of gray amid the black, and the three of us look up.

"Bye, Joe," Juniper whispers.

The birds flock, building momentum. Like dominoes falling, but in reverse, each following the last up into the dark sky, until there are thousands of crows above us. And then tens of thousands. The sunrise is crimson, reflecting off the black feathers until it looks like the crows are burning as they rise, like a hundred thousand phoenixes soaring over Auburn.

It is a new day. A new year.

It is like ending a nightmare and waking up to a new world.

Campbell and Juniper come to stand on either side of me, each slipping a hand into mine, and I feel something shift inside of me. That winged thing in my chest settles. Silent. Safe.

We're home.

AUBURN, PENNSYLVANIA
JANUARY 1

CROW POPULATION:
0

Acknowledgments

Just a short time ago, this was not a book. It was only book-shaped. And it would have stayed as a book-shaped thing (and not a real book) if not for the help of some incredibly talented and gracious people. Time is precious, and they spent a great deal of theirs reading and advising me on how to make this messy work-in-progress into a story. I'm so grateful for each read-through, every note, every suggestion that made a lightbulb flicker on for a part of this story that was missing or dark.

First, a heartfelt thank you to the entire team at Pitch Wars, who make writing dreams come true. It's a first stepping stone, but it's a huge one, and I've met so many wonderful people through the community you've created. Thank you to the 2017 Pitch Wars group, which feels like home. It's the place I come back to when I'm feeling lost (and when I'm lost in my feelings).

Thank you, Kate Karyus Quinn and Mindy McGinnis, who plucked this story from their inbox and told me everything that was wrong with it. Thank you for answering a thousand questions, and for helping me muck through the hardest parts of writing it. Your humor, insight, and countless notes have made me better at this, and I'm so grateful for the time you gave to this story.

I'm also so thankful for my incredible agent, Suzie

Townsend, and the entire, overwhelmingly supportive group at New Leaf. You make it feel like joining a family. Suzie, I think there were moments you believed in this book more than I did—thank you for being the greatest advocate a writer could hope for.

Thank you to my insightful editor, Ben Rosenthal, for reading this book *so many times*, and still loving it. Thank you for catching all of the strings I dropped and helping me weave them back into the story. Thank you to the rest of the team at Katherine Tegen Books for the warm welcome, and for lending your many incredible talents to this book.

To the writers of *The Great Noveling Adventure*—you created the first writing community I felt I belonged to. Thank you for helping me shape the first 1,000 words of this story. Jenny Perinovic, my fellow Pennsylvania Senator, I have no idea where I'd be without you. Thank you for the encouragement, the writing dates, and for being my friend. I'm so grateful.

Thank you to my high school English teachers and my college sociology professors. The former taught me how to find my voice, and the latter taught me how to use it. Thank you, Pat and Jill, for everything.

Thank you, Natalie, for being my dearest friend for almost twenty years. You've helped me navigate so many hard decisions. I'm so glad that I found, as Anne "with an e" would say, a kindred spirit. Adiah Wren, I hope you know how much I look up to you. Whenever I start to forget, you remind me that our voices matter *so much*. I can't wait to read more of what you have to say. Jacqueline, thank you for being one of my earliest readers and earliest friends, and offering endless support from day one.

To my huge, wonderful family, extended and in-law included, you are the net that catches us. What an incredible gift it is to have the security of your love. I've never taken it for granted. A special thank you to Aunt Molly, for the Oreos and *Gilmore Girls*, and to Uncle Matt, for the Nintendo. Really, this is a thank you for showing up when you did—it meant the world. Grandmom McCauley, thank you for lending me your home, and your tenacious hope, when I needed them most. And thank you, Mom, for being my North Star. I'll always look to you for guidance. Loved you first.

Kayleigh, thank you for answering my panicked phone calls, for being the first, fiercest advocate for this story, and for reading this book start to finish more times than I did. Thank you, Katharyn, for making me laugh so hard I cry. You two are my best friends in the world, and I'm so lucky to have you in my life.

Finally, to Andrew. You treated this book (and all of my writing) like it was inevitable, and never the impractical, inconvenient dream I thought it was. Thank you for believing when I didn't, and for chasing our little monster children around while I wrote. Thank you for being the first person I've turned to since we were sixteen years old, leaving Straylight Run lyrics on our AIM away messages for each other. I love waiting for the train with you.

Author's Note

At its core, *If These Wings Could Fly* is a survival story. But instead of taking place on an island or lost in the wilderness and removed from human contact, this story takes place at the heart of it: in a small town, in a house that is shaped by domestic violence.

I wrote the book I would have liked to read when I was fifteen—when I didn't know it was domestic violence. No one had ever described it that way, and I'd certainly never seen it in a book. As an adult, I turned to advocacy, volunteering at a domestic violence intake center, and studying the sociological roots of violence. But the more information I gained, the more fervently I wished I could share this hard-wrought knowledge with the version of me that needed it the most.

Then I realized that I don't need time travel to find readers who need the message now. In writing a story that centered domestic violence, I knew that I had to show how the threat of violence hangs like a sword overhead, and how the fear can often feel worse than the fall. A story in which the thing you are afraid of looks very much like someone you love, and how confusing that can be. It makes domestic violence very difficult to navigate from the inside, and incredibly easy to misunderstand from the outside.

This story has some magic in it, too. I've always felt that there was something surreal about domestic violence, like it exists in this strange absence inside a home, where time slows down, and the outside world feels so far away. A parallel universe. In writing, I could make that feel tangible, in the form of an unkind house that hides signs of violence. It also meant that I could write in the rebuttal—in the form of a magical force of a hundred thousand crows who arrive to protect the girls. My goal was always to tell this story through the lens of hope, and to pass the urgency of that hope on to a reader who needs it most.

Resources

There are many wonderful organizations working to raise awareness, provide leadership in legislation, and offer support and information for victims of domestic violence. Below is a list of resources related to advocacy and safety planning. *Please keep in mind that abusers can track your browsing history. Only access these websites from a safe device and location.*

The Hotline: The National Domestic Violence Hotline has trained advocates available 24/7/365 to answer calls and provide information and resources. The website has a live chat feature to message with an advocate, an escape button if you need to quickly exit, and Spanish translation.

www.thehotline.org

1-800-799-7233

1-800-787-3224 (TTY)

<u>Love is Respect</u>: Highly trained advocates offer information and support for young people experiencing dating violence. Also provides resources for concerned family members, friends, teachers, counselors, service providers, or members of law enforcement. Free and confidential phone and texting services, available 24/7. This website has an escape button, live chat feature, and Spanish translation.

www.loveisrespect.org

1-866-331-9474

1-866-331-8453 (TTY)

Text: "loveis" to 22522

<u>National Coalition Against Domestic Violence</u>: Education, advocacy, policy, and resources related to domestic violence. Hosts "Action Alerts" to help users engage in policy action calls related to domestic violence legislation and VAWA renewal, including graphics and suggested language to use on social media to raise awareness and call political figures to action.

www.ncadv.org